The
NAKED
SEASON

'Sharp, witty and entertaining . . . Hope for the "girl-power" girls after all!'   Stella Duffy

'A modern novel with ballsy characters, bags of punch and a quirky style'   *The Bookseller*

Born in Essex in 1977, Kira Cochrane studied American Literature at the Universities of Sussex and California before moving to London to work as a journalist. Now based in Brighton, she writes regularly for *The Sunday Times*. *The Naked Season* is her first novel.

The
NAKED
SEASON

Kira Cochrane

POCKET
BOOKS

LONDON • SYDNEY • NEW YORK • TOKYO • SINGAPORE • TORONTO

First published in Great Britain by Simon & Schuster, 2003
This edition first published by Pocket Books, 2003
An imprint of Simon & Schuster UK
A Viacom company

1 3 5 7 9 10 8 6 4 2

Simon & Schuster UK Ltd
Africa House
64–78 Kingsway
London WC2B 6AH

www.simonsays.co.uk

Simon & Schuster Australia
Sydney

A CIP catalogue record for this book
is available from the British Library

ISBN 0 7434 4103 6

Typeset in Plantin by M Rules
Printed and bound in Great Britain by
Cox & Wyman Ltd, Reading, Berkshire

To Tessa, Frazer and Avril

1

Me and the Showgirl

'She was a showgirl, your real mother, all sequins and blue eyes. A fading beauty' – my mother pauses – 'fading fast. She had slightly hunched shoulders, a stooped back and she seemed somehow – I don't know – collapsible. She had the look of someone who's waiting for the wrecking ball, just staring at the clock, about to be demolished, like one of those tower blocks you see on TV. Wired up, detonated and crashing to the ground – boom.' She claps her hands together happily and smiles. 'Crashing to the ground and then bouncing in her own dust, almost imperceptibly, like a shrug.'

My mother takes a long drag of her cigarette, licks her finger and smooths it across my right eyebrow. She stretches out on the bed.

'That's better. Anyway, your mother was unhappy. Depressed. Not unhappy like you or I might be, Molly. Not unhappy like the other day.'

I look at her, confused.

She continues, 'The other day when I sent you to school with that ice-skating sprain—'

'Fracture,' I say.

'OK, that ice-skating sprain that turned out to be a fracture – but properly unhappy. Reno, Nevada unhappy. It's not like being an unhappy kid here, you know, Molly. Not unhappy like a Sunday in London when you can still see a film or go to the library. There's no place quite like Reno if you want to be depressed. I think it's the dust.'

My mother runs a hand through her hair and lights another cigarette. Her voice is dry and nicotine-brittle. I've been asleep for a couple of hours and my eyes adjust slowly to the light from the hall. I yawn pointedly. She ignores me.

'It was the summer of seventy-five when I found you, and me and Ellie had been on the road for almost a year, driving across America on a lecture tour. We had packed up our place in Oakland the August before, the apartment we had lived in while I taught at Berkeley. It was a great little place,' she sighs, exhaling a dragon-puff of smoke. 'White-slatted on the outside and a bit dilapidated, but not too near the industrial part of town. There was a good community, tinderbox politics – it was exciting. We had two bedrooms, one we used as my study, and a shared garden where all the residents grew tomatoes and industrial-strength pot brought down from Humboldt.' She smiles. 'Such great pot. There was an iron fire escape that ran down the back of the house and sometimes Ellie and I would perch on the steps after dinner smoking or sharing some wine and the neighbours would come out and join us.'

My mother sits up, stretching over to rearrange the Minnie Mouse doll that's sitting on my pillow. She crosses her legs, head tilted. 'We had a huge party just before we left,' she says, 'huge. We'd got the whole place stored away that day, all my books boxed up ready for shipping to London. I'd tied an old offcut of curtain around my head like a pirate while we packed' – she leers at me and laughs, doing her best to look piratical – 'and before the party Ellie and I had gone to bed, hoping to rest for an hour or two.

'Anyway, having drunk a couple of bottles of wine in between the stacking and lifting, we fell asleep, curled up together, the humidity creating a kind of' – she waves her hands vaguely – 'metallic fug in the room. Hours later we woke up, legs flailing in the air, to find one of my women's studies students, Jen, tickling our feet with a peacock feather. We had given her the key to the apartment – she was going to live there until the lease expired – and she had let herself and a bunch of friends in. I'll never forget it. Me and Ellie huddled together, laughing hysterically, kicking each other as we pulled our feet away, surrounded by Berkeley students. Grateful Dead T-shirts and denim everywhere.' She pauses. 'There was a lot of hair in that room.'

She takes a long slug from a glass of water that's sitting beside my bed, rocks her head back and gargles.

'Mmmm. Anyway, the party was great. Memorable.
There was a wooden table out back which was laden with
barbecue food – kebabs, salad, burgers – and Jen and I
had sex beneath it, great sex, while the other guests
helped themselves to sweet pepper couscous.'

My mother smiles and strokes my head. 'The next
morning Ellie and I set off along Highway Eighty, straight
to Salt Lake City and right on through the Midwest, with
packed halls at every stop. All these students nodding
lazily in the theatres, as if they were at a rock concert, as
I spoke about motherhood and paternalism and sex roles.
We went through Cleveland to New York, past
Philadelphia and the Carolinas, sloping around through
Texas. There were seductions all along the way of course,
a string of affairs – the physics professor who fucked me
in a turban' – my mother grins – 'she kept quoting de
Beauvoir in bed. There was the dean's wife at a private
college in New York, all mahogany skin and blonde hair.'
She sucks contemplatively on her cigarette. 'I should have
snaffled her for good. There was the eighteen-year-old
literature student, away from home for the first time, who
said I was old – old! – at thirty, and that she couldn't
believe she had gone to bed with someone famous. She
made me autograph her pillow.

'And always, at the back of the hall, Ellie, knitting the
longest scarf in the world, the striped one that's on the top
shelf of your wardrobe. It's faded now. She was drifting
along as usual, playing the guitar and writing poetry on
envelopes and drawing. Stars, she kept drawing, and tiny

portraits of me in profile. They drove me mad, littering up the car. She'd bought *Blood on the Tracks*, that album about Bob Dylan's divorce, and I swear she played it a zillion times. It was like water torture. God. It was like that time in the bath when you wouldn't stop singing "Yellow Submarine" and I had to gag you with your flannel.' She laughs. 'Bob Dylan's whine coupled with the fact that the songs were all about relationships ending, nothing upbeat. There was this vocal tic on one of the songs that just drove me mad' – she bangs her foot against the bed – 'a stress on the final word of each line, a complete over-emphasis, and after a while I began to believe that he was doing it just to torment me, Augusta Flynn. I started having delusions, nightmares, that Bob Dylan was torturing me. Rock and roll schizophrenia. Anyway, it wasn't music for the road and it only stopped when I snapped the tape in half and slung it out the window in a potato field.'

My mother's stomach gives an alcoholic gurgle and she pauses to swallow.

'So,' she nudges me, 'when the tour ended, we stopped in New Mexico for a while, in Taos, and rented a house for the winter and spring whilst I wrote a thesis on Georgia O'Keeffe. *From stamen to semen*, it was called I think,' she laughs, 'very subtle. Come May, when the heat really kicked back in, we decided to carry on through to San Francisco, see a few friends and head home. Back to London after nine years.'

She pushes a strand of hair off my face, hooking my

fringe behind my ears. She kisses me gently on the fore-head.

'Hey there, beautiful, you still listening?' I nod sleepily. 'Good. So as we were getting close to Reno we decided to make a stop. We had been talking about seeing some showgirls for a while and we figured that it would be cheaper than Vegas, more accessible. We decided that we'd find a gambling den, hunker down for the night and watch some high-kicking women.' She sighs softly. 'It would be just like the Folies Bergère.

'We were just outside Reno when we found a revue in a tiny shack by the roadside. You could see the Sierra Nevada, all snow-peaked in the distance, but apart from that the place was completely barren. Just dust bolls and dry grass. Desert. A metal sign was propped against a wall – "God Bless America" – and there were some dis-used petrol pumps out the front too, still showing nineteen-sixties prices. The old man on the door was cleaning his fingernails with a penknife and there was blood just pouring from his hands. It reminded me of the first meeting between Picasso and Dora Maar,' says my mother, 'when she skewered her hand to the table with a kitchen knife.

'Anyway,' she continues, 'the blackboard beside the entrance said "Nude girls tonight, eight pm" and so we decided that we might as well stop. We paid the old man a dollar each and then went right in.'

My mother shifts on the bed, pulling the covers away from my chin. She turns her face to me. 'The place was like something out of a Western inside – silent, with sawdust on the floor and men playing cards. It could probably have been in *The Dukes of Hazzard* – she prods me – 'that dumb TV show you like, it could probably have been in that. Anyway, it was really dark, foggy with smoke, and the women were at the back of the room, performing behind chicken wire to stop the men molesting them.' She takes a drag on her cigarette. 'All the men there were disgusting, just pigs, with this wet, fatty quality about them, like the residue left in a frying pan. They were just meat really, those men, flesh and gristle. Me and Ellie were getting drunk and laughing behind our beers as they watched the girls dance, digging their hands into their crotches. It was horrible really, their erections so obvious, but we found it funny after a few drinks. You could tell that the girls were bored, because their kicks were always a little behind the music, lethargic, and their heads rolled back, like this—' My mother's head lolls onto her shoulder, just the whites of her eyes visible beneath the lids.

She goes to stub out her cigarette and spills ash over my blankets.

'Mum,' I say, whining, and brush it onto the floor.

'Shhhh,' she says, putting a finger to her lips. 'I'm telling you a story, Molly,' and she lies across the bed and winks at me.

'So there was this one girl in the revue, this one girl who both me and Ellie liked. She wasn't the most beautiful – her skin was lined, leathery, even though she couldn't have been more than about twenty – but she had a dusky quality, a darkness.' My mother pauses, thinking. 'Like the cadences in a blues song, the clusters of minor chords. She was wearing an incredible outfit – the Southern Cross picked out in sequins on a tiny leotard – and her hair, which was blonde, was piled right up on her head, all ready to topple over.' She smiles. 'She reminded me of Dolly Parton.

'Anyway, I caught her eye and nodded at her, holding up my beer. And when she smiled back it all fell away. The sleaziness, sawdust, the men and their hard-ons, Ellie. It was just me and her.' She starts singing throatily, 'You're just too good to be true,' before coughing. 'Her smile was full of light and happiness and,' my mother sighs, 'and sex, I guess. But not the seedy kind. No. Carefree sex. Timeless.' She pauses and rolls onto her back. 'I'll always remember it.'

She's crushing my legs and I push at her from under the covers until she props herself up on her right elbow.

'So after the show me and Ellie went out to the back of the bar and found the girl sitting there, head bowed, on a step beside the bins. There was a chicken, scrawny and almost featherless, pecking at a rubbish bag, the contents spilling out around it. Broken beer bottles, Oreo wrappers, an old, used porn mag. "I was waiting for you," she said, and she took both our hands and started marching us across the wasteland. It was really late by then and once we were away from the bar, far from the lights, it was pitch-black and unknown in the way that only the early morning hours are.

'We slowed down after a while and started talking, and when she found out that we were British the girl was ecstatic. She kept cupping her face and squealing, "It's perfect!" before grabbing our hands again and hugging them to her stomach. Ellie and I were laughing obliviously, giggling all the way back to her home, which turned out to be a trailer propped on a few pieces of wood. The wheels had been stolen years ago. Inside, the place was decorated with cross-stitched homilies and when I asked her about them she pointed at one that said "Love thy neighbour" and screwed up her nose. "My mom made them but I ignore that one. My neighbour is a fat fuck called Wayne who tried to pimp me when I first came to town." Then she lowered her voice and whispered, "He also has crabs, which is not a sign of godliness."'

I find this interesting, since I don't know anyone who keeps crabs as pets and I can't see why God would mind. I'd spent the whole of the last summer holidays catching crabs on Frinton beach – sometimes as many as fourteen a day – letting them swim around in a water-filled bucket and then freeing them out into the sea. I almost ask my mother about this, but I'm tired and want her to finish.

'So we were looking around her trailer which, let's face it, didn't take very long, when she went to an open drawer in the corner and brought out what looked like a rolled-up towel. Holding it to her breast she edged towards us, looking sort of worried and excited. "This is Molly," she said, "my daughter," and we saw that nestled in the towel was a tiny child, days old, with tendrils of hair splaying

out like a halo and huge limpid eyes. They were like fish
eyes,' she says, laughing, 'wide and goggly. The girl sat on
the edge of the bed and held the baby on her lap and Ellie
and I just glanced at each other, nervous. We were concerned about the situation but we were also drunk and we
ended up sitting on either side of the girl, taking turns
holding the baby, stroking her hair and making her smile
by pulling faces.' My mother lunges at me, gurning, her
fingers holding her eyes up at the corners, her mouth
open, tongue out. I can't help laughing.

She smiles widely, her eyebrows rising, and strokes my
hair. 'There you go. And so we all ended up going to
sleep that night, fully dressed, the four of us on the
double bed, with you between me and the showgirl. It
should have been one of those nights when you hardly
sleep and find yourself dreaming a lot, conscious here
and there. But it wasn't. We were all completely comfortable. And in the morning, when we were still groggy, the
girl asked me to take you to London. "I've heard about
England," she said. "I've heard that you still wear sack-
cloth and that you don't have electricity, but that you're
good to each other, real civilised. The other day I was
reading about your royal family too, and they seem
great."' She pauses. 'And so me and Ellie brought you
home.'

My mother stretches out again and after a few seconds
I realise that she's asleep. I kick her, gently at first, and
then violently, she comes to and I get out of bed and pull
her, stumbling, into the next room. I start to undress her

and, unable to reach the shirt buttons, I sit her down on the bed.

'Molly,' she mumbles, 'are you glad I adopted you? You are, aren't you?'

I smile. 'Yes, Mum.' I undo her bra, take it off and put her pyjama T-shirt on. In big black letters on the front it says, 'Choose life, lose Thatcher.'

'Ellie'll take you to school tomorrow, Moll, OK? She should be back from work at about eight in the morning, so she can walk you. Don't wake me up or anything, because I haven't got lectures until the afternoon.' I lift her legs and pull the duvet across before kissing her on the cheek. 'I love you, Molly Flynn,' she calls after me, 'even if you're not my girl.'

I reach up and turn off the landing light then climb into bed, tucking my blankets in on either side. As I'm drifting off to sleep I wonder whether I am really adopted. It seems unlikely since everyone says how much I look like my mother – same olive skin, strong jaw, dark eyes – but maybe it's true. Maybe my mother's not really my mother at all. For years now she's been telling me these stories. That I'm the daughter of Mormon missionaries, students at Brigham Young University, who were posted to Africa, had a love affair and concealed my birth. That I'd been born to a Vietnamese woman, the product of a forced relationship with an American soldier. That I was the bastard child of a Protestant woman and a Catholic man in Northern Ireland, both of them later kneecapped.

She's made even more outrageous claims about my

provenance – that I'm the child of Elvis and Jane Fonda, of the Pope. There was the story about me being the daughter of Fidel Castro, a love child, who'd been born in Cuba and smuggled out in a fishing boat, only for my mother to find me abandoned on a beach in Key West. When I was very young she'd told me that I'd been found in a seashell and that as I grew up I would notice scales on my arms and would start finding it hard to breathe. My toes and fingers would grow webbed and my legs would meld together. Eventually I'd be unable to survive outside water and I would discover the secret of my birth – that I'd been the product of a mermaid mating with a human. Lost in the ocean, I would find my way back to Neptune.

My real parents are revolutionaries and saints, rock stars and visionaries. 'You were never mine,' my mother always says after a few drinks. 'I know I'll never keep you,' and after this she tends to pass out.

2

Forecast: nasty

I hear a rustle behind me as I stand on the sidewalk, the slap of skin against concrete. Turning, I see a skateboard career past the dirty-video store on my right, propelled by a man whose body has been amputated just below the navel. I watch, apprehensive, as he throws his torso forward, pulling his fingertips along the ground and picking up speed.

'Impressive,' says the taxi driver, following my gaze.

'Yeah. More dextrous than me.' I heft my backpack up the steps to the hotel entrance, stumbling slightly at the top.

As the taxi driver steers away, I walk back onto the street, peering up the hill. He has brought me from Sea-Tac Airport to First Avenue, Seattle, site of the cheapest hotel in the city. I had stayed here with Tom six years ago when we were first together, and had come to appreciate its piss-stained stairs, the unexplained stickiness of the outside walls. 'This place is a dump,' Tom had grinned when he'd first seen the decaying sign, 'The Landor', its vowels having toppled off years ago so that the hotel's name was spelled out in shorthand. Seeing the prices, his smile had stretched wider. 'Let's stay here,' he'd said, running his hand protectively through my hair until it got caught in a stray clump near the bottom.

Opposite the hotel is a porn cinema, the Lusty Lady, complete with furtive men outside, talking in whispers. The film programme lies beneath a neon outline of a naked woman, her eyes clenched. It reads simply, 'Forecast: nasty', the time of showing, 'anytime'. I look up at the sky, a muggy, low-riding fog stealing its way in. Could be right, I think.

Exchanging pleasantries with the manager, I book into a room on the fifth floor, go upstairs, dump my bags and stretch diagonally across the king-sized bed. I am sweaty from the flight, greasy-haired, my stomach heavy with airline food – chicken medallions and potatoes dauphinoise, mashed sweetcorn and swede. I climb under the covers, pulling them up to my chin, and switch on the TV. Flicking through the channels – sport, sport, religion, sport – I come to an infomercial in which a paunchy, bubble-haired man is selling exercise videos. He is sitting beside a woman who had been 500 pounds overweight until she started his disco-cise programme. 'It was awful, wasn't it,' he says, patting her hand, 'not being able to play with your children or run up the stairs.' She nods tearfully. At the top of the screen is a white-lettered title, 'Great American Transformations'. A small-print message at the bottom notes 'Results not typical'.

I start flicking again and settle on the flashing fuchsia logo of a programme called *Ex-Games*. The ads have just ended and, returning to the show, the camera pans to a girl on an orange couch, looking shell-shocked. She is backing away, just perceptibly, from the host, who is goading her to criticise her ex-boyfriend. 'Come on, Kelly,' he says, the sheen of his hair glinting under the studio lights, 'you can tell us his good points after the bad ones.'

In a faltering voice, Kelly starts talking about Paul, her recent ex-boyfriend. She's polite, tentative, a young Californian girl with neat hair and manicured nails. After a few minutes of encouragement from the host, she starts to list some minor gripes that she had had in their relationship. There's the waxy Q-tips he left in bed, the used tissues down the side of the couch, the half-eaten hot dogs she'd find in her utility cupboard. She mentions the stains on his underwear, his dirty fingernails. Then, as the host leans in for more, her voice speeds up. Suddenly she's launching into a catalogue of sins.

There's his snorting laugh, the hair on his back ('he made me pluck it – it took hours!'), the way he used to moon waitresses in bars when out with his frat-boy friends. There's his habit of getting her drunk and then trying to ease the condom off while they're having sex, so that he 'has more feeling'. I imagine him whistling unassumingly and covering Kelly's eyes – 'let your fantasies roam free, baby' – whipping off the rubber in one fluid movement and heading back in. There's the time he slept with her twin sister, Shelley, who was so wasted that she passed out during the act. And finally there's the herpes he gave her after a three-way with some girls in a West Hollywood brothel.

The host is laughing breathily. 'Geez,' he says, winking at the camera as Kelly pauses. 'You sure haven't tamed him yet!' The audience laughs enthusiastically and applauds. 'Well,' says the host, 'have we got a surprise for you today, Kelly.'

She looks confused and smiles, her face round as a downy-skinned peach. 'What's that, Ray?' she says, and the host takes her by the hand.

'Well, what we didn't tell you is that your ex, Paul, is in an isolation booth offstage and he's come here tonight to win you back!' Kelly claps a hand to her mouth, gasping, as Paul walks through the doors at the back of the stage, his arms outstretched.

I turn the TV to mute and start running a bath. All the hotel fittings are old, slightly chipped, and the bathroom includes an ivory tub with clawed feet so detailed that it looks ready to jump alive. I arrange my shampoo, soap and razor carefully on the curved side and take my clothes off, kicking them into a dusty corner. My hearing is still blocked from the flight and I drill my fingers into my ears, inhale and swallow. Watching myself in the mirror, my mouth pulls into a taut, concentrated line, cheeks billowing painfully. After a few minutes I give up, cupping my breasts and stepping into the bath.

Water laps over the side as I sit down, spreading puddles across the linoleum. I soap up my armpits and shave them carefully then start in on my bikini line. I push my hips out of the water, lathering and then shaving in one swift move before the foam washes off.

As I shave my right leg, the razor snags, the skin rippling prettily through the blades – a concertina ruffle – leaving a huge, bloody gash. I peer through the water as bright red curlicues start snaking away from the cut. It mirrors the scar on my other leg from the first time I shaved. That was when I was eleven and Andy, a boy who could burp the alphabet, had told me that I had 'legs like a gorilla'. He had then belched Tarzan's call of the wild. I had run to the school toilets and, pulling my socks down, inspected my legs. Although I had never thought about it before I had to concede that it was true. I was a Yeti. It's official, I thought, I'm a wildebeest. And suddenly a vision had come into my head, a magnified image of a fly, its legs stout and stunted, covered by something as coarse as dachshund fur. On the way home, I'd stopped at the local corner shop and used my lunch money to buy a pack of ten disposable razors.

Heading upstairs, I had locked myself in the bathroom and gone to work with a determination previously reserved only for Boggle. I was going to be smooth, depilated, perfect. Not realising that it was better to wet my legs and the razor before shaving I had pulled the blade firmly up my left shin, sending blood spurting over my school uniform and the white bathroom suite. After a few minutes trying to staunch the bleeding with a succession of towels, I had gone downstairs to find my mother.

Augusta was sitting cross-legged in her study, eyes closed, head bowed. It was difficult to imagine that someone as aggressive as her could actually meditate and so I had always suspected that this was just an act designed to convince me, Ellie and herself that she had a core repose, an intellectual stillness. I burst in to find her playing a tape of whale song, the pained, incoherent yelps forming a perfect aural backdrop as I presented myself – her wide-eyed, wounded daughter.

Blood still spilling onto the floor, my mother opened her eyes and looked vacantly at me for a couple of seconds. Then she fell forward, hiccupping with laughter. 'Fucking hell, Ellie,' she crowed, 'get in here.'

Ellie came in from the kitchen wiping herself with a tea towel, her black dress covered in floury handprints. 'Oh Christ,' she said. 'It's a scene from *Carrie*.'

I wash my hair in the pink water, pull the plug and get out of the bath, soaking up the blood with wads of toilet paper. When it doesn't stop I stick a huge plaster over the cut and watch as the blood seeps slowly through the fabric. I pull on my red dress, low cut at the front and backless. Taking the TV off mute I see Kelly and Paul walk into a superimposed sunset, their fingers curled together, bemused. 'Well,' says the show's host, his smile almost a grimace, 'that's another triumph for *Ex-Games*, another couple back together.' Kelly – framed in a love heart – turns to the camera with a worried smile.

I scrape my wet hair into a ponytail and head out. Sitting by the hotel entrance is a group of men who glance up as I leave the building. 'Can you lend me a hundred thousand dollars?' says one, young and tidy, with a checked shirt and well-trimmed beard, drinking from a bottle of Colt 45. I shake my head – 'Sorry.'

It's early evening and further into town I find that the bars and restaurants, the endless coffee shops, are filling up. Walking along Third Avenue, I pass the place where Tom and I had eaten on our first night in Seattle. A functional cafe, with wipe-clean tables and cheap Mexican food, we had spent hours there, chewing our way methodically through nachos drenched in cheese and beans. Two days earlier we had left Australia with a shared hangover and this was the first food that we'd been able to digest. Licking our fingers we had sat there for an hour, stomachs distended, laughing at a warring couple at the next table. It was the smug, satisfied laughter of a new relationship, and it only stopped when the couple stood up and started ripping chunks out of each other's hair. At this point we'd snaked gingerly outside.

I come to a second-hand bookstore, a table outside heavy with its cheapest offers. Although I've travelled from Seattle down to LA before, I decide that I could still use a guidebook, some information on public transport. Tom, a California native, had been driving last time and I had looked on past the redwoods, the coastline, the unpredictable hills of Oregon, with the split-mouthed happiness of the passenger. 'Look,' I had said to Tom, as we passed a North Korean Presbyterian–Methodist Alliance, 'another strange Christian ministry.' As he sat reading maps beside me I had wondered at the prolifera- tion of dream catchers, windsocks and chimes on American porches. It was as though wind alone just wasn't quite enough. The residents needed to harness its entertainment value.

I find a recent guide to the US in the travel section and pass into fiction, picking up the latest Tom Robbins novel. Flicking through biographies, I decide on a life of Zelda Fitzgerald and Virginia Woolf's letters. I head for the till, situated at the back of the store, passing rows and rows of books on the way. I won't look, I think. I've done my browsing. I bow my head and keep walking. If I look, I think, she'll be there, filed away in a corner, waiting to pounce. I pass social studies, psychology, self-help, my resolve firm, eyes trained ahead.

On the last stretch though, the final few metres, I weaken and find myself glancing to the right. There, in ten-inch-high cut-out capitals, is the heading WOMEN'S STUDIES, and below it I catch sight of the giveaway scarlet spine, the heavy black lettering. Without think- ing, I go over and pull it off the shelf, my mother staring back at me, unflinching, implacable. She's everywhere, I think. This book is in every bookshop in the world – new, second-hand, big, small. Jakarta, Beijing, Sydney. I could go to the furthest kibbutz, a Tibetan monastery, an ashram, and the book would be there on a shelf, willing me to pick it up. I run my hand across the cover.

It's the fifteenth-anniversary edition, published in 1989, and there is a picture of my mother on the back, a full-length portrait in black and white. Her hair is cropped short and she's smiling, hands on hips. She's wearing a suit, tie and a tweed trilby pulled low over her left eye and she looks challenging, attractive, her whole body resting on a bone structure that is almost too fine. I stare at her for a second, remembering the Christmas that she had worn that suit to dinner. She had drunk a bottle of vodka before we sat down and had launched unsteadily into a story about a girl at college, one of her students. 'She's gorgeous,' she had said, laughing, 'the prettiest lips.' I had just had time to scrape a teaspoon of cranberry sauce onto my plate before Ellie ran out into the snow.

I turn the book over. 'MATERNITIES,' shouts the cover, 'the book that shook the world!' The description under my mother's picture is almost as histrionic. 'With this manifesto Augusta Flynn sounded a wake-up call to both women and men, forcing readers everywhere to reassess their gender roles. Through essays, storytelling and biography she argued that motherhood was an occupation for all – female, male, gay, straight, old, young. In the introduction to this fifteenth-anniversary edition she explains how the book changed people's lives – including her own – and why a sense of universal maternity is needed in our nuclear age. Be enlightened!'

As I stare at my mother's picture, the words start to distort. There had been a slew of profiles in newspapers and highbrow magazines a couple of years ago when Augusta's latest book had come out, looking at her influence and her recent re-emergence on the cultural frontlines. A few were illustrated with pictures that I'd never seen before, including a glut from the late sixties when my mother had been writing her doctoral thesis at Columbia University, New York. There was Augusta at a national conference of radical women, wearing a monocle and shouting at a mousy girl who'd been advocating celibacy. Standing outside an underwear shop on the Lower East Side with members of her feminist co-operative, the Super Flying Femmes, all dressed in jeans and black leather jackets. Marching at the Miss America protest in Atlantic City, holding a cardboard cut-out of a bikini-clad woman.

Other pictures were old family favourites. The photo of Augusta swearing at a police officer during the Stonewall riots, for instance, had been framed on my bedroom wall since birth. And I was thrilled that a few editors had included the one of her in a Greenwich Village restaurant, 1969, standing on a table, surrounded by women, thrusting a speculum into her vagina.

As the profiles noted, Augusta had been all but excommunicated from the New York radical scene by the early seventies, and had escaped to a teaching fellowship at Berkeley. The reasons for her falling out with the feminist community seemed muddy and various. First, in 1970, had come her split with the Super Flying Femmes. This was prompted by an ordinance agreed by the other fifteen members that they would all become lesbians – regardless of their genuine sexual persuasion – and live in a commune in Woodstock. Augusta had been apoplectic. 'What could be worse for a woman than ending up with a political lesbian?' she'd fumed, in an infamous television interview with Dick Cavett. 'Can you imagine being with someone who views giving head as part of the struggle for women's suffrage? How romantic. Or someone groping your breast because she feels an affinity with Elizabeth Cady Stanton? Can you imagine that?' Cavett had bowed his head. He clearly couldn't.

After burning her bridges with the lesbian separatists, Augusta had gone on to outrage the rest of the sisterhood. Feminists had just started holding speak-outs against rape, large communal gatherings where women could talk publicly about their experiences. The organisers hoped that these would expose the widespread incidence of sex attacks and their significance as a patriarchal tool, a way of keeping women, quite literally, on their backs. At a large anti-rape rally Augusta had stepped onstage with her usual aplomb and prompted brutal heckling by suggesting that the violence involved in a rape was of more import than the actual penetration. 'By focusing on penetration,' she had said, 'and implying that it's the worst fate that can befall us, we credit every man's penis with an unassailable power which those tumescent pieces of gristle just don't possess. We reinstate the idea of the erection as the ultimate symbol of dominance when, in fact, it's not the penis that's the problem. It's the fists and the guns and the knives.'

Following the rally, feminists from various radical groups had joined forces against Augusta, maligning her in the *New York Times* and publishing long tirades in their free sheets. In the years to come, my mother would always contend that her contemporaries had been waiting for an excuse to vilify her and that what had really annoyed them was her growing stardom. In a movement that prided itself on its non-hierarchical structure, her regular appearances on late-night talk shows, her scattershot debating style and burgeoning career as a *Village Voice* columnist had caused a ripple of sniping that was fast becoming tidal. By 1971, Augusta had accepted that she'd never be a joiner. California would be her resurrection. Her chance to shine. Alone.

The journalists had continued by noting the huge success of *Maternities*, followed by the downward curve of Augusta's career during the eighties. As the world sped into the Reagan era, her view of gender – once so positive – had sunk into a mire of recrimination. Back in Britain she had started her ill-fated porn project which sought to prove the thesis that all men were misogynists.

There were discrepancies in some of the profiles, differences of opinion and fact, but however they were organised and written, each had ended with the same question. How the hell had Molly Flynn come into being? What was the provenance of this shock-headed copy of

Augusta Flynn? Could the outspoken lesbian have inseminated herself with a mug of sperm and a chicken baster?
Had she had sex with one of her powerful male friends,
one of the small coterie of men she had stayed close to
since her incarnation in the early sixties as a boyish, New
Left Cambridge student? Was there a chance that she had
faked the pregnancy and adopted Molly – picking out a
dark-skinned reflection of herself? After all, wasn't it just
a bit convenient that her baby had turned out to be a
girl? Wasn't the wide-eyed, chubby little child she had
toted through the late seventies just too ideal an adjunct
to Augusta Flynn's life? Could it be that she had been
taken on as an accessory, a sign of just how far Augusta
would go to immerse herself in the world of women?

None of the authors had been able to answer the question. All quoted distant friends, or 'anonymous sources'
with varying theories. There was one Sarah McFadden,
who had apparently been at university with Augusta ('she
must have been fucking boring,' said my mother, 'since I
can't remember a thing about her') supporting the
chicken-baster theory. 'Augusta was always a self-starter,'
she said in the piece, 'always firm in the knowledge that
she was independent and capable of getting whatever she
wanted, when she wanted it. I remember her having a
big group of male friends at Cambridge – far more male
friends than female actually. There was still a lot of sex
segregation at the time, and there was an awful fuss when
the authorities realised that she'd been dressing in
trousers and eating in one of the male colleges for

months. She loved male company. But even then she would never have slept with a man. Never. I think she probably convinced one of her friends to provide some sperm and then inseminated herself. The perfect feminist conception.'

An unnamed source disagreed. 'I think that Augusta's lesbianism is a pose that she took on to make her famous. Think about it. At the time that she emerged onto the cultural scene in the late sixties – already streaks ahead intellectually – the fact that she was an out lesbian was audacious. It was unheard of, basically, to be publicly lesbian and voracious with it, and that gave her an infamy she was able to parlay into a career and a role as a figurehead. It set her apart. Beneath that, I think, is the fact that she's probably lived as a bisexual her whole adult life. I know of a few men from her circle who claim to have slept with her, and I think it was probably one of them who fathered Molly, agreeing that all details of her provenance would remain secret and that Ellie would be the co-parent.'

My mother had particularly enjoyed this theory. 'That'll be my amazing bisexual doppelgänger,' she'd commented sarcastically in a TV interview. And then, warming to the theme, 'She's a lovely woman – lives in Belgium – who's taken my name and had her face surgically corrected to match mine.' She ran a finger down the side of her face and brought it to rest coyly against the corner of her mouth. 'It's a nightmare really, the way that woman sullies my good lesbian name by sucking cock.'

I open the book. I'd forgotten that there was a tribute

in this edition. 'To Molly, who took me by surprise.' I decide to buy it and go up to the till where there's a sweet-looking girl serving. She has black chin-length hair pulled into two short plaits, and is wearing a pair of spangled glasses, a floral tea dress and wedge sandals. She looks through my books. 'You're travelling, huh?' she says, picking up the guidebook and grinning. 'Fantastic. Have you been to the States before?'

'Oh yeah, I've travelled around a bit.'

'Great.' She nods. 'Are you just staying in Seattle or are you seeing more of the West Coast?'

I look down. Sometimes my mind just goes blank, panicked, when called on for small talk. 'Oh, I have a few people I need to see in California, so I think I'm going to head down there.'

'Cool.' She puts a hand on my arm. 'You have to travel down the One, Highway One. It's really curvy – there are parts that might make you puke,' she laughs, 'but it's beautiful.

'Oh, I love this book,' she says, coming to the Tom Robbins. 'He's so great.'

I raise a smile. 'Yeah.'

She flicks through, punching in the prices, and then gets to *Maternities*. 'Oh my God!' she says. 'Have you read this before?'

I smile wryly. 'No.'

She laughs. 'God, this is just the most amazing book. It changed my life. Wait a minute' – she pauses – 'you're British, aren't you? That accent . . .'

I smile. 'Yep.'

She looks at me askance. 'So have you met Augusta Flynn?'

I laugh, hand over thirty dollars and start loading the books into a bag. 'Augusta Flynn, no. I just heard about this book from a friend and thought it sounded good.'

The girl's face falls. 'Oh.' Then she perks up. 'Do you know Angela?'

'Angela?'

'Yeah, I met this girl called Angela the other day in the coffee bar around the corner and she was British too. Are you two over here together?'

I laugh again. 'No, I don't know Angela.'

She touches my hand and smiles. 'Maybe you should get out more.'

3

Peanut butter and death

Putting a hand against the mirror to steady myself, I feel my fingers smear up and across the glass. I am standing in the toilets of a basement club in Seattle, leaning over a clogged sink, fighting the urge to retch. My head bowed, the nausea finally seems to subside and I prepare to celebrate conquest. Raising my arms tentatively above my head, still staring at the hair snaking around the plughole, I strike a pose that could be read in two ways. 'Victory,' it could say, or, 'There's a gun at my back.'

I look up, my mouth wide and coy, the expression I've used in the mirror since I was five. Gazing at myself all I can think is: Picasso. I look like a Picasso. My nose swims eerily to the side of my face, lips distorting like candy shoelaces. One of my eyes bulges, staring to the right, the eyeball clear in three dimensions, while the other looks into the mirror. This is it, I think. I'm cubist.

And staring at my face, I realise through the fog and

distortion that there's a level of inebriation at which everyone becomes fat Elvis. There's no dignity there, no repose. No pretence that you can achieve anything tangible, like crossing the room and refilling your glass. Just the eiderdown comfort of shame.

Reaching for the gum and deodorant arrayed at the side of the sink, I run my tongue around my mouth. It tastes of decay in there now, the first rot of decomposition. I can sense bacteria breeding, leeching off the alcohol and nicotine in thrilled symbiosis. Sticking my tongue out, I scrape at it with a clipped fingernail. Towards the back, it's covered in a thick layer of scum, like the mossy liver we used to be given for school lunches. I feel my gag reflex set in, rest both hands against the mirror and lean over. Retching, nothing comes. Oh well, I think, and stand up uneasily, a physical stutter. I'm like a Petri dish. Let them breed. I fold three sticks of gum into my mouth and pump my jaw mechanically.

The taste won't go away though. It's like death. I think of the pub lunch I'd had with my old schoolfriend Jason a few weeks ago in London and how he'd talked about a girl he'd picked up on a one-night stand. When it came to foreplay he'd ducked gamely between her legs before rearing straight back up. 'She tasted of peanut butter and death,' he said, 'peanut butter and death,' and his bottom lip had folded down, inside out, at the thought. Shovelling a forkful of peas into my mouth I had felt my nose retract and then laughed, 'What was her name?' and he had shrugged, and that somehow made it funny and I didn't feel bad for her, this girl whose identity had been reduced to the most basic thing: poor hygiene.

I throw my gum into the bin, and my tongue lodges in the roof of my mouth. The taste is still there – like the contents of an overflowing ashtray – but it's masked now by a thin wash of menthol. I spray on some deodorant, leaving stark white patches on my dress (red and white, I think vaguely, never send red and white flowers) and walk as confidently as I can through the cloakroom door.

The club has filled up, a heaving mass of bodies advancing and retreating like an army. Against the wall opposite the bar people are sprawled out on flat velvet cushions, eating the Moroccan food they serve here, picking noncommittally at rice and chicken. They stare at the dance floor with a blank-faced stillness, a strange kind of suspension.

As I walk through the dancing crowd, a man pulls me aside, reaches around and retrieves a string of packing tape from the back of his collar. It's covered in pills and he offers me a couple, holding my shoulders, his face so intense that I panic. Fuck, I think, and I see the image that always surfaces in these situations. Me falling down some stone stairs – medieval bricks, like those of a castle – toppling in slow motion, headfirst to the bottom, my face splitting apart and blood spreading around it, like a sped-up film of a poppy growing.

I push the man away, 'No, no,' and carry on to the bar. Leaning my face against it I feel relieved, the cold marble surface like a kiss. I stretch my left arm on there too and the cool stone makes me feel instantly better. Like morphine, I think.

I'm lying there for a few minutes, considering climbing onto the bar, pulling off my dress and stretching out like an effigy. A nerve has started twitching rhythmically in my right eyelid, and views of the dance floor flash past. In a corner close to where I'm sitting, a group of people are bobbing lazily to the music, petulant in their bleach-splashed designer jeans, slugging occasionally at bright bottled beers.

A glimpse of one of the girls (her hair tied in tight plaits, face sombre, cigarette held loosely at her side) reminds me of the party in Sydney that May, seven years ago. This girl and her friends look like the media types who'd been there that night – part of the same distant tribe. A people possessed by the surface of things, the tribe can assess an individual's worth at ten paces, based purely on their footwear, ostracising anyone who hasn't achieved just the right level of non-conformist conformity. The tribe knows best. I was only seventeen at that party, I think as I cling to the bar, desperate to stay upright. Seventeen.

A boy walks by with some fried food and I recall the smell of the burger place on Bondi Beach where I'd worked for eight months after arriving in Sydney. Burnt rubber and synthetic beef. All the kitchen staffers had hated that stench and the way that it clung to us, sweating constantly through our pores, as though our veins pumped the purest chip fat. It had been Shulie, one of my nylon-clad colleagues there, who had coaxed me along to the party. I remember her battling through the tired heat of a whole afternoon shift trying to convince me to join her.

'It's for the launch of this new magazine,' she had said, her voice rearing up in an antipodean roar as I emptied a large sack of chicken nuggets into the deep-fat fryer. 'It's called *Slit*, I think' – she had scrabbled in her bag for the invitation – 'some new women's magazine. Josh got the tickets, but he can't come.'

God, Josh, I think, picturing his face and standing up a little more confidently. Josh was Shulie's boyfriend, a lumpy-skinned thirty-year-old who had been trying to break into photography after years of managing the burger bar. There was something sickly about him, his pallor pasty, face a little bloated, as though his earthly purpose was to prove every nutritional warning about fast food. He'd quit the café before I arrived there and, ever since, Shulie had been supporting him on her grease-slave wage. Not that she seemed to mind. She would spend hours regaling me with stories of his searing wit, gentle hands and bewildering sexual staying power. 'It's like he has an engine,' she'd say, a low purring sound at the back of her throat as we stood side by side flipping the ground-meat patties. 'It's like he's fired by a special fuel.'

At nineteen, Shulie was sure that she and Josh would be married within the next few years, with at least three kids by the millennium. 'Do you really think marriage is a good idea?' I'd asked one day in December as we emerged from the fatty heat into the humidity of the street.

'Of course,' said Shulie, laughing as she pulled off her uniform cap. 'It's security, isn't it?'

With Josh covering a student fashion shoot that night, Shulie was desperate for company at the *Slit* party. Brought up in a distant suburb, she had come to central Sydney a year earlier in the hope of becoming a make-up artist. This would be a good chance to network. 'It'll be great,' she shouted as I liberated the last nugget into the boiling fat, 'there's free booze.' I nodded my acceptance over a panpipe rendition of 'Dancing Queen'.

Later, as we got off the bus in Paddington, I realised that free alcohol was a necessity. At just past eleven the venue was crammed with media people, all of them dressed in designer clothes, many air-kissing indiscriminately. I regretted wearing converse boots with my denim dress, I realised, almost as much as I regretted coming. Having decided to showcase her make-up skills, Shulie was in full plumage, her face a riot of colour. Green eye shadow vied with orange blusher and she had pulled a stern strip of pink lipstick across her mouth. 'How do I look?' she said nervously, sliding open a hand mirror. 'Striking,' I said, 'striking.'

Holding the invitations out to the doorman, Shulie barrelled into the room and started eyeballing the crowd, her head moving slowly from left to right, as if scoping out enemy targets. Leaning into me, she had shouted names while I smiled, clueless. 'I can't believe they're all here,' she said.

I looked over at the throng encircling the bar. 'We need drinks,' I observed, touching Shulie's shoulder. 'Shall I go and get some?' She nodded, silent. For the past ten seconds her eyes had been trained on an unlikely-looking middle-aged woman in pedal pushers and a padded headband.

Scything my way towards the bar, I decided to have a drink – a double – and then leave. I noticed a girl just standing up and bulldozed over to her empty seat.

Sitting down, sighing, I looked around. The competitive boredom in the room was incredible, most of the people so expressionless that it looked like they'd been mainlining muscle relaxants. I heard an Englishwoman talking to her companion. 'I can't believe that they're using this bar for their launch. This area's been over for so long now.'

Next to me, pouring the remnants of a large jug of cocktail into his mouth, was a boy, about mid-twenties, wearing an old T-shirt and sand-blasted shorts. As he slammed the jug down, I noticed that his eyelids were almost closed. 'What's that?' I said, nudging him.

He sputtered and looked at me. 'I'm sorry?' His voice, with its American edge, sounded genuinely apologetic.

'That's OK,' I laughed, 'I just wondered what you were drinking.'

He had smiled, shrugging. 'I think they call it a Blue Lagoon. I chose it for the alcohol content, but it was pretty good.'

'Do you want some more?' I motioned towards the

bartender and he brought over another pitcher and some tall glasses. I filled them both.

The boy's head had fallen forward, sun-bleached hair brushing across his cheeks. He looked ready to leave.

Downing my drink, I turned to him. 'So are you having a good time?' He didn't need to answer.

'This isn't really my scene,' he said, gesturing vaguely at the crowd. 'A friend of mine works here and he said to come, but I think I should have stayed at the beach.'

'Bondi?'

'Yeah.'

'You live there?'

'For now, yeah.'

'Me too.'

We sat in companionable silence as I downed a second glass. Finishing it, I felt a woman shove viciously at my stool. She slammed a hand hard onto the bar. 'I need a fucking drink.' Her other arm was clasped around a female friend. As the bartender started making some cocktails, she began talking in an overstated whisper. 'For fuck's sake,' she said, 'there's no one here. It's a washout. Did you see that girl with the blusher trying to talk to me? So embarrassing. She looks like she should be working on a make-up counter.'

Handed their drinks, the two women flew off, splashing me with a backwash of blue alcohol.

'Shit.' I patted at my chest with a tissue.

'Bitches,' the boy was laughing. 'What's your name?' He held out his hand.

'Molly,' I said. 'Molly.'

'Huh.' He stroked his fingers lightly across the back of my hand. 'I'm Tom. It's good to meet you.'

As he pulled his arm away, fingers curling back around the glass, I had looked up at him properly. I couldn't tell quite what it was, but something made me stare at him vacantly. It was his frame, I realise now, as I balance my head on my hands, elbows pivoting unsteadily against the bar. It was the musculature of that arm as it bent slowly, the skin ballooning, unexpected and graceful. He was much bigger than me, tall, and I remember wondering drunkenly whether I would ever need sunscreen out there on the burn of the beach, if I had him for shade. Was I no better than Shulie? I think now, as my right elbow skids forward and my chin falls hard onto the polished wood. Had it all come down to security? An epiphany based on his size? All the conversations that my mother and I had had since I was a kid about the bullshit of romance, the fallacy of male strength, the myth of girlish dependence – had they all been blown away by the mere presence of a well-muscled arm?

He had been talking as I stared, telling me about his work as a surf instructor these last few months, work he'd qualified to do while studying in San Diego.

'. . . just for a while,' he was saying, 'I don't want to be here too long really, maybe until July or something.'

I had snapped back in. 'Were you studying before you came here?'

He grimaced. 'Oh no. I finished college a couple of

years ago. I was working in the Peace Corps up until
February, on a project in Ecuador.'

'Wow,' I'd said, not quite sure what the Peace Corps
involved, but knowing that it sounded worthy. 'What were
you doing there?'

'Oh,' Tom had shrugged, 'it was a farming project,
trying to help out some people in this little village.
Renewable resources, that kind of thing. Small-scale
really.'

'It sounds great.' I was impressed by his conscience.
'Did you like it?'

'Well, it was OK,' he laughed. 'Right up until I plotted
my escape.'

'Your escape?'

'Yeah,' he said, his face still caught in a smile. 'After a
while I couldn't stand it really. I don't know. Some of the
projects set up by the Peace Corps aren't so well thought
through.' He sighed. 'I ended up spending most of the
time in my hammock getting tan. The people in the village had their own farming methods, what the fuck did I
know? I'd try to show them what I'd been taught and
they'd just come up with a much better way of doing it. It
was embarrassing.'

'Oh,' I said. I tried to smile encouragingly. 'But I bet
they appreciated your efforts.'

'Maybe. I felt really self-conscious, though. Like I was
some kind of imperialist. A bit of a' – he paused – 'well, a
bit of a Nazi, I guess. So I left.'

I started to refill Tom's glass. 'Just this one,' he said,

'then I should really get going.' He turned. 'Do you want to get the bus back to Bondi with me?' His eyes were pleading. 'Not for anything funny, you know, but it's probably not so safe for you to go back on your own.'

'I'll just have to check with my friend.'

Shulie was embroiled in conversation with a photographer as I approached, discussing a shoot he was assisting the next week. She smiled when I said I was leaving, nodded, kissed me goodbye.

I'd caught up with Tom in the doorway. 'You got everything?' he said.

I try to stand up straight again, the edge of the bar having dug a ridge across my stomach, and think of that night. I had moved in with Tom right then, had only been back to my studio flat once to pick up my suitcase. There's nothing like the cluttered hormones of the first three weeks of a relationship, I think, nothing like those heady jealous times. We had both been high on the speed of it.

Closing my eyes, I picture the cockroach that I had seen in the cloakroom a few minutes ago, scurrying through a puddle of water. A month after Tom and I had met, we had decided to get out of Sydney for a few days and had gone to visit a friend of his from college, Phil, who was living in a tiny village three hours away. Arriving at dusk, we had downed a bottle of vodka, getting quickly drunk before Phil's girlfriend offered us some acid tabs. It was the first time I'd tried it, but Tom had used them regularly through college and as the

chemical diffused on our tongues he had bundled me
into our rented van and driven the two of us out into
some woodland.

The ground was slippery with fallen leaves and twigs,
hard round seeds. Sliding down a hill we had come to a
ravine, and Tom had taken off his trousers and shoes to
paddle through the few inches of water. I sat down, legs
dangling over the edge, and tried to work out whether the
detritus of the woodland floor was running down the hill
towards me. There seemed to be a movement there
whenever I turned around, the first loosening of an ava-
lanche. Tom was skipping now, laughing and pulling me
in. I felt the water as it seeped through my canvas sneak-
ers and wondered whether this was what it would feel
like to be encased in a rain-filled coffin.

As Tom trudged through the mud of the ravine, I had
pulled away from him and started back to the van.
Getting into the front seat I had bent over to take off my
shoes before looking up and seeing them crawling over
the dashboard. They were everywhere, I realised, looking
around, a herd of huge cockroaches scurrying about.
Running over the humped steel of the hollow behind the
front seats, up the white walls, their brown metallic shells
glistening softly. There were about ten on the window
beside me, another throng bursting up over the back of
the headrest, plummeting through my hair. I thought of
the theology I had studied at A Level, the Old Testament
swarms of locusts, the plague on Job's house. This was it,
I thought, a plague on my house, and I watched

fascinated as they patrolled endlessly around the leather-clad steering wheel.

I had never been able to work out whether that swarm of cockroaches was real. An hour or so later, as I sat still gazing patiently at them, Tom had come back. As he opened the door to the driver's seat, they had seemed to stream from the van, a great pulsating horde of insects funnelling through. 'There were cockroaches,' I said to Tom, 'a huge swarm,' and he had laughed and stepped on the accelerator.

Could they have been real? I think, as I look up to see the barman approaching. I climb grudgingly onto a stool. It wobbles. 'What would you like?' he says, and I bite my lip, the bottles swimming in front of me, blending and separating. 'I don't know,' I say, thinking, shit, I really don't know, and he starts mixing a cocktail. He pours a variety of clear spirits into a long glass, filling it four fifths of the way, and then adds a splash of cranberry. 'There you go, I'll add it to your tab,' and he holds up my credit card – which I had no idea I'd given him – and I smile in what I hope is a knowing way, and nod.

Beside me at the bar is a group of men in black suits who have obviously come straight from work. They're all talking together, laughing and necking beer. From their conversation (which involves percentage points and share options and equity) I gather that they are bankers. Just as I decide that it's time to drag myself back across the dance floor, sit on one of the cushions, nurse my drink and consider getting back to the hotel, one of the men turns to me and sticks out his hand. 'I'm Michael,' he says, and his friends laugh, and I hold on to him, mute at first, before remembering my name. 'I'm Molly,' I shout.

And then everything changes and it becomes one of those odd, drunken nights, where nothing fits together and everything happens – and is remembered – in pieces. Broken shards of light. Discontinuous, disjointed, Super-8 scenes cut haphazardly together. Here we are on the dance floor, my left hand raised as I lean back on my stilettos and almost fall, Michael pulling me to him, his friends dancing around us. Here we are at the bar again, ordering tequilas. I'm explaining to one of Michael's friends how he should bite into the lemon after the shot and he keeps shouting, 'What?' We're drinking the tequila and ordering more, more rounds, until it doesn't taste so much of lighter fluid, doesn't taste of anything.

And then we're in a car, a red car, Michael's friend is driving and there are four of us squashed together in the back, laughing. Michael's hand is on my thigh and Seattle is flying by, we're going up a hill slowly, and speeding down. A few people are walking along the streets, mainly couples, but it's hard to make anyone out. Everything becomes blurred lights, like vision pared down to its most basic form, temporary blindness.

I jolt awake, my head hitting the back window, and realise that the car is stopping, pulling in. We get out and Michael's holding me, we're walking up a hill, very slowly, the effort more and more pronounced. Midway I realise that his friends have gone and it's just me and him, and he turns and kisses me and I think, it's OK. 'You're perfect,' he says, with all the romance that comes with tequila and an erection, and I smile.

We're at his door and he's struggling with the key but we get in eventually and both collapse on the sofa, kissing, hands everywhere, and suddenly we're naked and I'm laughing, really laughing, and he's smiling, kissing my neck and breasts, two fingers up me, and just as suddenly we're passed out.

The Blue Mountain

I take my stiletto off, inspect the torn skin, nod, and push my toes through the mud. It seeps between them easily, rippling and soggy, oozing up, over and around. A perfectly balanced family is walking through the rain towards me – a father, mother, young son and daughter – dressed in identical waterproofs, their pointed hoods speaking ever so slightly of Southern bigotry. I pull at my red dress, now wet and clinging, then hug my muddied legs to my chest. Glancing over at me the parents avert their children's gaze with a deft hand movement, almost as though I am naked.

The children peer back after a few seconds, curiosity piqued by their parents' concern, and I give them a grin and wave my muddy hands manically above my head. The gesture is somewhere between a welcome and an SOS. Scowling and with a just-audible hiss the father turns his children away again, steering them along the riverbank as fast as he can without slipping. I feel a stray drop of rain run in a rivulet along my collarbone, between my breasts, past my navel and down, rerouted on its way like a ball bearing in a pinball machine. My laughter follows the family until they are well past the slatted bridge.

I start spelling the alphabet out with the heel of my shoe, the letters dissolving in turn. The ground had been hard when I was last here, blue skies, good camping weather, and Tom had persuaded me that it might be fun to stay at Mount Rainier for a few days, an extra pit stop on the way to California. After hours of wrangling he had convinced me that it wouldn't be like the childhood camping trips with my mother – which had always involved a protest march – or the school excursion I had taken as a teenager, when I'd wound up in a tent with two stinking boys while a snowstorm raged through the Pyrenees. 'It'll be great,' he said, 'fucking great,' and he'd thrown me that huge, insidious grin of his, the deal-making grin he was so proud of. 'I can't believe that you don't like camping,' he said, 'it's going to be amazing. We can roast marshmallows.' He had paused. 'Or you can roast marshmallows anyway, like a girl,' he laughed, poking my right breast lightly, 'and I can go out and hunt bison or something.' He had growled enthusiastically, swinging his hips as he stood naked by the wall, showing off in that happy, boyish way and hammering his chest with his fists.

And I had laughed, almost won over, and pulled him back into our hotel bed by the hair – the hotel being the piss-drenched Landor in Seattle. And later, much later, we'd gone outside to a second-hand bookstore and he had bought me a first edition of a minor Kerouac novel and I, in my eighteen-year-old way, had simultaneously sworn, blushed, kissed and hit him. And at that moment he knew he had triumphed. There was no need for argument now, no need to ply me with drink or drugs or oral sex. We were going camping.

I look over at the car park where a group of people are unloading their van. Stickers crowd the glass of the back window, most depicting fish, and the side is painted with a huge yellow sun under the slogan 'Jesus wants you'. What for? I wonder. He has quite an entourage already. It reminds me of a story from an anthology of feminist fantasies I had read last summer, the account of a woman who wanted to assuage her Catholic guilt. The idea was that she would fuck her priest in the middle of his sermon, mounting him on the altar as the congregation looked on. This, she thought, would compensate for her years of repression. It sounded like a shaky proposition. I watch as a tanned man in tiny khaki shorts heaves equipment from the back of the van, until each member of the group is laden. Tripods, sleeping bags, tents, tent poles, saucepans, hiking boots, rain macs, Bibles, baked beans. Thermals, running shoes, paddles and a canoe. I look at the muddy uphill path to the car park, more sodden now than when my bus had pulled in. I contemplate my stilettos.

Tom had been prepared of course. He'd amassed a

huge range of camping equipment while travelling in Australia, and had picked up some supplies in Seattle too. On our way to a bar one evening we'd come to an outdoor adventure store and Tom had stopped wordlessly, motioning me in with a bow and a big swirling hand gesture, like a high-class doorman. Walking through the shelves I had been incredulous at the paraphernalia it was possible to buy. The freeze-dried food, the maps, the thirty varieties of thermal gloves. Tom had spent most of the time in the navigation section, squealing at each compass, before moving on to the next. After he had shown me a couple ('look how precisely it moves') I had started to question whether Jack Kerouac was worth a camping trip. Wasn't it Truman Capote who had said that Kerouac was just a typist? Watching Tom dance wild-eyed through the aisles, his gaze training ferociously on one gadget after another, I had found myself wondering whether any gift was worth the potential boredom of camping. Was a first-edition *Catcher in the Rye* worth this? What about a Cindy Sherman? The original manuscript of *Herzog*? A sketch by Egon Schiele? Sylvia Plath's unedited diaries – the ones only Ted Hughes had seen – were they worth this?

But hungover the next day, Tom had driven me off down Highway 90, whistling thinly for the first hour, until I had turned the radio on in desperation. Scrolling through the country stations I had come to Stevie Nicks, growling out a live version of 'Landslide', and we had both sung along, wilfully tuneless, our voices cracking in mock heartache. 'I took this love and I took it down,' we wailed, hands clasped to our necks, nails clawing at our faces, laughing.

As we drew near to Mount Rainier – its bulk looming in the distance – I had started to worry again, tense at the prospect of three days hiking and fishing. 'Isn't this what boy scouts do?' I said to Tom. 'One of those challenges they endure to win a special badge? Isn't this something that parents make their kids do on the premise that it'll make them better people? Happy camping' – I enunciated the syllables slowly – 'happy camping is just an oxymoron like friendly fire really, isn't it?'

Tom had sighed, put his hands up like claws and done a careless impression of a bear. 'Molly, stop analysing this, OK? We're just going to go and put up our tent, catch some fish for dinner and light a fire. It's the good life, it's getting back to nature. You'll love it.'

'If nature's so great,' I had said, 'then why does eighty per cent of the world's population choose' – I paused for added emphasis – 'choose to live in cities?'

Tom laughed. 'Jesus, do you have an answer for everything?' Then he'd cupped my left breast, raised his eyebrows and changed the subject. 'Those really are great breasts.'

I had stood, drink in hand, looking on sulkily as he put up the tent, hammering the pegs with his boot and pulling the fabric taut. 'It'll be like having a den,' he was saying, 'like when you were a kid and you'd make dens in the garden with boxes and blankets and shit.'

I had grimaced and taken a large mouthful of vodka. 'I

was an only child. My mother was crazy. I didn't make dens.' I laughed. 'Unless you count the time that I hid under my bed for two days and Ellie smuggled food up to me.' I paused for effect. 'I don't like dens. I like hotels.'

He had gone silent then, had given up for a while. When the tent was finished though he opened the flap at the front and gestured me in. Crawling through I found it glowing inside, the sun beaming bright through the cloth and the space lit up like an alien ship. He followed me and we lay there together, quiet for a while, the groundsheet not down yet, ants crawling through our hair. 'You like it, huh, admit it?' And I had shrugged and smiled.

Later he had insisted that we go for a hike, 'just to explore the place, come on,' and so we had sallied forth, him in his hiking boots, me in my flip-flops. Tom had pointed out details that I wouldn't have noticed – certain trees, flowers, the erosion of the riverbank, a tiny, shuddering bird pausing at a purple flower. He started climbing, fifty metres ahead of me, and I hurried along behind him, flip-flops flapping hard against my feet like half-hearted applause.

And as he pushed on higher and higher, smiling with satisfaction, pausing only to take big theatrical breaths, I had given up and sat down on a rock. It was too hard. I could feel the pressure expanding in my chest like a rogue airbag and I was panting uncontrollably. Too hard. Walking fast uphill was a pastime for masochists, I decided. It wasn't for literate, intelligent adults. Not for me.

Still striding along like a tour guide, a scout leader, Tom had looked back and made an arching hand movement, beckoning me on. I crossed my legs, tilted my head on my shoulder and lit a cigarette. Tom cupped his hands to his mouth and yelled, 'C'mon, Molly, get off your ass and get up here.' Closing my eyes I noticed that his tone was strikingly similar to that of my secondary school PhysEd teacher. I took a long drag, looked back and shook my head.

Within seconds he was down the hill, slipping slightly and steadying himself against a tree. 'What are you doing?' he said, leaning against the trunk and offering me a lazy smile. 'Come on, it's great up there. You'll feel much better if you keep going. Stopping makes it harder.' He skipped a few steps forward and went to put out my cigarette.

I pulled my hand away. 'Don't think so.' I took another drag. 'I don't mind waiting for you here, it's fine, but I just don't think all this climbing is really my thing.' I'd motioned down the hill. 'I think I'll just go and get my pad from the car and do some drawing.'

His smile had lapsed, muscles loosening so that he looked tired, slightly wrinkled, the shadow of what would one day be his jowls hanging about his face. I watched as his mood spread like tar across a beach. I'd seen this happen a few times now and knew the pattern. He would be leaden for hours, immovable.

And so the coaxing started, me running uphill behind him, Tom spiting me with the length of his strides. 'I didn't mean it,' I said, trying to get in front of him, 'come on,' and I pushed the hair off his forehead, tracing my finger along his bottom lip. 'I didn't mean it. I love it out here.' I took a long, overstated breath. 'Mmm, country air, it's great.' I danced on ahead of him as he stood there silent, contemptuous. 'I love the countryside,' I said, whirling around, my arms flung open. 'It makes me feel like Julie Andrews. Tarka the Otter. One of those rabbits in *Watership Down*.'

Tom had pushed roughly past me then and on up the mountain. 'The rabbits died,' he said without irony, and I had laughed and realised that my attempts to lighten the mood were fated to a sudden and embarrassing death. Mortification.

I set off back down, feet scuffing along the ground, dust gathering beneath my toenails. Looking around, I saw Tom receding in the distance until he was unrecognisable – far enough away that you couldn't make out the slight bandiness of his legs, the hairless bulge of his upper arms, the heavy width of his shoulders. Too far to make out the weight of his steps, the way his muscles stayed so strangely tense.

I sat by the river, a few metres from a bridge where happy couples kept stopping to take photos. I had a huge blister on my right foot and as I pulled at it a bubble of clear liquid oozed out. After draining it I pushed the flap of white saturated skin flat against my toe. I knew that Tom would be down in a few hours and that he would be fine. I'd seen these mute spells regularly over the last three months and I understood their ebb and flow. Seeing Tom in this kind of mood was like catching his disposition in negative. The angry white light of snow-blindness.

Three hours later Tom had come down the hill to find me sitting on the riverbank, an A4 pad balanced on my knee, drawing a tiny flower. He had pulled me up with a laugh – 'wouldn't you rather draw me?' – and had led me back to the tent, the fug having lifted. Kneeling on the ground, our backs stooped, he had pulled off my top and unhooked my bra. I had felt between his legs and unzipped him, pulling off his shorts, and we had lain down – this not being a space for gymnastics – and started. Biting, scratching, an uprooted tent pole later and my legs were around his back, ankles locked together. I started to push my index finger into him gently and a look of determination spread across his face, his mouth closing into a thin, concentrated line. Just as we were almost there, rocking, he shouted, 'Perineum!' and I laughed at this word we had discussed a few weeks earlier, a word that sounded so much like a flower. I crooked my index finger.

I push my stiletto heel through the mud in a lazy circle. Six years ago that had been the scene at Mount Rainier. That had been the situation. 'Damn my husband,' I say, and some of the Christians, who are passing on the way to a campsite now, look at me, worried. I grin, put on my stilettos and tear unsteadily down the bank, slipping a few feet as I run. 'Just passing through,' I shout over to them, waving hard.

5

Uncommon women

'I worry about Augusta.' Hattie takes a long drag of her roll-up and watches as my mother strides through the crowd, Ellie lagging a few paces behind her. It's Easter weekend 1983 and rather than celebrate with egg-shaped chocolate, Augusta has brought me to join the throng of women and children campaigning on Greenham Common. Earlier today the crowds had been swelled by journalists sent to record the women as they embraced the nuclear base, hands joined around the wire fence, singing the usual protest songs.

Now people are starting to disperse, distributing pamphlets, still singing. As she walks through the camp like a passing dignitary my mother's face is arranged in the fixed expression of concern and empathy that she saves for this kind of event. Retreating into the throng, shaking hands as she goes, I see reactions to her range from the jubilant hug of a young bald girl to the curled-lip distaste of a group of older women, dressed in long floral skirts.

I had watched this afternoon's protest from the edge of the camp, sitting in one of the makeshift shelters – plastic sacks balanced on bamboo – eating shortbread animals and playing patience. Augusta had planted me there as soon as we'd arrived, laying a new colouring book and pencils on the blanket in front of me. 'Happy Easter,' she'd said, kissing my hair lightly, 'you'll have more fun over here.' Last year she had brought me to stay at Greenham overnight and I had been woken at two am by the shrill alarm of screaming. Lifting a corner of our plastic sheeting I had seen a woman emerge through the darkness splattered with manure and pig's blood, a small group of armed guards standing to one side, laughing. She had been attacked by some residents who objected to the Common being occupied, in their words, 'by those fucking commie lesbians'. 'Slings and arrows,' my mother had said dispassionately, hustling me back into my sleeping bag, but I could tell she was worried that I had seen the shit these protestors attracted. She had touched me and Ellie quite tenderly then before disappearing towards the wire fence around the arms bunkers, a jagged pair of shears swinging awkwardly from her belt.

'I worry that Augusta will be remembered for those epigrams of hers, the funny comments,' says Hattie, and I watch as the lines on her face expand and contract, etched across her skin like a code. Esther nods, pulling thoughtfully on her cigarette. My mother had grown up with the two of them and often leaves them to look after me when she and Ellie are off campaigning.

'Yep,' says Esther, 'she'll probably end up the Dorothy Parker of academia, won't she? Another brilliant woman written off as a witticist.'

Hattie laughs. 'It's true.' Perched on the rug between Esther and me, she stretches her arms across our shoulders. 'She isn't going to be celebrated by the women's movement, that's for sure. They've hated her ever since she started stealing the limelight.' She grinds her cigarette into the ground and takes a slug from her hip flask, before offering it to me. I am staring at a girl about ten metres away who has the neatest plaits I've ever seen, tied at the ends with shiny pink ribbon.

I smile, pulling at a persistent knot in my hair. 'No thanks, Hattie.'

She shrugs. 'You don't like whisky, huh?' Hattie and Esther turn to each other laughing, the crevices deepening around their eyes.

'She isn't her mother's daughter, is she?' says Esther.

Hattie ruffles my hair and laughs. 'Certainly not. We could tell even as a kid that Augusta would grow up to be all about whisky and women, you know, Molly. It was a safe bet.' She squints out into the distance and I feel a brisk tug away from me as Esther pulls her arm tight around Hattie's waist. Hattie smiles. 'She was a total original from day one, wasn't she? That's why so many of the women here dislike her.' She pauses, watching as a long-legged bug dive-bombs Esther's hair. Hattie fishes it out carefully, letting its legs flail before it floats uncertainly away.

'Look at her,' says Esther, motioning over at my mother, who has almost disappeared into the throng. 'Augusta could never accept being part of the crowd. She's always been distinctive' – she pauses and smiles – 'superior, I suppose. She's no good with all this collective decision-making that they're so fond of.' Esther turns to Hattie. 'Can you imagine Augusta living in a commune?'

Hattie's head rocks back. 'It would be a dictatorship within days.'

I close one eye and peer shyly up at her. At eighty-one, Hattie has a presence almost as powerful as my mother's, and is well known in artistic circles as a painter of wild, colourful abstracts. Every time I see her she seems to get a little taller, more wiry, like a beanstalk stretching up into the sky. A couple of years younger, Esther is quieter, reserved, but she's always poised ready to help Hattie and come to her defence.

'Augusta grew up on your farm, didn't she?'

Hattie smiles at me. 'That's right, Molly.' She pauses. 'Has she told you about it?'

I shake my head, despite the garbled stories of sheep and pigs I've heard when my mother's arrived, half-cut, in my doorway. Hattie is a good storyteller and I like to listen to her almost as much as I do Augusta. 'No.'

'Oh well, it was just great.' A smile plays across her face as she grabs Esther's hand, clasping it to her chest. 'It was fabulous, wasn't it?'

Esther grins. 'A wonderful time.'

'You never met Augusta's parents, did you, your grand-parents?'

'No.'

They look at me intently, heads tilted, mirrored like bookends. 'Well, they were wonderful,' says Hattie. 'Her mother, Ann, was a great girl. Quite lovely. She came to work on our farm just after she'd found out she was pregnant with Augusta.'

'That's right,' says Esther, 'that's right. It was towards the end of the war, wasn't it?'

'Yes, it was before she married John – do you remember?' Esther nods and Hattie turns to me. 'She was so worried that her boyfriend John would be suspicious about the baby that she just started to panic. He'd been at home for a month in – what would it have been? – well, the winter of 1943, before shipping back out to fight. I remember Ann saying to me that they'd only slept together a few times. She was so worried.'

'God, I remember that,' says Esther. 'Her face wore this pinched look for months' – she sucks in her cheeks, puckering – 'months!'

'I know,' says Hattie, 'it was horrible. I wondered at the time whether all the worrying might affect the baby.' She takes another gulp of whisky and passes it to Esther. 'There were these rumours flying around at the time that women whose husbands had died in action were giving birth to deformed children, that their pregnancies were being disrupted by stress. Do you remember?' Esther nods. 'The cases of mental retardation in children were rumoured to have risen hugely.'

Hattie pauses to roll another cigarette, fingers moving with the deft grace of a spider. 'That was all we could talk about for months, wasn't it?' she says.

Esther strokes a finger across Hattie's hand. 'Absolutely. The two of us would lie in bed at night, Molly, and just talk and talk about the situation, running through all the problems of having this child in wartime, of looking after it. We were worried, but I think' – she pauses – 'I think we were really excited for her, weren't we, more than anything?'

'God, yes,' says Hattie, and she licks the cigarette paper with expert precision, puts it carefully in her mouth and hands me the lighter. 'Light it for me, Molly.' I oblige and she takes a huge gulping toke. 'That's great. It's always nicer to have someone light it for you.' She adopts an aristocratic drawl. 'Makes one feel like a lady.' Esther yelps with laughter, and Hattie punches her playfully on the arm. 'One does want to feel like a lady sometimes, you know, Esther. You're not the only girl in this relationship.' They shake briefly, wheezing, their eyes tearing up.

'Anyway,' says Hattie, shudders subsiding, 'where was I?' She pauses thoughtfully.

'The farm,' says Esther.

'Ah yes, the farm. So while she was pregnant with Augusta, Ann started working for us. The farm was down in Devon, south from here, and Esther and I had been living there a while.'

'About three years,' says Esther.

'That's right, about three years, and we had managed to cultivate all kinds of produce' – Hattie pauses – 'tomatoes, cabbage, potatoes, runner beans.'

'Animals,' says Esther.

'Yes, animals – chickens, cows, a big old bull' ('Magnus,' sighs Esther) 'and about twenty sheep. Ann looked after the cattle mainly.' Hattie plays with a lock of my hair, feeding it through her fingers. 'She was a natural actually, really wonderful.'

'Well, you would say that,' crows Esther, her voice teasing. 'You had a bit of a crush on her, didn't you?'

'No!' Hattie pretends to look affronted before falling forward, laughing. 'Esther and I had this running joke that I was in love with Ann because I always used to comment on how good she was at milking the cows. Sometimes I just used to stand and stare at her as she tended them, and Esther would creep up behind me and whisper, "Sorry, she doesn't like women" before running away, laughing. Not that I think she would have been bothered by me watching.'

'Oh no,' says Esther. 'She was a very open-minded girl.' She pauses. 'Just not open-minded enough for you.'

Hattie laughs and swats at Esther. 'You're so naughty!' she says. They giggle softly, leaning against each other and supping from the hip flask.

Hattie blows a billow of smoke over my head and pulls me tighter. 'So we were talking about Ann. That's it. Anyway, so when Ann first came to us she was living with her parents about five miles away, and she would walk to us from their house every day.'

'Oh yes,' says Esther. 'It seemed to be a terrible winter that year. I don't know whether it was just the fighting, the fact that the war was dragging on, but the cold just seemed to go on for ever.'

'That's right,' says Hattie, 'it was freezing. Sometimes Ann would arrive at the door soaked to the skin, and the next few days she would have to work through a cold or flu – she spent the entire winter with a red nose. We would always offer her a bed.' ('Of course you did,' says Esther, nudging Hattie. 'Our bed.') Hattie laughs. 'And we said that she could visit her parents on her days off, but she used to say that it would be too much trouble.'

'Yes,' says Esther. 'She never wanted to impose.'

Hattie nods. 'Too polite for her own good. In the end, though, her parents forced her hand. A few months into her pregnancy her father found out about it – I don't know how – and he just went mad. One night, it must have been two am or later, she turned up at our door with her shoulder all bent out of shape, dislocated, and a gash down her face.'

'It was awful, wasn't it?' says Esther. She leans over to me. 'It went septic, Molly, never really healed properly.'

'Yes,' says Hattie, 'she had this raised scar all along the left side of her face, you've probably noticed it in photos.' I nod. 'It looked really painful.' She pauses, pinching her arm. 'So after that she stayed with us.'

A girl approaches with leaflets about upcoming

protests. 'We'd love you to come,' she says, pushing some pamphlets at Esther.

'No thanks,' says Hattie, and when the girl persists, she swipes at her hand, flicking it away. 'I said no thanks.'

The girl walks off grumbling, before turning to us again. 'Give peace a chance,' she says, voice wavering somewhere between sarcasm and sincerity, and Hattie and Esther laugh, grimacing.

Hattie leans towards me. 'These young girls, Molly, they don't have the courage of their convictions. They just want to feel part of something bigger than they are.'

Esther nods. 'They want an identity,' she says.

Hattie laughs and gives her a fluttering kiss on the cheek. Then she turns back to me. 'Don't get me wrong, Molly. I agree with the peace movement but some of these girls, with their vegetarianism and ugly clothes, they just bore me. It's the older women who are really radical.'

She leans over and opens our cool box, now fairly tepid, scrabbling inside for something to eat. After a few seconds she emerges with a chicken sandwich, its contents hanging limp out of the bread. 'Sorry,' she says, as I inspect it at arm's length, 'that doesn't look so good.' She sighs, bringing her face close to mine. 'Your mother asked me to give you dinner though, so if you could just try and eat a few bites.' She tickles me, hands squeezing under my armpits. 'We'll go to a pub for lunch tomorrow, OK? We can have a nice hunk of steak.'

I nod, laughing, and bite into the bread, sucking it to the sides of my teeth as it melts forlornly.

'So we were talking about Ann,' says Hattie. 'Oh yes.' She tilts her head back, thinking. 'John came home – when was it? – I guess about May 1944, a couple of months before Augusta was born, and he and Ann got married.'

'Was it a big wedding?' I say.

'Oh no, nothing special,' says Hattie, 'just a quickie at a register office.'

'It was lovely,' says Esther.

'It was fun.' Hattie nods. 'Good fun. Luckily it turned out that Ann's worries came to nothing. John was shocked about the pregnancy' ('Do you remember that scream he let out?' says Esther – Hattie laughs) 'but he seemed thrilled. I remember him saying that everything had fallen into place. He'd been spared the slog of pregnancy, the nine-month waiting game, and the whole process had been shrunk down to two months.'

'Those months before Augusta was born were brilliant, weren't they?' says Esther. 'I just remember John leaning against the barn, smoking, grinning from ear to ear.'

'Yes,' says Hattie, 'they were both so happy. We'd offered John a job on the farm as soon as he arrived back, and he jumped at it. It was good for us, because he took over all the manual work that Ann was too pregnant to manage.'

'So what happened when Augusta was born? Did she help out on the farm?'

Hattie laughs. 'Not exactly, no.' She looks out into the crowd, eyes watery. 'Right from the first day it was obvious that Augusta was' – she pauses, and Esther interrupts – 'quite different.'

'That's right,' says Hattie. 'There was this incredible' – she searches for the right word – 'well, intensity about her, she never seemed to blink. And her face was always so serious – handsome. It was strange. You don't see many handsome babies.' Hattie strokes my arm. 'She wasn't called Augusta when she was first born, you know, Molly.' I look up at her, surprised. 'No. That was the name she gave herself when she was about seven, after I'd taken her to see some of Augustus John's paintings up in London. She was christened Susan, which never seemed quite right. Too feminine. I remember catching Ann and John in a quiet moment once when she was a baby, cradling her, and they both had this look which was a mixture of surprise and love and' – she rummages in the cool box and pours me a glass of milk – 'well, panic really.'

'She just seemed so different to them, didn't she,' says Esther. 'She didn't even look anything like them.'

'Oh yes,' says Hattie. 'Neither of them was good-looking. They had a' – she pauses – 'a dignity, I suppose' – Esther laughs – 'but they were ugly really. John had an underbite, which made his bottom row of teeth stick out, and his nose was pointy, much too long. Ann had beautiful skin, really milky and clear, but her eyes were set too wide apart and she had such thin lips that her mouth just looked like, well, like a slit in her face.'

'Like this,' says Esther, pushing her lips together until they turn white and disappear. She smiles.

Hattie sighs. 'I loved the two of them' – she turns to Esther – 'they were our family, weren't they, but I have to admit that they weren't pretty people.'

She pours two glasses of wine from a screw-top bottle and takes a sip. 'Mmm,' she says, 'vinegar.' She and Esther clink the glasses together, each taking a gulp. 'Oh well,' says Hattie, 'we were talking about Augusta, weren't we. Do you remember what she was like as a kid, Esther?'

'Of course, of course. She was cherubic, wasn't she, a very beautiful child, but' – she yelps with laughter at a memory – 'completely bizarre.'

'I'll say.' Hattie is laughing too. 'Christ. She was really odd. Very, very bright. Since Esther and I never had kids I wasn't quite sure how fast a child should develop, Molly, quite what the usual rate was, but even I noticed that she was forming sentences quickly, picking up a vocabulary. I used to sit her on my knee and read stories with her, like I do with you, not children's books, but proper novels – *Jane Eyre*, *Moby Dick*, *Martin Eden* – and by the time she was two, she was following words, shouting out phrases. She was obviously very' – she pauses – 'perceptive. By the time she toddled off to school she could read perfectly. The teachers just didn't know what to make of her.'

'She used to get into lots of trouble, didn't she,' says Esther, 'with teachers not believing her stories, thinking she was too adult for her age.'

'God, yes. I remember her first teacher, when she was five, sending Augusta home after she said that she'd read

Little Women the night before. They always thought she was telling lies.'

Esther rises slowly to her feet, stumbling a little. 'You carry on with the story,' she says, laying a hand on Hattie's shoulder. 'I'm just going to go and get washed and ready for bed.'

'OK,' says Hattie, 'I'll see you in a moment.'

Esther walks over, kneels down and kisses me on the cheek. 'Good night, Moll.'

Hattie turns to me as Esther retreats, patting the ground between her legs. I go and sit there, snuggling my back against her.

'Of course,' says Hattie, 'we didn't know how to treat Augusta either, we were all quite concerned about it, the responsibility of looking after this kid. Every time one of her school reports came in, each time it was broached that Augusta might be quite gifted, Ann and John just reacted with shock. This prodigy had landed slap bang in their lives, and they were like this' – I hear her jaw click and look round to see Hattie open-mouthed, tonsils silhouetted against her throat. 'By the time Augusta was about seven or eight' – she hugs me tighter – 'about your age, they'd given up trying to tell her what to do, trying to discipline her. She was just such a wilful child,' she sighs, 'that it was really pointless to try and get in her way. Once they'd realised that, Ann and John acted as caretakers really. They made sure your mother was clothed and fed, well looked after, but other than that they left her to her own devices. It was a good decision, I think. Augusta was always a wild kid, a bit of a scavenger. She liked being out on her own. She knew what she wanted to do.'

'So did she live with you until she went to Cambridge?' It's getting chilly and Hattie starts rubbing my arms.

'Oh no.' Hattie smiles. 'I don't think I could have coped with that. Just after I turned fifty I was given a big retrospective in London which brought me a lot of attention, a few new collectors.' She pauses. 'It was a great time really and Esther and I decided that it would be best for us to buy somewhere quiet for me to work, somewhere by the sea. Along with the money from the exhibition I had also been left quite a large sum in my mother's will and so that bought us our house on the coast in Hove. We left the farm for Ann and John to look after. Augusta was about ten, I suppose. After that she just used to come and visit me for occasional weekends or a week here and there in the school holidays.'

Hattie roots around in her bag, finds a brush and starts pulling it through my hair, concentrating on a particularly matted clump. 'I remember a great visit while she was at Cambridge when she came to stay for about a fortnight. She turned up on our doorstep after midnight, about three in the morning, shouting up at the windows, saying that she'd been suspended, rusticated, from university. The next day she told us what had happened, explained that she'd been dressing as a boy and eating with some friends at an all-male college. It was a huge scandal at the time, big news on campus. The college was worried that it was a challenge to their authority, that it suggested a new permissiveness at Cambridge, and I guess it did really. Although their idea that Augusta had been having sex with the boys was obviously a bit wide of the mark. She just liked male company. I remember Augusta talking about the Cambridge suffragettes and saying that they were all far too bluestocking and middle-class for her. She wanted to meet wild people, radicals, people with her sense of abandon, and I guess that there were more boys like that at Cambridge than girls. It was the men who ran all the major political societies. She felt lonely as a girl, I think. Peerless.'

A squabble is breaking out by the wire fence, a tiny, bespectacled woman haranguing one of the guards. As she shouts, he looks straight at her, face stolid and impassive. This goes on for a few minutes, the guard's mouth finally distorting, lips rolling back on bared teeth. The woman carries on, oblivious, her thin, sinewy arms held out, hands balled into fists. Suddenly, unexpectedly, the guard raises his hand and lets it fall, swatting the woman away with the graceful, fluid curve of a dancer. The whole scene plays out like a rehearsal. The woman falls to the floor, equally graceful, and a hive of people surround her.

Hattie and I look on intently, her sipping at wine, me at my milk. 'These women don't realise what they're up against,' she says, peering at the bottom of her glass before picking up the one left by Esther. She takes a gulp. 'They have no idea. I mean, Molly' – her voice is beseeching – 'I think the peace movement is important, maybe even essential. It would be great if the world was a more caring place, safer, without the fear that we're all going to be annihilated by whichever nut they have in the White House or Kremlin at the time. That's reasonable. Absolutely.' She kisses me gently on the cheek. 'But I don't expect men to lie back and give up without a fight. I mean, men have biological imperatives as strong as ours.'

She pulls gently at a tangled knot of my hair, trying to tease it apart. 'It's crazy,' she says. 'The fact is that women are always going to be more nurturing than men. We're built with wombs, we're built to incubate, to care for other people. Our sexual nature is receptive, accommo-dating. Men' – she pauses, and sighs – 'well, men are something very different. Men were made to penetrate. Sex, whether it's rape or love or plain unsullied fucking – I'm sorry to use that language, Molly – but it's nothing but a way for a man to colonise a woman's body. Both in the act, and then in the possible consequences.'

She pulls me tighter. 'So have you ever slept with a man?' I say.

Hattie looks at me for a moment as if she's never seen me properly, as if I'm a stranger, and her eyes widen with surprise. 'You're eight years old,' she says, shaking me and laughing. 'Eight years old! What kind of a question is that?' She pauses. 'I'm sorry, I shouldn't have been talk-ing to you about these kinds of things.'

We both sit there enjoying the warmth, and I can feel her rocking slightly with a laughter that rises up from her stomach. 'I can't believe you asked that. You're very naughty. But since you did' – she pauses – 'and since I like the fact that you're the kind of kid who'd ask, then yes, I have slept with a man.'

I look around and up at her. Hattie is staring out through the teeming people. 'I did sleep with a man a long time ago.' She pours the last of the wine into her glass and takes a mouthful. 'I need a drink to talk about this. Christ, I can't remember the last time that I spoke about Abel Mazursky. It certainly can't have been during the last few decades. No. Not for a long time.'

She lifts me up under the armpits and sits me down next to her. 'There you go. Are you sure you want to hear about this?' I nod. 'I mean, I could just read you something.' She looks through the books that Augusta has left for me – *Middlemarch*, a collection of Adrienne Rich poetry and Augusta's own latest treatise, *Misogyny: A case study*. 'Maybe talking about Abel Mazursky would be the best idea.' She looks at the books again. 'Yeah. I think so.'

'So who was Abel Mazursky then?' I ask, excited. 'Was it someone you just slept with once?'

She laughs. 'What are you trying to imply, Molly Flynn? Are you trying to say that I was a slut in my youth, a floozy?' She pulls a roll-up from her top pocket and lights it. 'No, he wasn't someone that I just slept with once. No. He was my first love, I suppose. The first person I couldn't shake off. One day you'll meet someone like that, Molly – someone who seems more special than they really are.

'I met Abel when I was eighteen. It was' – she pauses to

think – '1920, and I was living in Paris with my parents. You probably don't know this, I can't think that Augusta would have told you, but my parents were very important people in Britain at the time, very high up in the establishment. My father had been sent to Paris to work as a diplomat, and we were living on the Left Bank, having a fantastic time. Post-war Paris was brilliant, a ball, and there was a huge, artsy expat scene that everyone wanted to be a part of.

'Anyway, being young, rich and gorgeous,' she giggles, and suddenly I can imagine her at eighteen, sitting at a table outside a café, hands fluttering, animated as bird wings, a beautiful dress swaying around her, 'it wasn't difficult for me to finagle my way into that scene. Within months of arriving in Paris my life had become a regular whirl of absinthe, poetry and dancing. It was quite, quite wonderful.'

She reaches down for my hand and clasps it tight. 'So one day I was walking along the street with some of my new friends, discussing our plans for the evening in broken English, when a book dropped through the sky and landed in front of me. A collection of Rimbaud. I looked up, worried that this might be like the plague of frogs I'd heard of recently – a hail of great literature – and saw a young man standing at an upstairs window in the house next to us. "I've hurt my leg," he called, "could you bring my book up to me?" And so I told my friends to carry on, that I would meet them later, and started climbing the stairs.'

She begins packing away the cool box. 'Do you want anything else? I think there's another chicken sandwich if you're hungry.' I shake my head. 'Don't blame you. Anyway, I didn't come down from that room for two days. It turned out, of course, that the man at the upstairs window was Abel and that he'd neither hurt his leg nor accidentally dropped the book.' She lowers her voice. 'It was all part of a nefarious plan.'

'So what was he like? What did you like about him?'

'Where do I start?' She pauses and looks up. 'Abel was a thinker, really, a philosopher – he liked to figure things out. He was a New York Jew who had signed up and fought in the First World War. He was supposed to take advantage of a special scholarship he'd been given when he arrived back in America, a bursary to study literature at a college in upstate New York. He used to say to me though that studying seemed a little too' – she pauses to think – 'a little too sedentary, I guess, after the war. He couldn't really see how he could move from something so momentous to something that would involve picking through the minutiae, the finer symbolism, should I say, of Shakespeare's sonnets. It all seemed too – I don't know – diminutive to him. So he decided to settle in Paris and live the wild life for a while.'

'And so you started seeing each other?'

'Oh yeah, we were together pretty much all the time after that first meeting. He was making a living teaching English to rich Parisians, and he would meet me for lunch after the three hours of lessons he gave in the morning, and then I would be with him until dawn.' Hattie's arm circles my waist and she squeezes tight. 'At first I managed to convince my parents that I was just staying out at late-night parties, but after a few of their friends said that they'd seen me around town with a dark-haired man they cottoned on to the situation. My father – who was huge and not noted for his tact – followed me to Abel's apartment one day, rang the doorbell, came in and told Abel that we either had to split up or he would have to marry me. It was obviously a bid to make us end the relationship, since my father certainly didn't want me, his beautiful blonde daughter, marrying a Jew, but it backfired. Abel got down on one knee and asked me to marry him, and I said yes. My father stormed off' – she pauses, laughing – 'and we had sex on Abel's kitchen table.'

'Had you had sex before?'

Hattie looks at me. 'You and your questions, young lady. I'm shocked. But yes, we had had sex before. We'd had sex the first day that we met and every opportunity after that. He was a fantastic lover with – how shall I say this?' She pauses diplomatically. 'Well, there's no good way to say it really. He was huge.'

She sighs, and smiles, and for a moment her face is girlish. 'So after our engagement party Abel started working all hours and we scraped together enough money to buy a tiny apartment. My parents had agreed that they would pay for a small wedding and all the furnishings we needed for the place. We were ecstatic. I remember sitting with Abel in cafés and bars, just pawing at him for hours, desperate to get him home. He was gorgeous, black hair falling over his temple above these wide brown eyes. All his features were really pronounced and he had great symmetrical veins that ran along each of his biceps. I would spend hours just looking at him naked – the triangle of muscle around his pelvis, the tight, sculpted lines of his calves. It's safe to say that I was obsessed with him. I think he felt the same.'

She goes quiet for a while.

'So what happened?' I say, almost whispering. 'Did you divorce?'

She laughs, her mouth a sour half-smile. 'No, not quite. One day we were over at our apartment, getting ready to move in, painting our bedroom an eggshell blue. We had been there all day, just painting and having sex – I remember burning our skin as we knocked over a tin of paint, rolling around in it, worrying later about the imprints on the floorboards. Anyway, when it came to early evening I left to meet a friend, and Abel stayed on, just finishing up, painting the final inch where the walls joined the ceiling.'

Hattie starts to plait my hair, thinking.

'As far as we know he just fell off the ladder and broke his neck. When I came into the apartment the next morning I found him lying on the floor, his lips blue and the tin of paint spilled all over him.'

We see Augusta approaching with Ellie, waving to us before stopping to speak to a few people. Hattie gets up and starts packing away our rug and glasses. 'Come on, Molly.'

I shake out my blanket and fold it carefully. 'So you never slept with a man after that?'

'No, that was enough of men for me. I met Esther a couple of years later when I was studying in Dublin, and she was so charming, so funny that she really made me face up to something different. Not that I don't think it would have worked out with Abel, it might well have. I remember thinking that it was ironic that he had been through a whole war – had been shot at, charged with bayonets,' she laughs, 'or maybe not – and it had come to that. Slipping off a ladder. At least it would have made him laugh.'

Augusta hovers five feet away and Hattie reaches down to hug me. 'I worry about your mother,' she says.

6

The life model

'Y'all listening back there?' The bus driver locks eyes with me in his rear-view mirror, my lips turning up in a self-conscious smile. He clears his throat, choking forth a wad of saliva, and spits it into a Burger King cup. 'Because you know what happens to people who don't pay attention, don't you, folks?' Everyone nods wearily. 'They fail my test.'

He starts in on another of his monologues. 'So, people, here's the thing. I was driving along one day, just me and another bunch of passengers, when I noticed something small and pink lying beside the barrier on the edge of the freeway.' He points to his left. 'Just there. I was going fast as usual, trying to get the people where they needed to go, and at first I couldn't make out what it was, but' – he pauses – 'I'll let you have a guess. What do you think it was?'

There is intimidated silence, a spatter of shrugs.

'A pig,' he says. 'A pig!'

I glance out at the approaching sign: 'Irwin County: Grass Seed Capital, USA'. Quite a boast, I think.

'So I stop the bus' – the driver keeps talking, as relentless as he's been for the past few hours. 'I get out and go over to stoop beside the thing. It's cute, you know' – he catches my eye again – 'you still laughing?' I grin, accommodating. 'And so I take the piggy home with me to the wife.'

He stops for a moment and, when it feels safe, I hunch down in my seat and stare through the window. The sky is dense today, a canopy of white clouds distending low over the mountaintops ahead. Along the freeway's central reserve groups of teenagers in black plastic ponchos are picking up rubbish with clawed sticks. Signs trumpet Oregon's youth litter partnerships. Beyond them, in another field, a flock of tiny birds has gathered on an irrigation pipe that runs through the land. Every few seconds one of them flies an inch or two into the air before plummeting back to the pipe, as if simply making a point.

The driver is grumbling mildly now as we catch up with the only other vehicle on the road, a van creeping along at thirty miles an hour. The trailer that it's towing holds a blue portable toilet, creaking vulnerably from side to side, anchored with a collection of ropes. I wonder, briefly, what it's like to be the driver for a toilet firm and just how responsible you're expected to be. If that Portakabin upended, rolling clumsily across the freeway, its contents spilling out over the Oregon landscape, would the driver have a duty to clear it up? Who would blame him if he simply gathered his strength, pushed the toilet into the nearest gutter and abandoned his home state for ever?

'Jesus Christ.' The driver is panting now, slamming his hands on the steering wheel as we veer to a halt. Despite the delay I am pleased for the break in his latest monologue. He has been regaling us with his well-rehearsed stories since Portland, humiliating anyone who doesn't meet his gaze or laugh during the right pauses.

Closing my eyes, I curl uncomfortably on the seat, covering my legs with a denim jacket, ankles balanced on the far armrest, feet dangling in the aisle. The two girls behind me have been quiet so far, flicking zealously through fashion magazines, but as I drift off I hear one of them break out in asthmatic laughter, like an excitable long-distance runner.

'I can't believe I hadn't told you that.'

'I can't believe it either.'

They start whispering urgently as I fall asleep and I am woken a while later by their howls. Glancing at my watch I shift my head away from the damp patch of drool that has spread over my seat and think about the dream I've been having, a pregnancy dream. These recur quite frequently, usually when my belly is bloated after a big meal, sitting in my hands like a medicine ball. As always, in this one, I had found out about the pregnancy very late – eight months down the line. The realisation had hit me while out skiing, my centre of gravity more than a little off balance. It was a breach birth, one month premature, and I found myself stirruped on the hospital bed, Ellie holding my hand. 'Molly,' she was saying, 'just try to remember who the father could be.'

Racking my brains and pushing, I just couldn't work it out. 'I've been drunk a lot lately,' I said, and Ellie nodded sympathetically. 'That's probably why I didn't realise.'

'Try to think,' she says softly, and I pant in reply.

'There was that boy from school who I slept with, and' – I am pushing, pushing – 'and another boy at a party.' I gasp.

I'm still trying to work it out later when Ellie's gone and the baby lies beside me, pawing the glass of its iron lung. It is bug-eyed, too small to cuddle, but taking it out of the case I hold it loosely to my breast. Puckering its lips it tries hard to suck, but there's nothing there. Instead the baby bites down on me, clenching, and I cry out with pain. Looking down I see blood.

The girl behind me is still laughing, yelping. Peering through the slit between the bus seats I see that she is lank-haired, about eighteen, and is sitting next to an attractive, pink-cheeked blonde. From their accents I realise that they are British too.

'You know what I'm talking about, don't you? The tiny white vein that runs from the head to the shaft?'

'I know the one you mean.' The girl is kicking uncontrollably at the back of my seat, her laugh a frenzied whoop. 'So you were giving him a blow job,' she is saying, 'and the vein ruptured.'

'Yeah,' says her friend. 'I was just under the covers doing my thing when I heard Joe sort of yelp, like this' – she lets out a strange seal bark – 'and I felt this tiny wet spurt against my face.' She pauses, laughing. 'I thought for a moment that, you know.'

Her friend pauses. 'No. You didn't think he'd come?'

She laughs, slightly embarrassed. 'Well, yeah. So I came up from under the covers and saw that Joe was sort of shaking, he'd gone completely white. I put my hand up to my face and I saw that it was covered in blood, dripping, and I screamed.'

Glancing back, I see her shaking.

'Having a good time, girls?' Their laughter slows as the driver stares at them. 'Joke you'd like to share?'

They shake their heads, tears sweeping across their cheeks. 'Well, that's a pity,' he says. 'I would have liked to have heard a story from the two of you.' He sighs. 'Anyway, we're coming into the bus station now, so it just remains for me to congratulate you on being such a good crowd today. Tips are welcome, and if any of you would like to hear the end of my pig story, then you'll just have to buy a ticket back to Portland.'

The bus creeks through Eugene and into the Greyhound lot on East Tenth Street. I hike my backpack from the overhead locker, pick up my portfolio, knot my jacket around my waist and climb down the steps. I give the bus driver a weak handshake.

'Hope you enjoyed the trip,' he says.

I smile. 'Yeah, great, thanks.'

The weather is much better here, brighter. I stand in the sun for a moment watching as people exit the bus, scurrying away, purposeful.

I put on my sunglasses and sit heavily on my bag. The map in the guidebook shows that I'm in central Eugene and suggests that 'Although short of tourist attractions, the city is a great place to visit. There's cheap local accommodation with easy access to the weekly markets and outlying nature trails. Just book a room, don some tie-dye clothes and find out why Ken Kesey and his Merry Pranksters made Eugene the HQ for the hippy revolution!' I look around. Not a hippy in sight. Just a group of students milling around outside a bookshop across the street, dressed in jeans, University of Oregon sweatshirts and waterproof walking jackets. The American campus uniform. I fold down the corner of the page.

I had originally planned this as a short trip – a week ideally, two at most. Fuelled by vodka and trite love songs on the radio, I had booked the Internet's cheapest West Coast flight, which happened to be to Seattle. Afterwards I had sunk into a bath, the temperature unchecked and scalding, a pint of vodka cranberry at my elbow. I decided vaguely that I would bus straight through to California, visit Tom and fly home. Lying back, tears sloping grace-fully past my chin (watching them hit the water I began to laugh), I reasoned that it would be the cleanest way to end things. I could check on Tom, exchange divorce papers and leave. Back to London. Decision made, I had vanished beneath the water, surfacing to sing paeans to freedom – my voice emphysema-croaky – the encore a rendition of 'Holiday' that my wizened hands applauded long and hard in a cold puddle of bath water.

I follow a few people into the next street. At the far end is a deli, its storefront lined with bright boxes of fruit. Glinting enticingly in the light, they seem slightly less tempting as I draw closer. I scan a tray for the most palatable apple, pluck it out and head inside.

I haven't eaten anything since leaving Seattle, which – including my stop at Mount Rainier – was over twenty-four hours ago. I grab a V8 and Diet Coke from the fridge and look around for something that might stop the nag of hunger. Stacked up along the inside wall is more wilting produce, displayed beneath a bright red 'Fully Organic' sign. Other than that, there's just a fishbowl of beef jerky, the glass dappled with mildew. I peer in at the dark, smoked meat, curling up and away from me, and settle for the apple.

Behind the counter is a man of about thirty, tall, broad, his stomach resting gratefully on the worktop. 'That all?' he says.

'Do you do sandwiches?'

He shakes his head – 'Nope' – and I hand over my cash. He slowly counts out the change.

'Actually,' I say quietly, not wanting to distract him, 'do you know of a cheap place to stay?'

He licks his lips absent-mindedly, tongue crawling over them like a slug, and sighs. His face is paunchy, childlike, his speech deliberate. 'Place to stay, huh?' He pauses thoughtfully. 'There's a motel just next to the Greyhound station, that where you've come from?' He motions casually to the right. I nod. 'Timbers, it's called. That the kind of thing?'

I shrug. 'I suppose so. I just came into town and thought that it might be a good place to settle for a few weeks.' I pause. 'Maybe a month.' Saying this I feel a pinch of surprise, eyebrows jumping towards my hairline.

He smiles broadly, turning so that his shiny plastic name tag, 'Arnold', catches the light, blinking at me. 'You're darn right there,' he says. 'This is a great place. I've lived here since I was born and it's the finest city in the world.' He leans over the worktop and I catch the smell of jerky on his clothes. 'My mom took me to Disneyland once, you know, California, and I cried all three nights.'

His enthusiasm is intimidating. I smile, impatient. 'OK, so it's just beside the Greyhound station then?'

He nods vigorously. 'That's right. Or if you do want to stay longer you could have a look at some of the summer leases.' He points at a corkboard propped in the far corner next to a box of stunted cucumbers. 'Some of the students advertise for people to live in their houses over the summer, and it doesn't usually cost much. I think most of the places are gone now, but there might be something left.'

I go over and kneel beside the board. Along with ads for second-hand computers and bikes ('ten years old, no wheels, reliable') are two for housing. 'Summer tenant needed for laid-back group house. Must be non-smoker, non-drinker, Buddhist. Must be clean and tidy. No dreadlocks, preferably no hair. Must be female.' Laid-back, I think. The second sounds more promising. 'Live-in housekeeper needed for large house on Hendricks Hill, half an hour's walk from downtown. Light cleaning in return for rent-free living. No contract. Spacious room. Men only need apply.' There is a name and address at the bottom.

I take the pin from the ad. 'Do you know anything about this one?' I say, and Arnold casts an eye over it, mouthing the words as he reads. Coming to the end, he laughs.

'Sure, I know him.' He points at the name on the paper, holding it up for me. 'Charles Carruthers the third. He's a funny old guy, must be about seventy now. He's been in this town for ever – has a couple of huge houses up on the hill, one he lives in and one he rents out.' He takes a long gulp of air. 'Strange guy. My mom's a hairdresser and she tells me lots of rumours about him. I heard he shot his neighbour's dog when it pooped on his driveway.' He shrugs. 'He's always been fine with me though.'

'So you think it's worth a try?' I point to the 'men only' clause.

'Sure,' he laughs, and I see that the corners of his mouth are coated with a milky white mucus.

'Can I pay for one of those cucumbers and pick it up as I leave?' I say, wanting to buy something in return for the advice.

He grimaces. 'Marrows. Those are marrows.'

There's no phone number on the ad, so I decide to find the house and prostrate myself. It's already July 14, I think, they'll be needing a housekeeper by now. The ad is written in fountain pen and has faded in the heat, the card curling up at the corners. The house will be getting dusty, I think. Plates growing mould in the sink. Before long they'll have cockroaches. Big, virulent cockroaches, the size of your hand.

Walking through the streets, past the university and out of town, I feel calm. There's a light breeze now and every so often I pass a group of hikers looking tanned, wholesome, untouched, with the glow of people who understand wheatgrass. For a second I imagine myself like them, a vision of well-muscled youth, my liver revivified and pink, blackened lungs breathed clean. I smile and my face contracts, becoming just slit eyes, upturned nose and a cavernous, widening gulch.

Trudging up the hill, I have to stop at regular intervals, sitting hard on the sidewalk to catch my breath. The community at the bottom, Riverview, had looked quite working-class – a collection of small, light-coloured bungalows, basketball hoops on some, fairy-light fringing on others. Moving towards the top though, the houses are much larger. Arriving at the address on the ad I step back. The house is huge, four-storey, pale blue with purple trim. Perched on the edge of the hill its driveway pushes steeply down to the garage, with a huge, fenced garden visible out back.

I stumble down to the thin-pillared porch and climb the stairs. The front door has a long window adorned with a faded sticker, 'Beware of the dog', which has been pluralised with a shakily penned 's'. Inside, the glass is covered with thick brown mesh. I cup my hand and peer through, just making out the shadow of a large stuffed bear to the left of the door. I consider turning around and going to the motel. Having stopped walking though, I notice a dull ache in my right shoulder. I heave the bag off my back, reach into my pocket, run my hand through the nickels and dimes and press the doorbell.

Three piercing rings chime deep inside the house, each a tone higher, the final one pitched at tinnitus level. It occurs to me that there might actually be more rings, the last ones just benefiting dogs and dolphins. Waiting for a response, I begin to count; 120 seconds, I think, and then I'll consider my options.

I am picking vaguely at a hangnail and trying to remember whether I'm at eighty or ninety-two when a barrage of noise crescendos from a back room. Peering again through the brown canvas I can just make out a figure at the end of the hall who I take to be Carruthers. Silhouetted in a doorway, his arms fly about like those of a venomous shadow puppet, piles of paper billowing around him. This lasts a few minutes. Then the banging and sighing, the violence, are replaced by a shuffle, and I see the figure hovering fast towards me. I take a step away. The right side of a man's face is pressed against the fabric, his eye unblinking through the mesh.

A thin stream of blood trickles down my thumbnail. I hold the want ad up to the glass. 'I'm here about the housekeeping position,' I say, the bulging eye staring back at me, impassive. 'I thought I could help you out.' My voice tails off.

The eye blinks decisively and the figure shuffles away. The papers flutter up as he goes through the door at the end of the corridor. He turns fitfully, and stumbles. 'Fuck off,' he shouts, and the door swings slowly, deliberately, shut.

I sit heavily on the porch and watch my upended bag topple over. I have the nothing-to-lose calm of the condemned man, and a smile still splits my face. I bite the loose skin away from my thumb and chew slowly. Mastication, I think. Suddenly I have an image of Tom, framed by the sun, on the steps of a houseboat we had borrowed three years ago during our first summer together in Britain. A messianic glow spreading about his head, his hair grown wild and tangling in thick Medusa strands around a face cradled by stubble. Naked except for the shorts around his ankles, me on my knees. My face scrunched, compacted, as I go down on him, eyes closed by the sunlight and effort, only glancing up to see him once, smiling, his hands resting gently – almost effeminately – on his hips. The wicked gleam of propulsion.

The skin tastes good in my mouth and I swallow. I

squint over at the house next door and watch as two men emerge from an old Honda Civic out front. One is about six foot four, with the loping shoulders of a giraffe and hair down to his shoulders. The other – dressed in a clown suit – is smiling beneficently and waving to the long grass lining the footpath. The taller man takes him firmly by the shoulders, glances over at me and smiles, steering him through the front door.

I step over my bags and ring the bell again. As I push my aching shoulders out and forward, my breasts recede, back broadens.

This time there is no waiting or counting. By the third ring the latch is juddering free and the front door opens. A short, prodigiously wrinkled man appears, a deep red kimono pulled tight around his waist. I can just make out some hair curlers beneath an off-white shower cap. I stretch out my hand, smiling. He recoils.

'You're looking for a housekeeper,' I say. My inflection rises, laughter floating broodily in my throat.

He takes a few steps away. 'No girls,' he says.

I step into the hall as he goes to close the front door and it hits my upper arm, a bruise – soft blue with black flecks – beginning to form.

'What are you doing?' he shouts, a nerve jumping testily in his eyebrow. 'You're trespassing.'

He sets off down the hall. Taking succour from the fact that he hasn't told me to fuck off I follow him. He stops at the pile of papers and sweeps them away with his foot, before going into his lounge.

'Don't fucking look at those, OK?' I glance down and see a man's face staring back at me. A thin black scar rests above his right eye, but otherwise he's model-handsome. He stares belligerently from a hundred identical prints scattered across the floor, his face caught in a sneer. I feel a sharp prod against my bruised arm. Carruthers takes his finger away, leaving a small white circle. 'I said don't look.'

He walks across the room towards a drinks cabinet, takes a long swig from a decanter of what seems to be whisky and turns to me, unsmiling. 'The house next door is all male,' he says, as if trying to communicate with someone in a coma. 'I don't allow women in that house, whether as guests or tenants. It's tradition.' He pauses. 'It's the rule.'

'But you need a housekeeper,' I say, 'and I'd like to help you out.' I hear my mother's arguments swishing around idly, mixing and conjoining. 'Sex segregation' – I pause for emphasis – 'is apartheid. It's wrong. I'm sure your rules aren't backed by law.'

'Darling,' he says, his face contorting, 'it's my fucking house and I can do what I like. If I want some boys to live in my property, rent-free, then that's my prerogative.'

'Rent-free?'

'Rent-free.'

I look around the room, fairly plain except for a glass-eyed boar that sits stuffed and sombre in the corner. The walls are lined with photographs: Andres Serrano's 'Piss Christ', some of Warhol's car crashes, a collection of five

Mapplethorpes. It includes his notorious self-portrait, Mapplethorpe penetrating himself with a whip.

I pause to look at the pictures and, still staring at one, ask quietly, 'So why don't you like women?'

He sighs. 'For Christ's sake, what a stupid question. I don't need to justify myself.' He sits down on the couch, sinking into the cushions so that his legs dangle far off the ground. Kermit the frog, I think. My eyes wander to a rifle that hangs ominously beneath a blue photograph of an electric chair.

'So do you hate women?' I say. He shrugs. 'You just don't like them? Is it a religious thing?'

Carruthers sighs again. 'Since you're so interested, young lady, I find women dull.' He toys with a stray curl and smiles. 'Boring.'

'And why's that?'

He laughs quietly. 'You tell me why women are dull.'

I cross my arms. 'I don't think they are.'

'My theory on it,' he says, ignoring me and pulling gently at a loose thread in his kimono, 'my theory is that women have no inner life and therefore nothing to say.' He leers up at me. 'They're just primal creatures.'

'What do you mean?' I say.

He laughs. 'You don't know what primal means?'

I scowl. 'Of course I know what it means. I just don't understand why you'd think that women are more primal than men. I would have thought that men' – I spit out the word – 'with their sexual urges, are far more primal.'

'Ah, that's where you're wrong,' says Carruthers, leaning his head back over the edge of the couch, eyes closed. 'Men, you see, have civilising vision. They create art, philosophy.'

'So do women.'

He holds a hand up to me. 'They don't really though, do they?' His head rocks back again. 'If you take any woman,' he says, 'there are only two ways in which she can be truly creative.' He pauses, mouth holding the barest twitch of a smile. 'The first is primal.' He points a finger at me. 'A woman can be a sexual animal and an incubator, by bearing children.' He is laughing. 'The second is aesthetic, in that a woman can objectify herself through cosmetics and clothes. A woman can transform herself into something beautiful if she really tries. From an early age girls are taught that their success depends on their appearance,' he sighs, 'which is true. If a woman isn't beautiful' – he looks me up and down in my paint-spattered jeans – 'she means very little. Very little indeed, because she has nothing else to offer. That's why women put so much energy into their looks because deep down they know that that's true. A woman's creativity is therefore entirely self-absorbed. Bearing children and mask-making. Women have no outer, civilising vision whatsoever.'

He smiles smugly as I stand, open-mouthed, in front of him. 'So women are just incubators and objects?'

He grins. 'Of course.'

We stare at each other and I restrain a smile as a drop

of blood falls from my thumb, staining his light wooden floorboards.

Carruthers walks over to the wall and gazes at the 'Piss Christ'. After a moment he starts to speak. 'If you really think women are capable of' – he pauses – 'abstract thought, then name me a female philosopher.' He turns quickly, another curl falling from his plastic beret.

I pause for a minute, before sighing. 'Simone de Beauvoir,' I say.

He laughs, the shower cap falling right off now, white hair cascading around his face. 'Simone de Beauvoir,' he says, shaking. 'What kind of philosopher was she?'

'She was an existentialist,' I say, mouth virtually closed. 'Some people called her a feminist.'

Tears rush down his face. 'A feminist!' He is almost hysterical. 'A feminist! If anything proves that modern women aren't capable of abstract thought it's the fact that the only philosophers amongst them are feminists. What's feminism except a concern with your own experiences as a woman?' he giggles, almost boyish. 'That's not philosophy, that's self-obsession. Philosophy should be concerned with universal experience, the human condition as a whole. Not just the female condition. As I said, women are incapable of thinking about anything but themselves. They have no vision. They're just' – he shows me his palms and shrugs – 'vessels.'

I start to walk up the corridor, seething, and dig my hands into my pockets. Fingering a dollar bill I stride to the front door, propping it open with a foot. Reaching over, I pick up my portfolio and march back to the living room. Carruthers is reclining against a feathery white cushion, puffing forcefully at a cigar.

'You're back?' he says.

I start to pull out some A2 drawings.

He snorts. 'You know what I think about female creativity. Keep it in your panties.'

I ignore him, lining the portraits carefully along the floor, until they cover his large white animal-skin rug. Watching, Carruthers turns quiet. Most of the pictures are of Tom, and they show his torso and genitals in minute detail, blown up three times their actual size. Receding from the body are his limbs, which taper vaguely towards the edge of the page, useless as bound feet. The fifth drawing I pull out is the only one to feature Tom's head, included after a few weeks' whining. 'Can't there be a face along with the genitalia?' he'd said and I'd laughed uproariously. 'It'll never sell.'

Carruthers leans forward, doubtful at first, before creaking to his knees. He starts to talk, faltering. 'These are' – he opens his mouth and then clamps it shut again – 'these are very good.' He turns. 'Are these really your work?'

I laugh. 'Of course they're my work.'

He traces his finger lightly over Tom's genitals. 'I want one.'

7

The artists' colony

Carruthers has told me to enter through the back of the house ('It's always open – they're such naughty boys') and so I sidestep a couple of turkeys pecking out front, open the gate to the yard and walk through. The house is clad in untreated wood, but otherwise it looks about the same as Carruthers' - four storeys, vast. Hefting my bags up some iron steps I prod tentatively at the back door.

It swings open on a spare white kitchen. Plates of congealing food sit with beer cans and half-empty coffee cups, as though the residents have run away at the sound of footsteps. For a second I feel like Goldilocks. I stand, watching as a crowd of silverfish congregate happily in the thick orange grease of a bolognese.

Leaving my bags on the cleanest stretch of floor, I venture out into the hall. Just beyond the heat and plastic of the kitchen the ground floor is surprisingly dark, and a layer of smog hangs low over the furniture. With mahogany walls, greying curtains and the occasional sepia photograph, it's like walking onto the abandoned set of a horror movie. Goldilocks gets gutted, I think. A cluster of overstuffed armchairs sit in the lounge, each wrapped carefully in polythene. The chime of the grandfather clock rings out like a punchline.

The air thickening, I shrug and head back to the kitchen. My portfolio is hanging slightly open and as I pull idly at the zip, my head turns towards the oven, set in the far corner of the kitchen. Steam is billowing from each side of the door. Running over to open it, I gasp, an aborted scream. As the oven door swings shut I see a slab of blackened meat on a baking tray lit up like a birthday cake by a small yellow flame. The iron handle glows a faint red.

Coughing from the fumes – steak fried in Windolene – I go to look for help. As I jump up the stairs I think vaguely of the fireman who had given us a safety talk at school when I was thirteen. 'Never go upstairs if your house is on fire,' he had said. Like you would, I remember thinking, a curled-lip adolescent. I start to shout half-heartedly. 'Fire!'

A row of doors lines the hallway at the top of the stairs, and I push at each in turn. The first two are empty, and I catch just a glimpse of them – one bare except for a grubby-sheeted bed and the bones of a motorbike, the other full of furry toys, with a wilting helium balloon tied to the door handle professing 'I love you'. A clown suit lies on the bed.

Behind the third door is the tall man I'd seen earlier in the front yard. He is standing by the windowsill, flicking through some old records, the strains of Nick Drake eking through his speakers. 'Fire,' I pant, and he turns to look at me, quizzical, just smiling.

'What?' I see a lit joint in the ashtray and put a hand on my hip.

'There's a fire,' I say slowly, 'fire.'

His eyes widen, forehead corrugating. 'Oh,' he says, and plods towards me. 'That's my steak.'

I run down the stairs, and he lopes a few paces behind me. 'I'm sorry you've had to deal with this,' he's saying, 'all a bit of a mess.'

I turn to him. 'Can you put it out?'

He shrugs, bites his lip, the left corner of his mouth contracting with muted worry. 'I sure hope so.'

Getting to the kitchen, he reaches for the stained tea towel that's hanging on the back of the door and pulls at it so that the sticky patches smooth out. He uses it to open the oven and then throws the towel over the flames. It catches alight. 'Could you get water,' he says, coughing a little. 'I'm so sorry.'

I start filling pint glasses and, since his eyes are weeping, he covers them with his left hand and throws the water blindly. After five pints in quick succession the flames jump defiantly before crackling down. 'You're OK,' I say as he peeks through his fingers, reaching for another glass. 'It's out.'

He gives a whoop of laughter then looks sadly at the

oven. 'I think it may have cooked its last.' He puts a hand on my arm. 'I'm so sorry about that. I'm Lenny.'

I start to laugh. 'Molly.'

'Good to meet you,' he says, and I notice that the creases around his eyes make him look almost permanently bewildered.

Using a spatula, he fishes the steak from the oven, prises the tea towel off (it's welded, in places, to the meat), grabs one of the dirty plates and sits down. His lips make tiny smacking noises as he chews the fossilised steak. 'Thanks so much for helping me save this,' he says. 'I was going to cook a sauce for it and prepare some baby vegetables too' – he looks down at the plate, contemplative – 'but it's fine. Delicious.' He makes an 'O' in the air with his right thumb and forefinger. 'Perfecto.' There is silence for a minute as he chews thoughtfully. Then he looks up, stricken. 'I'm sorry – how rude of me.' He holds his fork out. 'Would you like some?'

I sit down at the table opposite him. 'Well, it looks tempting,' I say. Lenny cuts into a blackened corner, which disintegrates sadly onto the plate. He holds the fork out again.

'I'm OK,' I say.

'Well, thank you.' He smiles. 'That could have been nasty.'

I laugh. 'Well, I would have been out of a job if the place had burnt down.'

He gulps at the meat and looks at me, head cocked. 'Job?'

'I'm the new housekeeper.'

He splutters a little, and I hit him softly on the back, embarrassed. 'You're the new housekeeper?' Lenny stares at me, incredulous, eyes poring over my face. I nod. 'Wow.' He takes another bite. 'That's great. I thought Carruthers wanted a man.' He swigs at a glass of water that's obviously been there a while (a fly floats lazily on the surface) and grimaces. 'Oh God.' Lenny jumps up, spits into the sink and then goes to the fridge. 'It'll be great to have a girl around. Great. You should have met our last housekeeper. He was in his sixties, a complete kleptomaniac. I walked into his room one day and he was lying in a pile of my dirty underwear.' He turns to me. 'It was disgusting. I had to buy all new boxers.'

There's a short silence before he pulls out a beer. 'Do you want one?'

'I'm OK.'

He peers into the fridge. 'I've got an open bottle of wine here as well.'

'What colour?'

'White.'

'Sure.'

Lenny finds a tumbler, wipes it with a piece of kitchen roll and pours me a glass. 'Here you are.' He looks at me thoughtfully. 'Do you want to bring that up to my room?' He waves a hand around. 'I don't usually eat in here, it's so' – he pauses – 'unsanitary really. It's more comfortable upstairs.'

I nod. 'Sure, OK. Shall I bring my bags up?'

He shakes his head. 'Oh, leave those here for now. They'll be fine – I'll come down and get them later.'

Lenny pulls a few more beers from the fridge and puts them in his trouser pockets so that his waistband sags at the front. 'Lead the way,' I say.

'My room's a little bit cluttered right now,' says Lenny, as we climb the stairs. 'I've been meaning to get it tidy for a while.' As he throws open the door I notice that Nick Drake is still whirring on the stereo. 'This is a great album,' I say.

'You know Nick Drake?' Lenny looks surprised. 'I just found this record in a thrift store the other day.'

He pats the room's only chair, next to the wall, beside the window. 'Do you want to sit down?' He perches on the windowsill and saws off another bite of steak.

I rest the bottle of wine and my glass on the floor and motion at the bookcases lining his wall. 'Are these yours?'

He smiles, talking through a mouthful. 'Yeah. They seem to keep breeding.'

'Can I?' He nods as I go to take a look.

Scanning through the books, I realise that they've been alphabetised and then split into categories. Fiction, philosophy, art, poetry. The shelves bear everything from *Tales of the City* to *Lolita*, Nietzsche to Andrea Dworkin. All look used, well-thumbed, loved. Stacked beside the bookcases are a couple of huge boxes, also full.

'So have you lived here long?' I say, picking up a dusty copy of *The Iliad*.

His hair sways gently about his face as he looks up. 'Oh yeah,' he says, 'it must be' – he puts the plate down and counts on his fingers – 'six months now. I was in California before that.'

'Oh really? Whereabouts?'

He smiles hazily. 'Oh, it was a small town, I don't think you'd have heard of it, in the southwest corner. There's not much there,' he says, 'apart from the ministry. It doesn't make the tourist maps.'

'Oh.' There's a short pause. 'I used to live in California,' I say, a little lamely.

'Where?'

'Davis, university town.'

'I know it,' he says. 'Were you at college there?'

I look down and am struck by the clear white band of flesh around my ring finger. I had never noticed quite how stark it is. 'No, an old friend of mine lived there.' I pause. 'Well, he was a boyfriend really. I lived with him in California for three years.'

'And then you split?'

I smile, my mouth twitching. 'Yeah.'

Lenny takes a noisy gulp of beer. 'So do you like it here in Eugene?' I say, swilling some wine around my glass.

He nods, face animated. 'Eugene's OK,' he says. 'It's OK. I don't know. I'd heard a bit about it before I came, you know, in all those accounts of the sixties, and I thought it was going to be more exciting than it is, a bit more radical.'

'There's not much happening?'

He laughs. 'No. I don't know where Ken Kesey's hiding, but I sure wish he'd come out.' He sighs. 'I suppose it's probably like a lot of college towns, probably like Davis, you know, the students just seem vaguely' – he pauses – 'boring.'

'In what way?'

'Oh God.' He squirms slightly on the windowsill, pressing his back against the glass. 'I don't mean it horribly, I'm sure they're all very nice, but they never seem to go out dancing, or get drunk. They're big on sport – you might have seen the Os in some of the windows on your way up' – I nod – 'they're for the Oregon Ducks, but apart from that they're not very social. Most of the time when you see them out somewhere it's on a study date.'

'They do that here too?'

'Oh yeah, they did it in Davis?' I nod and he laughs. 'Well, they're big on study dates in Eugene. You see all these students congregating in Quizno's or one of the pizza places, having a soda and poring over their books. It's weird. There are good restaurants here, really cheap, but you never see students in those. They're too dark for them to read their books while they eat. A place that's not well lit has no chance in this town.'

'So there's not much in the way of nightlife?'

He smiles. 'Not really, but I've had some fun, so.' He takes another swig. 'Do you have any plans while you're here?'

I go to sit down. 'Not really, nothing special. I think I'll probably just stay for a month or so and get some work done.'

'Right, right.' He gets up to change the record. 'And what kind of work do you do?'

I watch as he pulls a Joni Mitchell album carefully out of its sleeve, trying to think of a good answer. Artist sounds so pompous. 'I draw.'

'Great,' says Lenny, 'that's great. I'm a writer' – he gives a nervous chuckle – 'when I'm not stacking shelves at Albertsons.'

'Oh, cool,' I say. 'What do you write?'

'Well' – he pauses – 'I'm in the middle of my first novel at the moment.'

'Wow, that's great,' I say. 'What's it about?'

He laughs. 'Oh, I can't talk about it, it's too embarrassing. When I describe the plot out loud it just makes me feel kind of weird.' He looks down. 'I'll let you read it when it's done.'

I shrug and smile. 'Oh, OK.'

As he plays with the volume on the stereo, I wander over to the other side of the room where there's a tiny print, an Egon Schiele nude.

'You like Schiele?'

'Oh yeah.' The first few bars of 'Blue' chime out. 'I really like his drawings. I like portraiture.' He sits on the floor cross-legged. 'Is that the kind of thing you do?'

I look at the picture, a woman lying on the floor with just a skirt ruffled around her thighs. 'Well, not exactly,' I say. 'I'm not obsessed with painting prostitutes,' I laugh, 'but I do draw nudes.'

He nods. 'Men, women?'

'Just one man so far.'

'Oh,' he smiles, rolling a joint. 'So are you looking for people to pose?'

I walk back over to the chair and sit down. 'Sure, if they're willing. Why' – I nudge him with my foot – 'do you know of some potential models?'

He lines the tobacco along the cigarette paper. 'Sure, I can think of a few people who might be interested.'

'Like who?'

Lenny picks up the magazine that he's been resting on and puts it down beside him. He pulls a beer from his pocket and levers the top off. 'Oh, there are probably some guys in this house who wouldn't mind.'

'Really?'

He leans his head back, gulping the beer. 'Sure,' he says, 'there are some exhibitionists around here.'

I laugh. 'What do you mean?'

'Oh,' he says, 'some of the people in the house are' – he wipes his mouth – 'a bit unusual.'

'Like how?'

'I don't know.' He goes to stand by the window. 'Not in any bad way. I mean, I get on with most of the people in the house really well.'

'How many are there here?'

'Well, with you, it'll be up to eight,' he says.

'And do most of them work?'

He smiles. 'Most of them are artists of one sort or another. Carruthers established this place as an artists' colony a couple of decades back, but I guess its reputation has dwindled over the years. It still attracts some good people though.'

'But not everyone's an artist.'

'No, the two guys who've been here the longest – Ed and Matt – they're not.'

'So what do they do?'

'Well' – Lenny's mouth moues into a hoop – 'I think you saw Ed this afternoon.' I look at him blankly. 'The guy in the clown suit.'

'Oh.' I pour out another glass of wine. 'That was Ed?'

'Yeah.' Lenny sighs. 'He's a very sweet guy, probably about thirty, I guess, but he has quite serious mental problems, a low mental age. I'm not quite sure why Carruthers took him in, but I think he might be a relative – a nephew maybe.'

'And where is he at the moment?'

'Oh, I think he's been taken back to daycare for the afternoon. He goes there every weekday.' He walks over to one of the bookshelves and holds up a lumpy pot. 'He made this for me.'

I smile, 'That's gorgeous,' and take a sip of wine. 'So does it cause any problems having him here?'

Lenny sits down on the bed. 'No, not really. Everyone's pretty fair and we all take turns driving him around. There are only ever problems when he brings his friends home.'

'Does he have a lot of friends?'

'Hordes' – I laugh – 'honestly. And he's always picking up new ones. It can be a bit freaky when they stay over. They're always hiding in cupboards and things, jumping out when you walk past. It can be dangerous.'

'If you're drunk,' I say.

'Exactly.'

'And what about Matt?' I bite my lip. 'Carruthers warned me about him.'

'What do you mean?'

I laugh. 'He told me that if I touch him I'm out.'

Lenny leans over. 'He said that?'

'Yeah.'

'Doesn't surprise me.' He looks up. 'You'll have got him running scared.'

'Why?'

'Oh,' he smiles, 'we all think that Carruthers is in love with Matt.' He picks up the magazine to finish rolling the joint. 'He's certainly obsessed with him. I don't know what Matt's story is, but he's been living here since he was about sixteen. Carruthers has been trying to get him into modelling for years, but I just don't think he's got the temperament for it. Too surly.'

'What do you mean?'

'Oh,' Lenny laughs, 'you'll see. He's beautiful, but' – he pauses, head tilted – 'he never really says anything. Occasionally you'll get a grunt out of him, but that's about it. There are either some very deep thoughts going on behind that pretty face of his or Matt's just stupid. A beautiful, silent Neanderthal.'

'And does he have a job?'

'Yeah, he's a mechanic, works locally.'

He puts the joint on the window ledge and takes a slug of beer. 'Do you want me to show you your room?' he says. 'You're right next door.'

'Sure.'

We walk to the adjoining room and Lenny throws open the door. 'Here we are,' he says, 'it's my favourite.' It's sunset by now, the sky a gaudy flamingo-pink, and a stretch of light splays across the floor. The room is plain – dusty windows, white-painted walls and a huge pine bed. Lenny claps his hands together. 'It's great, isn't it?'

'It's amazing.' I walk over to the windows and look out on the back yard. A bird flies close past the window, before swooping off into Hendricks Park.

Lenny lights up the joint and holds it out to me. 'Do you want some?'

I take a few tokes. 'This is great.'

We head to the kitchen for my bags, running awkwardly down the stairs in the dark. Coming to the bottom, I stumble into someone, putting a hand on their arm to steady myself. 'I'm sorry,' I say, laughing, my eyes getting accustomed to the light.

'Hi, Matt,' says Lenny, 'had a good day at work?'

He gives a grunt and shrugs. 'Sure.'

'This is our new housekeeper.' Lenny nudges me a little way into the hall, where a light reaches out from the kitchen. 'Molly.'

'Hi,' says Matt. I look at the scar above his right eye,

more pronounced than it had been in Carruthers' pictures. He stares at me for a few seconds, before pushing past us and upstairs.

'Well,' says Lenny, reaching down for my backpack, 'that's Matt.'

8

Porn dollies

'Oh, lovely. It's like a mass grave in there, isn't it.' My mother peers into the box of Barbies. 'All those naked, hipless little bodies.' She sucks her cheeks until they meet in the middle, her lips puckering, the outline of her teeth undulating beneath the skin. She looks up at Jane's mother and her mouth thwacks suddenly open, before widening into a smile. 'Thanks so much for bringing these round. I'm sure you and Jane will have fun with them, won't you, Molly?' Standing beside me on the porch, she tickles me between the shoulder blades. 'Oh yes,' I say, giggling. She bends down and holds out the box to me. As I pick up one of the dolls by its hair the head comes right off in my hand, leaving just a ridged stump. My mother claps her hands together happily. 'Decapitation!' she says.

Christine, Jane's mother, shudders, her toe tapping an offbeat rhythm. She bends to kiss Jane goodbye, before licking a screwed-up tissue and wiping the lipstick off her daughter's face. I see Jane gag. 'I'll be round to pick you up later, sweetheart, have a good time.' Christine turns to Augusta, her eyes hooded. 'Jane can't eat broccoli,' she says, 'or nuts.'

Augusta smiles. 'She says that now.'

Her face contemptuous, Christine stands, mute, and holds out a second box, this one full of neatly folded Barbie clothes. A purple polyester nurse's outfit sits on top. 'They're ironed,' she says. It is the first time I have heard conviction in her voice.

'Thanks,' says Augusta. She ushers us inside and closes the door abruptly. 'Obsessive compulsive,' she says quietly, and then repeats herself a little louder. 'Obsessive compulsive.' Steering us towards the sofa, she puts a hand on Jane's shoulder. 'Tell me, how many showers does your mother have a day?'

'What?' says Jane, a deep indentation appearing on the ridge of her nose, right between her eyes.

'Nothing,' says Augusta. 'Time for TV.' She hands me the remote and disappears into the kitchen where she starts singing loudly.

Jane and I sit in silence, eyes trained ahead. My mother is off-key, her voice soaring shakily through a rendition of 'I shall be released'. 'My mum says Augusta is a freak,' Jane comments, as though stating a fact – the world being round, grass green. 'She says that your mother's kind should be sterilised.' She roots through the box of Barbies and pulls out my favourite, Aerobics Barbie. Jane strokes the doll's long brown hair and yanks her legs violently into the splits.

'Sterilised?' I say.

'Yes, sterilised.'

'What does that mean?'

Jane pauses and starts to plait the Barbie's hair. Her head tilts to one side. 'I guess it means that they should be cleaned up. Properly cleaned up.'

'Like sterilising milk?'

Jane looks confused. 'Suppose so.'

We are silent for a second.

'My mum says Augusta's a dyke. I heard her say to my dad the other day that she's a dyke who sleeps with women.'

I frown. 'So what if she sleeps with women?' I say. 'I bet you've slept with a girl before.' I pause, thinking. Then, triumphantly, 'We slept together last summer, round at Poppy's house.' I point both hands at her, my fingers held up like guns. 'We shared a sleeping bag.' I mime shooting her and then blow gently across my fingers.

Jane eyes me lazily as she pulls a cheerleader's outfit from the box. She says nothing for a few moments, and I watch as she pushes the Barbie's arms up, pulling the tiny dress over its head. She has been irritating me for a few weeks now, ever since we began work on a maths project together. Right from the start I could tell that she was confused because she kept craning her neck to look at my work, scribbling, then smiling smugly. Jane's face in these

instants reminded me of a picture I had seen in an ency-
clopaedia of a dead boar on a serving plate, its mouth
stuffed with an apple. After two weeks our group had
been told to reach a conclusion and Jane had insisted that
we give our teacher some answers she had worked out
with her mother. When I'd told her they were wrong –
really wrong – she had retorted that I was stupid. 'And
anyway,' she'd said, 'I'm nine and you're only eight.' We
had given her answers in. We were graded F.

She finally finishes fastening the cheerleader's dress
and looks up at me. 'Maybe I have slept with you,' she
says, 'but I had all my clothes on and I didn't touch your
foo-fee.'

'My what?'

'Your foo-fee.'

'What's a foo-fee?'

'You know.' Jane looks embarrassed. 'Your ladies' cha-
cha.'

I shrug, bemused. 'Nope.'

'It's the name for what you have down there, isn't it.'
Jane points impatiently at her crotch. She says 'down
there' in an undertone, inhaling slightly.

I sigh. 'Oh,' I say. 'A vagina.' There's a pause. 'Anyway,
who says that Augusta kisses girls?'

'Everyone.' Jane smiles and pulls out another Barbie.
'Everyone. I heard Miss Spry talking about it at school, so
even the teachers know. Your mother sleeps with Ellie,
doesn't she? They probably do proper kissing in bed, like
people in films.' She sticks her tongue out and leaves it

lolling around her lips. It's not seductive. She lowers her voice. 'I bet they frenchie.'

I hug my knees to my chest. Jane is so annoying, I think, and the phrase starts running through my mind on a loop, like one of my mother's mantras. Imagining that she's cleverer than me just because she's a year older. Not even that. I hold my fingers up. She was born in October and I was born in July, so that makes her . . . nine months older. Jane is staring at me suspiciously. I bet she doesn't even know how many months there are in a year.

And then, thinking about her mother, I realise that she probably doesn't know how many months there are in a year either. She's stupid. And Jane thinks she's better than me because she has a mother who sleeps with her father. Stupid, stupid. She's not better. Her mother smells of beef.

Jane is prodding me now, obviously a little bored. 'At least my father isn't a teacher,' I say. 'When you go to secondary school he'll be taking you for gym classes and everyone will laugh at you.'

'At least I have a father,' she snaps back, attaching pom-poms to the Barbie doll's hands with Velcro straps.

'So do I,' I say.

'Oh right.' Her voice has a sharp edge. 'What does he do then?'

I press the remote and turn the TV on, volume high. 'He's an astronaut.'

Augusta sweeps through the kitchen door with a tray of flapjacks, still warm from the oven and dripping chocolate. Ellie has been lost in a flurry of baking for the past few days, and Augusta keeps zealously feeding me cake. 'How are you two, having fun yet?' she says. She puts the tray on the table and stands for a moment, one hand resting on her hip. A group of teenage morris dancers are darting across the screen, legs flying violently at the camera. The music accompanying them is a strange high-pitched wheezing, like a pig squeezed in a vice. Pig juice, I think.

'What's this?' says Augusta. She puts a hand to her temple, her face scrunching into a pained expression.

'*Blue Peter*,' says Jane, her voice high and patronising. 'It's *Blue Peter*.' I can tell from the way her nose turns up – just slightly retroussé – that she's amazed by this question. I know what she's thinking. Any proper mother would know that this was *Blue Peter*. Any mother who didn't sleep with women would know the children's TV schedules by heart.

My mother rubs a hand over her eyes. '*Blue Peter*,' she sighs. 'Tell me one thing, girls' – she looks down at us wearily – 'tell me why they have to make a children's TV show sound so much like a porn film.' She kneels by my side and exhales. I catch the taste of gin on her breath and swallow greedily. 'Don't you think it's terrible, Molly?'

I smile. 'I'm sure you're right, Mummy.'

She climbs to her feet, flashes a grin and ruffles my hair. 'Thank you, darling.'

As she heads back to the kitchen, Jane and I sit staring at the screen. After the morris dancing is a new segment on how to make a Barbie bedroom from household waste. We both lean towards the TV, silent, our enthusiasm contained by mutual dislike.

While the presenter creates a dressing table – quite ingeniously – from a toilet roll, I hear noises in the kitchen. My mother's voice, as usual, is like a siren. 'I'm not going to tell her,' she's saying insistently. 'I won't do it, so you can fuck off.'

Jane is biting her lip. 'Your mum just swore at Ellie,' she says.

I keep staring straight ahead. 'Yes,' I say. The presenter is covering the cardboard with pink crepe paper and I am determined to concentrate. The finished dressing table is shiny, bright and sturdy. I will make one of those, I think.

There is more noise from the kitchen, banging this time, the sound of pans hitting the ground and a pained miaow. Nin, our cat, has been caught in the crossfire.

'What's going on in there?' says Jane, her voice more curious than concerned.

'They're making a pie,' I say distractedly. I am trying to think whether we have any spare shoe boxes in the house that I can use to make the Barbie bedroom. 'Ellie's making a chicken pie for dinner.'

Jane puts two fingers down her throat and pretends to retch. 'Ugh, I hate chickens. You can catch plague from them.'

'Rats,' I say.

'What?'

'You catch plague from rats. We did it in Miss Hanson's class last year.'

'Oh,' says Jane, surprised. 'I forgot that.'

She's so stupid, I think, really dim. Why was I ever friends with someone who – aged nine – thinks that chickens carry plague? 'Duh,' I say.

Jane looks angry for a second. Then her face softens. 'At least I'm pretty,' she says.

My mother is shouting now, her voice resonating through the house. It makes it impossible to concentrate on the TV (even though I'm keen to know how to make a Barbie wardrobe out of matchboxes) and I start trying to figure out what she and Ellie are arguing about. 'You're just the sodding babysitter,' my mother is saying, 'I won't have you telling me what to do.' Ellie's response, as always, is much quieter than my mother's. I hear her talking, but it's a low murmuring, unintelligible.

The noise finally stops and Ellie throws open the kitchen door. The handle hits the lounge wall as it has so many times before, and an even bigger hole is chipped into the paintwork. Ellie's eyes are swimming, her skin blotchy and burnt red on the right-hand side of her face. She runs upstairs, two at a time.

'She was crying,' says Jane.

'She's been chopping onions.'

'I don't think that's why she was crying.'

'Her eyes are always like that when she's been chopping onions,' I say firmly, but I am suddenly a little worried.

Last night Ellie and Augusta had had an argument. It

had started tentatively at about four pm with the three of us clustered in my mother's study. Ellie was in the corner, in the armchair, knitting, Augusta was at her desk and I was sitting by her feet reading a Judy Blume book. Everything was silent except the opposing tick of the clock and the knitting needles.

'So,' said Ellie, 'what does everyone want for dinner?'

Augusta had looked up, her head pulled back sharply. 'What do you mean?'

Ellie laughed. 'I just wondered what you wanted for dinner.' She paused, taking in Augusta's face, the way the top corners of her mouth had retracted in a worried sneer. 'It's not a metaphysical question.'

Augusta put her pen down. 'I thought you were working tonight. It's Friday.'

'Augie,' Ellie smiled as though addressing a small child, 'I've only been working one Friday a month for two years now. I don't have another shift until Monday.'

Looking up, I could see my mother's hand move slightly, hovering dreamily an inch above her desk. 'I've got a guest coming to dinner tonight,' she said.

'A guest?' said Ellie, her voice enthusiastic. 'Great. Who is it?'

I reached out to touch my mother's leg to see if it felt as tense as it looked. Her calf was like rock. She pulled away irritably.

'Molly, get off. I don't think you understand, Ellie. I'm having one of my students over for dinner. She's a PhD candidate and I want to have a good talk with her about her' – she paused – 'her thesis.' She looked over at Ellie, beseeching. 'I just think you'll be bored, you know.'

Ellie put her knitting needles down and gave a tight grin. 'I can't see that it'll be a problem. I can always cook while you two talk and then we can sit down to eat.'

'She's bringing takeaway.'

'Fine,' said Ellie. She threw Augusta a smile and I caught, for a moment, her joy and bitterness at gate-crashing the planned seduction. 'You'd better call her and tell her to bring enough for four.'

'Four?'

'Well, there's no point Molly eating alone.'

They had reached a standoff then, an uneasy truce. The rest of the afternoon had been spent in silence, my mother pretending to write while staring blankly at the wall, Ellie rattling around the house watering plants and cleaning the windows. As the sky darkened I had looked round to see her outside, wiping the smeary glass of the study, smiling at me and waving. Augusta had glanced over, aggravated, and stood up. A minute later the two of them were framed by the window and I watched as they bickered, motioning occasionally at me.

We had eaten lunch early that day – an unusually healthy chicken salad – and by seven pm I felt the sly ache of hunger. Climbing onto the work surface in the kitchen I scouted through the cupboards looking for bread or biscuits, but behind each door was a new stack of Tupperware, the plastic boxes laden with Ellie's cup-cakes. Despairing, I had gone to my room to read.

After an hour, my stomach felt so cavernous that I decided it was time to confront my mother. I found her sitting in bed, fully clothed, writing a report. A large glass of wine was held to her lips, like a sacrament.

'I'm hungry,' I whined, standing in her doorway, hands clasped together, 'but I can't eat more cake. I'm sick of it.'

'What's that, Molly?' She smiled sleepily.

'I'm hungry.'

My mother's voice was unsympathetic. 'Well, you know what to do when you're hungry and the cupboard's bare, sweetie.'

'What?'

'Go to bed.' She turned the page and started scribbling. 'You can't feel hungry if you're not conscious.'

My eyes had narrowed. 'I might starve though.'

'What?'

I spoke slowly and emphatically. 'I might starve.'

She snapped her fingers angrily. 'You won't fucking starve.' Putting her wine on the bedside table, Augusta threw the covers off and came towards me, arms held out. I stumbled, backing away. 'You'll go to bed now and I'll wake you up when Vanya brings the takeaway.' She clasped my shoulders and pushed me towards my room.

I had climbed into bed, muttering angrily as I drifted off to sleep. A couple of hours later I felt the tickle of my mother's breath on my face. 'Come on, Molly,' she said softly, shaking me. 'The food's here.' She sounded almost placid, sedated.

I walked downstairs heavily in my makeshift pyjamas –

my mother's 'If I can't dance it's not my revolution' T-shirt falling to my knees. I had the headachy, blurred vision that comes with disturbed sleep and as I walked down the hall I closed my eyes and started to suck my thumb. Striding ahead, Augusta turned around. 'Move it, Molly, and cheer up. One of my friends has bought us dinner. She won't want to see you looking like you're chewing wet liver.' I opened my eyes and tried to smile without moving my thumb. A dribble of saliva ran from the right corner of my mouth, hanging thoughtfully for a second before dropping to the floor. 'For God's sake. She'll think you're orally fixated.' Augusta took me by the hand and pulled me towards the lounge.

Ellie and Vanya were sitting on the couch, the coffee table stacked with takeaway boxes and tea lights. 'This is Molly,' said my mother, as I hoisted myself onto the leather beanbag in the corner.

'Hello,' I said shyly, waggling my fingers at Vanya before hiding the hand behind my back. I could sense tension, noticed that she and Ellie were squashed into opposite corners of the couch, a stretch of cushion between them. Looking at Vanya I guessed why. Her blonde pageboy hair fell around her face like a halo and she was clad in a clinging black dress.

'Hello, Molly,' she said, her smile blithe and beaming. There was a slight Swedish lilt to her voice.

'It's so lovely of you to have brought all this round,' said Augusta, loading a plate with egg-fried rice. She passed it to me with a fork and then squeezed between Ellie and

Vanya. 'It's just so kind.' I watched as Ellie rolled her eyes.

'Oh, it's not a problem,' said Vanya with the vague, clipped formality of second-language English. 'It's really a pleasure to be invited into your home. I'm so excited that you're looking after my thesis.'

'I'm thrilled too,' said Augusta. Staring over at the three of them, I began shovelling rice into my mouth, before reaching for a prawn cracker and sucking on it. I liked the light fizzing on the roof of my mouth before it dissolved into a thick layer along my tongue. 'Don't suck your food,' said my mother, raising her hand at me. I shrugged, embarrassed, and started in again on the rice.

'So what's your thesis about?' said Ellie, her voice laced with boredom.

'Oh,' said Vanya, 'this and that.'

I turned to see Ellie's face shift, incredulous. 'This and that?' she said. 'That doesn't sound very specific.' I saw my mother kick at her. Ellie persisted. 'I thought you were here tonight to talk to Augusta about your thesis. We were all looking forward to hearing what you had in mind.'

Vanya laughed, oblivious to the tension. 'Oh, I don't think you'd be interested in what I have to say.' She paused for a forkful of beef and chilli. 'My thesis is focusing on popular women's novels,' she said, pronouncing every syllable carefully. 'I'm examining Jackie Collins from a radical lesbian perspective.' My mother nodded approvingly.

'Anyway,' said Vanya, glancing at her watch. She wiped her mouth with a napkin printed 'Wong's', 'we should probably put the television on now, yes?'

My mother placed a hand cautiously on Vanya's leg. 'Maybe not,' she said, 'under the circumstances.' She looked pointedly to her left.

'What's on TV then?' said Ellie, staring back at Augusta. 'If there's something the two of you planned to watch, then that's fine.'

'You mean she hasn't told you about it?' said Vanya.

Ellie raised her eyebrows. 'About what?'

My mother leaned forward and loaded some sweet and sour pork onto her plate. 'It's not a big deal. Nothing important.' She took a bite. 'I've got the video set anyway. It's just that there's an interview about my porn project on now.'

'An interview?'

'Yeah,' said Augusta, 'I filmed it last week.'

Vanya hunched forward to address Ellie. 'It's a very important interview,' she said, nodding seriously. 'It's an hour long.'

'What's the programme called?'

'Oh,' my mother shrugged, 'it's in the listings as *Changed, a gende*r. I think they might have stitched me up.'

Ellie reached for the remote control, flicking through the channels until she came to the grey painted set of a discussion programme. I turned so that I could see the screen more clearly. Augusta was sitting on a black swivel chair in front of a poster that showed a man and woman holding hands, a great jagged tear painted between them. A presenter was perched to her right, her hair curled up into a crown, addressing the studio audience and introducing my mother.

'Do we really have to watch this now?' Augusta sighed, and I saw that she looked slightly nervous. 'It didn't go that well. I'd rather see it on video.'

'Shhh,' said Ellie, with a tight hiss of sarcasm. 'It's an important programme. Vanya's come round to see it.'

My mother bit her lip, put her plate down and grabbed a large handful of crackers. She began crunching loudly.

'. . . she's been a presence on the cultural scene for more than a decade now,' the presenter was saying, 'coming to major prominence in the mid-seventies with her book *Maternities*. In that work she put forward the popular thesis that male and female sex roles are determined by social construction rather than biology. She argued that a man brought up in a neutral environment might display feminine characteristics – might want to stay at home and look after children, for example – whilst a woman could evolve masculine behaviour. This view was shared by many feminists and scientists and reflected the optimism of the women's movement at the time, a sense that social hierarchies weren't imperative and could be deconstructed and rearranged.'

'Enough with the intro,' said Ellie.

The camera panned in for a close-up of the presenter, her face held in a fixed expression of concern. 'However,' she said, 'since then Augusta Flynn has changed her views radically. Through her latest and ongoing work – the controversial porn project – she is arguing that men's biology makes them naturally aggressive. She now believes that men have an essential, biologically programmed hatred for the fairer sex and that they are waging a war against women.' The camera backed away, and the presenter turned to my mother. 'Could you explain the porn project to us?'

Augusta folded her arms. 'What do you want to know about it?'

The presenter cocked her head to one side. 'Well, what premise is it based on? How's the experiment being conducted?'

Sitting on the couch, watching herself, my mother sighed again. 'What a question,' she said. 'How can you answer that succinctly?'

On screen, she started to respond. 'The premise, Mary, is that, as you said, I believe men have an essential hatred of women. In the book that accompanies the project, I argue that this hatred is controlled by a thin layer of socialisation and inhibition, a mask that men use to obscure their natural violence.'

'What do you mean?'

'Well' – Augusta paused – 'The process of civilisation has led us, as human beings, to rein in our natural urges and instincts, the biological natures that define us. In the case of men, their natural desire is to rape and pillage at every opportunity, whatever the situation. Over time they've been socialised – through moral and criminal law – into a level of restraint, a level of inhibition that keeps society from becoming disorderly and anarchistic. From an early age then, men are taught to hide their sexual hatred.' She paused to take a sip of water. 'It's not that their urges and desires diminish particularly, simply that they exist behind a veil. Men are still easily coaxed into violence against women, but they learn that it's best to exercise this urge only when there's little or no chance of getting caught.'

'So what does the porn project aim to do?'

Ellie turned to Augusta. 'I can't believe you didn't tell me about this. You haven't done any TV for years.'

My mother pursed her lips. 'Like I said before. I didn't think you'd be interested.'

'. . . by showing men a series of pornographic videos – ten over the course of a day – I think I've been able to induce a short temporary breakdown of these inhibitions. Obviously I don't like using porn, I'd like to see it banned, but it has proved a useful tool. The effect of prolonged exposure to pornography is that it normalises violence towards women and allows men to access their natural view of all women as sluts and whores. By surveying men straight after one of these bouts of pornography, I'm able to get a far clearer view of how they actually feel about women. Watching the scenes of intercourse and sodomy breaks down the moral niceties that men have had bred into them and allows me to record the true venom that they feel towards women.'

The presenter sighed. 'It's a long way from the views

you expressed in *Maternities*, isn't it? In that book you suggested that both men and women were free from biological imperatives and that it would be quite easy for them to break away from gendered behaviour.'

'I didn't say it would be easy.'

'No.' The presenter sat back in her chair, chastened. 'I'm sorry. That's wrong. You did say that it was a possibility though.' She flicked through some notes held in her lap. 'Shortly after *Maternities* was published in Britain your publisher also announced that you would be carrying out a study of swingers and sexual freedom in California. The publisher said that it would be' – she paused – 'and I quote, "a positive look at the way that both heterosexual and homosexual intercourse can enrich society". You had a very different view of human sexuality then, didn't you?'

Augusta pouted. 'There's no point in being an academic if your views remain fixed. Some of my ideas do contradict what I said in *Maternities*, but I think that's in the nature of pushing everything forward. The porn project's the most important work of my career so far.'

'Do you think so?' Augusta nodded as the presenter continued. 'Because when announcing the project, you made some very contentious comments, didn't you?' She glanced at her notes again. 'You stated last year that the only way for women to be truly independent was for them to live in all-female communities and to conceive through artificial insemination. "Veto the penis" – that was your phrase, wasn't it?'

Augusta leaned forward, spreading her legs slightly. 'That was my phrase, yes. At the time I wrote *Maternities* I believed, completely naïvely, that male and female bodies could be best understood as complementary. I was caught up in the notion that biology was irrelevant, and that men's urge to penetrate was matched by women's enjoyment of sex.'

'Yes,' said the presenter, 'you wrote quite a famous essay, didn't you, imagining how people might define the female body if women were in power. You said that rather than heterosexual love-making being seen as a colonisation of the female body by the penis, that it would be described in terms of the vagina "claiming" or "consuming" the male member.'

Watching herself closely now, Augusta groaned. 'Love-making and member. The woman sounds like a Mills and Boon.'

She looked less disdainful on screen. 'That's right.' She leaned over to put a hand on the presenter's knee. 'I was a lot younger then, Mary,' she laughed, 'a lot more optimistic and excitable. Luckily I've now recognised that what's most important is to be realistic, even if it does bring you enemies.' She laughed more loudly now, her voice crackling through the microphone. 'Then again, with forty-nine per cent of the human population as my enemy I guess I shouldn't bother worrying.'

'So what are the results of the porn project? Have they been what you expected?'

Augusta hunched over, rocking from side to side in the

leather chair. 'Mary, they've been more depressing than I first thought. I knew that breaking down men's social barriers would unleash some kind of force against women, but I didn't realise how strong it would be.'

'How have you been measuring this force?'

'A survey,' said Augusta. 'I put it together with a team of psychologists at the university and we've made sure that it's scientifically sound. I've done the test on over three hundred men now and the results have been startling.'

'They each have to watch the films alone, don't they?'

'Yes, that's right. They watch ten films on their own in a tiny room and then, immediately afterwards, they fill in the survey.'

'And could you summarise any of the results for us?'

Augusta pushed her shoulders back. 'Absolutely. I can't reveal all the data yet, but on the question of whether men find aggression against women sexually exciting, eighty-five per cent answered yes after the pornography.'

The studio audience – almost exclusively women – gasped.

'And that's not all,' said Augusta. 'Most of the men found depictions of murder in the porn films a turn-on. All of them made a positive connection between sex and violence and seventy-five per cent said that they would have no qualms about raping a woman if they felt sure they wouldn't be caught.'

The presenter looked shocked. 'That many?'

'Yes,' said Augusta, 'and I actually think that that's probably an understatement. I think that – as with hypnosis – there are some men who retain a sense of their social and personal inhibitions even after so much exposure to porn. In my opinion, the majority of that twenty-five per cent who said they were uninterested in rape were lying or deluded.'

Ellie picked up the remote control and pressed the off switch. Stretching over, Vanya tapped her on the shoulder. 'What are you doing? I was finding that very interesting. Very informative.'

Ignoring her, Ellie turned to Augusta. 'What was all that about? What's with the scare-mongering?'

'I don't know what you're talking about.' My mother leaned back and crossed her legs defensively. 'I was just explaining my research.'

Ellie laughed. 'And your research proves that all men hate women?'

'Absolutely.' Augusta nodded.

'And that includes Geoff and Bob?'

My mother looked serious, subdued. 'You might not want to believe it but I think that deep down, yes, it does. That doesn't mean that we can't get on with them on a surface level, but we could never really have a proper relationship.'

Ellie shrank back into the couch, her knees pulled to her chest, body turned towards Augusta. 'You've always had lots of male friends though. Most of your friends are men.'

'Maybe.' Augusta shrugged.

'Why are you doing this?'

'Doing what?'

There was a snap in their voices. Trouble, I thought, sucking on a piece of pork. Trouble.

'Why are you going back on what you said in *Maternities*?' Ellie paused, looking at Augusta intently. 'I remember when you were writing that book – you were so excited about all the arguments, so fired up. And look at you now. This project is the opposite. There's no debate involved, nothing – you're conducting this experiment to prove your thesis rather than to test it.'

Augusta stretched an arm around Vanya, leaning against her. 'I knew that you'd say all this, that's why I haven't explained the project to you before.'

'But it's crazy.' Ellie's mouth hung open. 'Just crazy. Look at you on that show, so severe and puritanical. That's not you. That's not what you're about. And anyway' – she paused – 'you've always liked porn.'

'Not now I recognise what it is,' said Augusta quietly.

'I am sure she has never liked porn, not really,' said Vanya. 'Not the pornography that shows heterosexual sex anyway, that shows women as sluts and whores and cunts. That kind of porn is just male violence on screen, even if they try and make it look loving. It's a war, a battle-ground. You watch that porn and you just see men hating women. Hurting them. Making them bleed.'

Augusta took her hand from Vanya's shoulder and held it in her lap.

'Is that what you think?' said Ellie.

'In a way,' said Augusta, 'in a way.' I licked my fingers slowly as I looked at my mother. She seemed depleted, spent. Staring at her I had the feeling that sometimes struck me of wanting to wrap myself around her, cling to her like a koala on a branch, protective. 'I don't think you understand,' she said.

'Maybe I don't,' said Ellie softly. She unfolded her arms and reached for Augusta's hand. 'I just don't think it's good for you to spend so much time convincing yourself that the world's a vast, violent conspiracy. I'm not saying that there aren't men who hurt women.'

'Well,' said Augusta, and her eyes grew watery, her knuckles white, clutching at Ellie. 'Go to bed, Molly.' Her voice was suddenly vindictive. I complied happily, heading upstairs, my thumb stuck comfortingly back into my mouth.

I am thinking about all this as I sit in front of the TV with Jane. I know that there is something wrong between Ellie and Augusta at the moment, something specific, but I can't quite work out what it is. It has to do with what they were talking about last night, but Ellie can't really be that upset about Augusta's porn project. My mother has done much crazier, more controversial things. I struggle to think what it could be, knowing that it's something about sex, something about men, but I just can't quite work it out. Maybe Ellie's just jealous about Augusta's affairs, I think.

Jane is pacing up and down in front of the TV, arms

swinging, fingers straight and tense, talking incredibly quickly. I have been ignoring her up until now, but suddenly I catch her words. 'Augusta is a dyke,' she's saying, 'Augusta is a dyke.' She keeps repeating this phrase, while I dress one of the Barbies in a stray Action Man outfit that has found its way into the box of clothes.

'Augusta's a dyke,' she says, as my mother sweeps through the kitchen door, all smiles, holding a tray of drinks.

'Yes I am,' she says to Jane. 'Anyone for lemon cordial?'

9

The father, the son, and the holy spirit

I watch, laughing, stretched out happily, as Lenny unpacks the picnic. I have been sitting on the back porch since six am hunched over my sketchpad, working on a couple of still lives that Carruthers has commissioned: a goat skull filled with flowers, some dead insects. For the past hour, I have been hovering, pencil ready, inches away from a beetle that had colonised Carruthers' house in 1972. Lenny has been in the kitchen, shelling prawns.

He had suggested a picnic lunch last night as we sat smoking on a fallen tree trunk in Hendricks Park. I'd said yes, expecting something modest – a few tortilla chips, some salsa maybe. As Lenny's fingers begin their slow pirouette through the foil packages though, I realise that he has gone to some trouble. 'I thought we'd be having sandwiches,' I laugh, 'with that orange squeezy cheese. What's it called – Velveeta?'

Lenny pauses. He is holding a bottle of olive oil, poised

ready to drizzle over an avocado salad. In amongst the lettuce leaves are ringlets of cucumber, chunks of basil and a clutch of cherry tomatoes cut into perfect imitation roses. Blinking a little, he swats an imaginary fly from his cheek and smiles. 'Don't you think it looks good?'

'It looks great,' I say quickly, noticing the curve of his lips. 'I just feel' – I scratch at a bite on my leg – 'I feel bad, I suppose. I didn't realise that you'd spend so much time on the food.' I pause. 'I would have baked a cake or something.'

Smiling, Lenny reaches behind him. 'No need,' he says, as a lacily piped chocolate cake emerges from his hamper, the sides laden with blue M&Ms. 'I made it last night after you'd gone to bed.'

'Wow.' I pull the cake closer. 'Where did you learn to cook like this?' I nudge him. 'It's a bit more sophisticated than that steak, isn't it?'

He unwraps the last of the food – a chicken, perfectly roasted, its skin glinting wetly and starting to fall away – and stretches out opposite me. We're in our vast back garden and it's a bright day, flaky clouds littering the sky like the white flecks on fingernails. 'The steak was an anomaly,' he says, 'I was stoned,' and he slaps the back of my hand, grinning. 'I used to do all the cooking at home when I was a kid. What can I say? I'm a pro.'

I've been living in Carruthers' house for a week now and have found that the housekeeping work is minimal, a relief. Lenny has been keeping me entertained, coming into my room to recite poems he's found and driving us into town for cheap Chinese food. I look forward to his hunched appearance in the doorway, his enthusiasm for peanut butter cups and Dylan Thomas.

Lying on his side, Lenny serves me a plate of salad, chicken and flatbread. 'First course,' he says, handing me a knife and fork.

'So where did you grow up?' I say.

He is carving a piece of chicken for himself. 'Iowa.'

'Des Moines?'

Lenny looks up at me and laughs. 'Oh, if only it had been the bright lights of Des Moines,' he says. 'If only it had been the heady romantic heights of the city.' He holds a hand mockingly to his chest and pretends to wipe a stray tear away.

'So not Des Moines?'

We are both laughing now. 'No, not Des Moines. Definitely not. I grew up in a small town, middle America, blah, blah, blah. A school, a church, a brothel on the outskirts.'

'One of those towns where they have a sign that says "Population two hundred and three" and it's being changed as you arrive?'

He nods. 'Oh yeah. Ours always stayed at around a hundred and forty-seven.'

We eat in silence. 'So did you like it there?' I say.

Lenny starts talking, his mouth full, tiny fragments of bok choy spraying across the blanket. 'I'm sorry,' he's giggling and we sweep the masticated salad onto the grass, 'but no, God. I hated it. It was just so' – he searches for the right word – 'so' – he struggles – 'boring.' Lenny pauses to wipe his mouth. 'Do you know what the big treat was each year, the major talking point?'

I shrug. 'What?'

He looks at me intently. 'Well, each year the town would hire three or four buses and we'd all pile in to visit this revivalist tent, you know' – he pauses – 'a faith heal-ing tent, about an hour away. That was the big event. The preacher was this old guy – he looked about eighty even when I was a kid – and he always wore this black suit with huge shoulder pads and leopard print brogues. It was a strange aesthetic really. He had all these young female helpers who'd come onstage with him, and he'd constantly be touching them, which I found a bit creepy. I remember noticing that the zipper on his trousers was undone once at the beginning of a show and feeling queasy for the whole evening.' He shrugs. 'I could never work out why people thought he could cure cancer.'

'So you were keen to leave home?'

'Shit, yeah. Everyone was.'

A black fly lands on the salad, huge and armoured, its shiny body segmented into several parts. Jumping to his feet, Lenny holds his hands up in surrender. 'Get away,' he says nervously, 'get away.'

I swat at the fly with my sketchpad and it hums off into some undergrowth. Lenny takes my hand. 'Thanks so much, Molly. I'm such a girl when it comes to that kind of thing.'

We lie down, silent. Lenny is still holding my hand,

stroking his fingers over my palm so gently that they feel like a dandelion wisping across or a ball of accumulated dust.

'So what about you as a kid,' he says. 'London must have been exciting, huh?'

I smile, thinking of the time that Augusta had insisted we paint our faces before going to the supermarket. 'We'll look like warriors,' she'd said, 'angry warriors,' and I had nodded, baring my teeth with a growl. Using some bright blue poster paint that Ellie had given me for Christmas, Augusta had taken great care over my face, filling every inch of skin, right down to my neckline. Aged six, I had done a slightly scrappier job on her (she wouldn't keep still), leaving bare patches on her nose and cheek. 'That's beautiful,' she'd said, looking in the mirror and kissing me. The moisture of her lips left a light imprint on my forehead. Holding hands, we'd run out of our front door, giggling, before marching through the supermarket and saluting the whispered horror of the cashiers.

'It was quite boring really,' I say. 'My mum was a housewife and my dad was an accountant. It wasn't very interesting.'

'Oh,' says Lenny, 'so did you miss them when you moved to California?'

I look over, my lips pursed, nose scrunching upwards. 'No, not really. We never got on that well. I haven't been in contact with my mother for a while.'

'And your dad?'

'Oh,' I say, 'he died a few years ago.'

Lenny is quiet, staring up at a hawk that's circling the parkland. 'I'm sorry,' he says.

'Not at all.' My voice is brisk. I let go of Lenny's hand and sit up. 'It's no big deal.' I cut into the quiche. 'What flavour is this?'

'Salmon and broccoli.' Lenny faces me. 'So is your mom glad you're an artist?' he asks.

I shrug. 'Oh, I don't know, we've never really talked about it.' I take a huge bite. 'This is brilliant,' I say, closing my eyes, 'yummy.' I pause. 'Anyway, what about you? Do you have any brothers or sisters?'

'I did have a sister,' he says, 'Tracy. She was a few years younger than me. I have a photo of her in my room sitting on the stairs with her stuffed toy, Mr Cow. I'll show you later.' He laughs. 'She was so sweet. She died when she was three though, falling off a climbing frame.'

We are quiet for a minute, respectful. 'And your mum and dad?'

'My dad works as an administrator at a construction firm and my mom' – he pauses – 'she stays at home.'

'And do you get on with them?'

He stretches out on the blanket, his feet tense and pointed. 'Not really.' He turns to me. 'I don't know. I used to really like my dad when I was a little kid but I think it was just because he was so tall.'

'How tall?'

'Six foot five.'

I nod, impressed. 'That's tall.'

Lenny laughs. 'Yeah.'

'And was he a fun dad? Did he take you out fishing and that kind of thing?'

'Oh no, not at all.' Lenny smiles. 'He made me join Little League and play baseball, but no fishing. He was no good at sports himself, a bit of a joke at school, I think, but he always used to coach me. He said I'd gain people's respect if I played well.'

'So when did you stop getting on with him?'

Lenny laughs. 'Oh, pretty young. About four, I suppose.'

'About four?'

'Yeah. It took me that long to realise that height was his only selling point.'

'But what made you dislike him?'

He shrugs. 'I don't know. He was just a bit of a control freak.'

'In what way?'

'All kinds. Like at home, when we had dinner, he'd say grace and then he'd start picking at the food, listing all the things that were wrong with it and getting my mom to write them down. When it was really bad, he'd just push his plate away and go and get a bag of chips.'

'How was your mum's cooking?'

'Well, my dad was kind of fair on that point actually. Her cooking was bad.' Lenny laughs. 'She's one of those people who just cooks the food until it melts, you know? She'd serve up the dinner and your vegetables would be like slush on the side of the plate. A steaming pile of slush. The leeks and zucchini, the carrots, they'd all have merged together, just fused into this big beige mess.'

'Is that why you learned to cook?'

'Yeah. When I was about seven, my dad banned Mom from the kitchen.' He laughs. 'He actually stuck these signs up on the door, in red pen, saying that he'd cut her housekeeping money if he caught her in there. She was allowed the occasional visit to make coffee or powdered soup, but that was all. It was weird.' He pauses. 'Then he'd take me shopping instead and we'd pick out meals for me to cook.'

'And how did your mum react?'

'Oh, she was OK. She just took root in front of the TV.'

'Oh.' We lie there, the sun fighting through some cloud cover, searing our faces. 'So your parents were religious?'

'Yeah,' says Lenny, reaching for the sunglasses that are holding my hair back and trying them on. They're huge Jackie O frames, orange and yellow striped, and they make Lenny look like a drag queen. 'Small-town people, you know. They thrive on frustration.' He pushes the sunglasses up over his forehead. 'Were your parents Christian?'

'No,' I say, 'Christianity's not all that big in Britain these days. We prefer soap opera.'

'Very wise,' he says, 'there's not much you can't learn from *Days of Our Lives*.' He looks up at me, his face a sudden frown. 'I hate religion.'

I throw an olive at him. 'Lighten up, Lenny, it's not

that bad.' He's still grimacing. 'Some people need religion,' I shrug, 'other people need UFOs.'

Lenny throws the olive back at me and I catch it in my mouth. Jumping up I clasp my hands in the air, holding them to either side of my head and grinning. Lenny applauds. 'Thank you, thank you.' I nod to the imaginary crowd.

'So what about your parents? Are they scary Christians?' I am laughing as I sit down. 'Do they have one of those pictures of Jesus on the mantelpiece, all white-skinned and oozing gore?'

He giggles. 'Of course. They have lots of icons. Just above the TV there's this painting of the Virgin Mary which shows her with massive hands, like a footballer's. They're huge. It was done by some local artist and he was obviously really bad at fingers. That picture always used to fascinate me. My favourite though is this dome they have with a little plastic figure of the crucifixion scene inside. When you turn it upside down, it rains bright red snow.'

'Great,' I say, 'you can't beat crucifixion memorabilia.'

'Absolutely.' Lenny reaches over for the chocolate cake and cuts a tiny slice. 'Just testing,' he says, folding it into his mouth. His eyes goggle as he chews. 'That's good.' He cuts a chunk and hands it to me, cradled in a swan-shaped napkin.

I take a bite. 'So were your parents bothered about you having girlfriends when you lived at home?' My voice is muffled by cake. 'Were they against sex before marriage and that kind of thing?'

Taking a slug of vodka and lemonade, Lenny splutters, laughing. 'Are you trying to make me choke?' He pats a napkin to his mouth. 'Just slightly. Completely. God, every Sunday the priest at our church would stand in the pulpit threatening people who'd had pre-marital sex or adulterous sex – anything like that – with death by drowning. It was terrifying. Christ.' Lenny shudders, remembering. 'It was awful. Every week he gave these really graphic sermons about lust.' He cuts himself a piece of cake. 'He always told us that we'd crossed over to the company of Satan, whatever we'd actually done that week, even if we'd given up masturbation for macramé.'

'So it was quite a fundamentalist church then?'

Lenny snorts. 'Definitely.'

'And people didn't have sex before marriage?'

Lenny has taken a huge bite of cake and his mulch-filled mouth falls open. 'Oh God, everyone was at it. Absolutely. There was nothing else to do. The big high-light of local life for me was the mobile library coming to town, but other than that there was no entertainment, nothing.' He pauses to swallow. 'I'm sure there's far more under-age sex and crack-smoking in small towns than anything you'd find in the city. Everyone's just so bored.'

Finishing our cake, we lie back down on the blanket. 'That was great,' I say, my head turned towards Lenny. 'Thanks so much for cooking all this.'

He reaches out and takes a strand of my hair between his fingers. 'That's OK,' he says, smiling.

We lie silent for a minute. 'So did you get a lot when you were a teenager?'

'A lot of what?'

'Sex,' I say, prodding his stomach. 'Did you get a lot of sex?'

Lenny sighs. 'Not really. I had a couple of girlfriends during high school, nice girls, but I never tried getting them into bed. I was too scared.'

'So when did you lose your virginity?'

'That's the question,' he says. He turns on his front. 'It was about a year and a half ago actually.'

'Really?' I say, my voice straying up an octave. 'So that would have made you, how old?'

'Twenty-two.'

'Wow.' Lenny looks embarrassed and I pat his arm. 'Sorry,' I say. 'What I meant was, that's so' – I pause – 'restrained.'

We are both laughing now. 'Oh, fuck off,' says Lenny, and he kicks me lightly. 'I know it was late, but I was a slow developer, OK?'

'What made you wait so long?'

He picks a blade of grass and pulls it carefully apart down the middle. 'Oh, I don't know. Part of me was scared of my dad, I suppose. He would have gone crazy if I'd got a girl pregnant.'

'Was he nice to your girlfriends?'

'God, no, he was nasty to them, horrible. I remember one of them refusing to come back to our house because he'd made so many comments about her weight.'

'Why was he like that?'

'I don't know.' Lenny pauses, his hand combing carefully for the perfect blade of grass. 'Jealousy, maybe.'

'Jealousy?'

'Yeah.' He picks a blade. 'You know, he didn't have any good friends himself, he was very' – Lenny yawns – 'closed off, and I think he wanted to keep my mom and me sort of annexed. He was very easily threatened.'

'He was like that with your mother?'

'Oh yeah, their marriage was so strange.' He stretches out again, sighing.

'And she did everything your father said?'

'Yep.' He pauses and wipes his mouth again. 'God, this is gross.' He turns to me. 'Can I tell you something horrible?'

'Sure,' I say.

'I haven't thought about this in a long time, but when I was six – it must have been just after Tracy died – I went into my parents' room in the middle of the night, wanting some water or something, I guess. Anyway, I put on the hall light, knocked on their door and walked in. My dad was shouting at me' – Lenny brushes the hair off my face – 'he was shouting for me to get out but his voice was all breathless, you know, and walking closer to the bed I saw that he was sitting on my mom's chest and his hand was moving up and down really fast. I didn't know what was going on, I couldn't work it out and then suddenly' – he sighs – 'I saw that he was coming on her face.'

'Wow.' We are both silent for a minute. The clouds are moving fast across the sky and I remember my childhood game of racing them, hedging my bets on which one would reach the sun first. 'That's horrible,' I say.

'Yeah,' says Lenny, 'probably more so now than then. I had no idea what was happening really, but I knew it was nasty.'

'Yeah,' I say, and I have that feeling in my throat that pre-empts tears, the rounded swelling at the back of the mouth. 'So who did you lose your virginity to?' I say.

'Back to my virginity?' he says teasingly, and then, 'It was quite traumatic really.'

'Traumatic?' I say. 'Did the condom split?' He shakes his head and I gasp, 'Was it bloody?'

Lenny laughs. 'No. I mean the actual sex wasn't traumatic, more the aftermath.'

'I don't think I've ever heard the post-coital glow described quite like that.'

He punches my arm. 'Don't be silly.' Lenny tries to sound authoritative, wagging his finger at me. 'Are you going to listen?'

I lower my eyes. 'Absolutely. Go on.'

'Well, it's kind of a long story' – he takes a deep breath – 'but after I left school I went to work at a construction firm, the same one as my dad.'

'What were you doing there?'

'Oh, you know, my dad was in charge of a lot of the admin side and I went there as the office junior. There were all kinds of basic jobs to do – sorting out payments, filing, that kind of thing. We worked out of a makeshift office, a plastic cabin, wherever the firm's biggest site was at the time.'

'OK.'

'So I'd been there for about three, three and a half years and it wasn't really going anywhere,' he smiles, 'I mean, there wasn't really anywhere that it could go. It was a boring job in a boring firm in the middle of Iowa. It was' – he pauses – 'very dull.'

'So losing your virginity was the answer? The only possible respite?'

Lenny laughs. 'I'm getting to the virginity part, young lady, give me a second.'

I smile. 'I'm sorry. You know me, always after the money shot.'

He hits my arm again. 'You're so bad. Anyway. I was getting really pissed off with the job, really bored. It was OK when the office was quiet because I could write, but it was a pretty successful firm and the phones went off all the time, there was always something to sort out. Most of the guys who worked there were great though,' he nods, 'really nice, so sometimes we'd go out for drinks after work.'

'Ah, they were showing you the way of the devil?'

Lenny puts his hands behind his head and smiles. 'In a way, yes.' He looks at me. 'There was this one guy there, Jeb, who I got along with really well. He was married.' He turns to me. 'He'd been married since he was eighteen, but we used to have a good time together. If there was no one else around we'd go out, the two of us, for drinks or to grab some food or something.'

My eyes start to widen and I reach out for his arm. 'Lenny, you didn't have sex with his wife?'

He laughs. 'No, of course I didn't. But after a few months of going out together things went a bit further.'

I bite my lip. 'I see where this is heading,' I say.

'Yeah, so we started, kind of slowly, to have a relationship.'

'Was he a muscle boy?' I say.

Lenny grimaces. 'He was great. Just great.'

'So what happened? Did his wife find out?'

Lenny laughs. 'No. Not at all. Thank God. No. One day after work, Jeb and I were getting ready to go out, putting on our coats, packing up our stuff. The place was empty – it was about seven pm – and I just leaned over and hugged him.' Lenny holds his hands up. 'Nothing really. The door opened though, and my dad came in and saw us.' He turns onto his side, facing me, and leans his head on his palm. 'I've never seen my dad move so fast. He put his hand flat on Jeb's face, kind of pushed him, and then dragged me to the car.'

'Were you trying to get away?'

'Of course, but he had a really strong grip and he was screaming at me. Capitalising on my surprise. He got me into the car quite easily.'

'Did you tell him he was being ridiculous?'

He pours a glass of wine for each of us. 'I didn't say anything. I was terrified. My dad's quite violent really.

Since I was about four he'd been coming into my room in the middle of the night, just straddling my back and hitting me.'

'That's awful.'

'Yeah.' He hunches a shoulder. 'Anyway, it was a Wednesday when he found me and Jeb together, and he told me not to go into work for the next two days. He left me and my mom locked together in the house.'

'What did your mum think about the situation?'

'I've no idea. She only talks about TV shows.'

'So did you go back to work?'

'Oh no. It came to the weekend and my dad packed me and my mom into our tiny car, him in the driving seat, and took us off to California.'

'What?'

'Yeah, I know, it seemed strange to me too, but he just wouldn't tell me what was going on. I had an inkling that we weren't headed for Disneyland or San Francisco though. My dad didn't really seem in the holiday mood. Still,' he laughs, 'it didn't take me long to figure out the situation once we arrived at the ministry.'

'The ministry?'

'Yeah, it was a Christian ministry and treatment centre. The people there sometimes called it a de-programming centre. My dad had gone to our priest for advice and he'd recommended it.'

'De-programming what?'

'De-programming homosexuals. There are a bunch of them across the country, lots in California. They've developed all these spurious therapies – conversion therapies, they call them, or reparation therapies – which are supposed to make gay people think like heterosexuals.'

'Oh yeah. I've read about them.'

'Yeah.' Lenny smiles, biting his lip. 'There was quite a lot of coverage about them a while back. I think one of the social work associations criticised them and there was a bit of a row.'

'So how long were you there for?'

'Oh well, my dad had gone ahead and signed me up for two years,' he laughs, 'two years! But I only lasted about a month. It was awful.'

'What was it like? What did they make you do?'

Lenny stands up, lunging forward to stretch his legs. 'God, do you really want to hear about it?'

I nod. 'Sure. If you don't mind. It's interesting.'

Lenny laughs. 'Oh, I don't mind. I mean, in retrospect some of it's quite funny.'

'Like what?'

'Oh well, like the guy who ran the place.' He sits down again, cross-legged, facing me. 'He was called Tony and, I swear, Molly, you have never met a gayer man. He must have been about forty, early forties maybe, and he had the most effeminate drawl you've ever heard. When we arrived he greeted us at the door, carrying a Bible, and he was wearing a tiny T-shirt with these tight, tight jeans that just kinda' – Lenny motions at himself – 'rode up at the back.'

'And was he friendly?'

'Oh yeah,' Lenny snorts, shoulders shuddering. 'The first thing he did was to introduce us to his wife, Maureen. His wife!' He sighs. 'She was this really dumpy woman, mousy, and he beckoned her over from the reception desk and told us that she was his life partner. He was shaking my hand, smiling, and he said,' Lenny giggles, 'he said something like, "I may not have found Maureen attractive when we first met, but due to God's healing love I've come to realise that she's my helpmate and destiny." Poor Maureen. They'd had five children,' says Lenny. 'It was depressing.'

'How weird.'

'Yeah. It was all very strange.'

'So what did they make you do? How did they plan to repair you? Did they start getting heavy with the coffee enemas?'

Lenny laughs. 'Molly, sometimes you're just really gross, aren't you?' I nod. 'No, Tony took me for a tour of the ranch owned by the ministry and then he showed me my living quarters.'

'What were they like?'

'Oh, you know, they just gave you a cubbyhole really in this huge dormitory, very spartan. They used these hideous blankets on the beds that were made of some kind of animal hair, all brown and itchy. They brought everyone out in a rash, which was attractive, and the whole living area was open plan so that no one had the privacy to do anything naughty. Anyway, so he showed me the cubbyhole and then he went through my luggage and started confiscating things.'

'What did he confiscate?'

Lenny looks up, thinking. 'There were some jockey shorts which he said were quite suggestive, T-shirts, a pair of jeans. He took a copy of *Men's Health* that I'd bought in the seven-eleven.'

'What was wrong with that?'

'Oh well, Tony flicked through and said it was titillating.'

'Well, of course it was titillating – he's a gay man who's been in a relationship with a woman for, how long was it?'

'Fifteen years.'

'Fifteen years. That's sad, isn't it?'

'Deeply.' Lenny pauses. 'The whole thing was just unfathomable. After he'd been through my bags he sat down and told me some of the rules.'

'Like what, like what?' I sit up and slam my hands excitably against the grass.

'Oh well,' Lenny's laughing now, 'everything was banned, just everything.' He looks at me. 'You weren't allowed alcohol, sugar, caffeine, porn, TV, disco music—'

'Disco music?'

'Yeah,' he says, 'absolutely no disco music. I asked Tony why it had been banned and he said that some of the older residents found that it reminded them of their gay lifestyle. "It's not the Lord's music," he said.'

'What is the Lord's music?'

'I don't know. Tony liked country.'

'So was there anything else that they stopped you doing?'

'Oh yeah. I mean one of their main concerns was that no one was allowed to masturbate.'

'Why?'

'Because any sexual activity that happens outside marriage is supposed to be a violation of Christian principles. That's the central credo of the whole operation really.'

'And what were the others?'

'Oh, there were hundreds of little rules and regulations. We had to have counselling sessions every day to get to the root of our gayness, all this awful cod-psychology about family relationships. They think that homosexuality is caused by a failure to bond with your same-sex parent during childhood. The idea is that gay men spend their lives just searching for the meaningful relationship they never had with their dad. The whole thing was embarrassing. I mean, I know I have problems with my dad, but I think in psychological terms that's about as reductive as it gets.'

'Fuck, yeah. I mean, how did they explain away the flamingly heterosexual boys brought up by single mothers?'

'Oh, they didn't. I think they just ignored all the holes in their theories. I tried to tell them that I liked women too and that I didn't really feel that the programme was for me but they just said I was in denial.'

'And where did they find evidence in the Bible to back them up?'

'Corinthians, mainly. There were a couple of verses that they used to chant all the time – "Such were some of you once, but now you are washed by the power of the Holy Spirit." They said that it proved that there had been homosexuals in the early Church and that it had been possible to cure them.'

'What bullshit.'

'I know. It was all horribly unscientific. A mess. Anyway, a big part of the therapy involved pairing men up and trying to create a non-sexual bond between them that would fill the gap in their psyche. Sort of like a surrogate father.'

'Sounds dubious.' I watch as Lenny shudders. 'Don't tell me – you slept with your partner, didn't you?'

He shakes his head. 'Shit, no. It was when I found out what he was in for that I decided I really had to leave.'

'He wasn't gay?'

'No,' says Lenny. 'After a couple of weeks I found out that some of the men there were paedophiles, pederasts. The ministry believed that it was possible to treat anything they saw as a sexual problem in the same way and that they could cure these men who'd been preying on kids for years.'

'Oh God.'

'Yeah. There were people there who just should have been in jail, there was no way that they should have been hidden away at this centre. Other men were being treated for addiction to Internet porn too, really violent stuff, all kinds of things. I just felt so sick when I found out. The idea that my dad had thought I should be subjected to the same kind of treatment as people who like to fuck animals. It was awful.'

'So you left?'

He sighs. 'Well, it was a little more difficult than that.'

'You couldn't just walk out?'

'No, my dad had stood over me when we arrived and made me sign an order that said I was happy to be restrained and brought back by one of the guards if I tried to leave.'

'So what did you do?'

'Oh, I snuck out in the middle of the night, walked to the nearest town and got the bus up to San Francisco for a few weeks. Then I heard about this place.'

'Have you been in contact with your parents since you left?'

'No, not really. I sent a postcard to my mum from Carmel, just to let her know I was OK, but I've left it at that.'

'God. And you didn't get chased by any guards on your way up here?'

'Oh no,' Lenny smiles, 'I can be quite subtle sometimes. I'd been scoping out escape routes since I arrived. I knew exactly what I was going to do.'

'So that was the end of the ministry.'

'Yep.' Lenny laughs. 'I was outta there.' He pauses, mischievous. 'I did look up their website on the Internet the other day though, just out of curiosity, and it turns out that Tony's been suspended as chairman.'

'Why's that?'

Lenny grins so widely, laughing, that his face resembles a split melon. He leans over and kisses me with a thwack on the cheek. 'He was caught by the LAPD with an orange in his mouth, tied up in the dungeon of an illegal S & M bar.'

10

Suspicious minds

Waking up, it takes a moment to place the source of the
bright yellow stripe on Tom's forehead, the circle of pink
on his cheek. The colours are so luminous, reflective, that
I just stare for a second, bemused, as they float on his
skin. Reaching out to touch him, I turn a little and my eye
catches the tiniest corner of a casino sign, glinting its invitation through our window. Las Vegas, I think. Never
wanted to come here. Always thought it would be ugly.
Welcome.

I pad to the window and look out onto the neon sea of
the Strip. It's five am but Las Vegas Boulevard breathes
activity and I watch as a steady gasp of people emerge
from one casino to be swallowed by another. Tugging at
the curtains I let out a mocking sob, realising they are
destined never to meet in the middle. The lights beat
relentlessly through the two-inch gap.

I go back to bed. Tom is asleep, the thin blue sheet

pulled up around his head like a veil. The Virgin Thomas, I think, smiling wryly. The motel we're staying in is insistently cheap, the air conditioning shot, and both of us are coated in a waxy film of sweat. Moving close to Tom's neck I catch the sweet glandular smell of beer, the faint sugary odour fighting through. I kiss him softly. I can just make out the rapid movement of his eyes beneath the lids, and wonder what images are ticker-taping through his dreams. Probably porn, I think. This room could only inspire porn.

Trying to sleep, my eyes refuse to stay closed, cast open again and again by the lights. I stare at Tom, his eyeballs still jostling, and notice for the first time a thread vein that throbs in his forehead. It runs at a right angle to the ridge of bone that crosses his brow and I can suddenly make out all the details of his skull, the framework of his face. As he rests on his side, I see the skin of Tom's right cheek sink into the open space above his jawline. I peer closer, noticing the signs of a rash amidst his stubble and the varying size of his pores. My eyes set an inch from his face, I examine the deep scar on the bridge of his nose, the badly grafted skin used to cover the bloody hole of a childhood accident. Raising my hand to touch it, suddenly fascinated by the ill-set ridges and discoloured stitching, I feel Tom's breath fall on my fingers. He exhales, coughs, and turns over, legs kicking at the sheet, sighing. I notice that he has dribbled on his pillow.

Scared to wake him, my hand stays poised in the air as he turns and, while it hovers, I look curiously at my ring.

We'd bought it in a souvenir store on the way to Vegas, a fat pink plastic band with an orange cut-out of California stuck to it. White glue oozes around the state like a milky sea and if I curl my fingers too fast San Diego gets caught on my knuckle. It is hideous. 'Perfect,' we had both said when we saw it, Tom paying the two dollars, putting it with the marriage licence in the pocket of his jeans and patting it gently. 'Perfect.'

Tom had seemed laid-back that morning, his usual scuffed-shoe self, but once we'd bought the ring his gait had suddenly changed. Climbing into the car, leaning low over the wheel, he had started to drive so fast, so possessively, that I had opened the window and nervously sucked down two packs of cigarettes. 'Why so frantic?' I'd said, a hand on his knee. 'My visa doesn't expire for two weeks.'

He'd turned to me then, smiling, guileless. 'Why would we wait,' he'd said, 'when we can do it all today?' and his hand had shuddered off the wheel to stroke my face. I had grinned then too, careful not to burn him, caught up for an instant in his happy, simple certainty.

The nerves had nudged me again as we drew up to the Strip though, the lights of the billion-dollar hotels like brilliant shrapnel, a swarm of fireflies. Arriving at a twenty-four-hour chapel just after midnight we had sat in the car, swigging at our whisky bottle, giggling. There was a while to wait – thirty minutes had been allotted for the three couples before us – and we stayed there, holding hands, barely talking. 'You're not nervous, are you?' said

Tom eventually, his voice breaking. He took another bolt of whisky.

'Not at all,' I said. 'I mean, we've known each other almost four months, right?'

Tom's laughter sounded a little demented, but he squeezed my hand hard. 'I'm sure,' he said.

The radio was playing a Sinatra tribute as we watched the couples process out, their faces happy, drunk, surreal. Something about the lights, the music, the seamless procession of brides made the whole scene flicker past like a silent film, a collection of stills. The couple before us had gone to some effort – she was wearing a puffed-sleeve dress, he was in a blue velvet suit – and they stopped as we walked in. The man, a small rat-faced guy, shook Tom's hand. 'A fine one there,' he said, gesturing at me and winking, 'very young.' I had grimaced whilst Tom laughed. Looking down at my Scooby-Doo T-shirt and khaki shorts I felt, for a second, a little underdressed.

The chapel was tiny, its ten-foot aisle traversable in five long paces. We shuffled up, trying to take our time, as the organist – a moustachioed woman of seventy – played a stunted version of 'Here comes the bride', a samba rhythm pulsing in the background. The pastor faced us moodily, asking the necessary questions in a Southern drawl, blankly professional. Edging the ring onto my finger, Tom and I shared hyena grins. 'You can kiss the bride,' said the pastor, unmistakably bored by the proceedings. He started to inspect his fingernails, scraping away at some dirt as Tom pecked me sweetly, respectfully on the cheek. 'She's not your aunt,' boomed the pastor, 'kiss her like you mean it, not like she's here for a green card.' He leaned towards us and I noticed the smell of vegetables on his breath. 'I want to see some kissing.'

Tom had raised an eyebrow at me and we kissed properly, a lingering whisky kiss. After a few seconds the pastor had tapped me on the shoulder and whispered, 'Move along,' and we turned to see another couple at the end of the aisle, faces red with impatience. We walked quickly to the lobby and signed the papers. Leaving the building I noticed that the muzak being piped through the air conditioning sounded distinctly like 'Suspicious Minds'.

I pull at the ring and realise that the heat and moisture in the room have created a vacuum. It's soldered to my finger. I go to the bathroom and sit on the toilet. I am tempted to have a bath, but something about the chipped, heart-shaped tub puts me off. I tug at the ring half-heartedly and wonder what Augusta will think. Her daughter, married at eighteen, annexed in America.

A few years ago, 1991, Augusta had written a damning book about the US that had prompted a renewed welter of interest in her personal life. Called *The Freedom Trap*, it had moved away from the subject of gender to offer up a broad-based critique of American culture. In it Augusta had argued that the triumph of individualism and capitalism, the inexorable rise of the self, was a movement that would allow the US to suck the world dry of resources. Within the next fifty years, she said, the effluent of self-help books, the me, me, me cries of the American people, would effectively end the human race.

British critics had been divided on the book, some praising Augusta's focus on environmental issues, others calling her critique shallow. Despite these differences though, all the reviews had picked up on the personal vein of hatred that Augusta was spewing at the US. Just beyond her arguments was a flood of rage, too searing to be dismissed and too personal to seep into the supposedly objective body of the text. Instead it sat on the surface like a stinking, stagnant pool. Most journalists had picked out a phrase from the introduction to emphasise the point. 'America seems to offer escape and beauty,' Augusta had written on the opening page, 'but I, like many others, found only emptiness, depravity and horror.'

I fill the toothbrush glass at the sink, take a gulp of the minty water and head back to bed. It's five-thirty am and the sun is vying with the neon. Both are winning intermittently. I lie heavily on my front, pulling my breasts up so that they are crushed more comfortably. Dozing, I dream of my mother and her reaction to my American husband.

A couple of hours later I wake to feel Tom holding me, gentle but insistent, turning me over, parting my legs. He starts to push a finger into me – I am dry – and then I feel his breath. His tongue, flat and warm, takes one long stroke.

I pull him up, kissing him, and detect the dank taste of me on his breath. He moves to go back down and I draw him in tight. 'Not now,' I say, kissing him again, diversionary.

When he pushes into me a few minutes later I am still dry, despite his efforts. Squeezing my eyes shut I struggle to conjure the orgies of flesh, the undulating bodies that might make me ready. As Tom strains against me a little while later I come with all the velocity of a sneeze. He pants, his body always somehow heavier, denser, after sex, and lies on top of me for a few minutes. Then he rolls off and sits up, smiling.

'How are you?' he says, picking some dust from the corner of my eye. He looks nervous. 'Are you OK?'

I smile reassuringly, laughing. 'Of course, Tommy.' I reach out my hand lazily. 'We're married.'

He beams, taking my hand and kissing it. 'I'm so glad,' he says, 'it's going to be fucking great, isn't it?' He looks at the ring. 'That's a beautiful piece of jewellery,' he adds, 'gorgeous, but maybe we should get you a better one.' He starts tugging at it and I yelp. The suction is strong. 'Maybe not right now,' he says.

I want to stay in bed – we had been drinking until three am last night – but Tom is excited about the tub. Leading me into the bathroom he points at it, clapping his hands together spontaneously. 'It's brilliant,' he says. I start to pull him back to bed but he insists. We each climb into a separate half of the heart, our feet entwined at the point.

'So,' says Tom, switching on the Jacuzzi feature with his big toe, 'do you want to stay in Vegas a few days or shall we go straight to Davis?' The bath whirrs a little, as if ready for take-off, and then lets out a thin stream of bubbles. 'Jacuzzi!' says Tom, and I find myself laughing at his unassailable glee.

'I don't mind really,' I say, thinking again of how I will tell Augusta. A part of me wants to call her from the motel phone, tell her right now when I can be sure of her anger. 'I suppose money-wise it might be worth going to Davis, but I don't know.' I put my head underwater a second to wet my hair. I turn to Tom, my eyes beseeching. 'What if your parents go mad when they find out we're married? What if they hate me?'

Tom laughs and starts splashing. 'They'll love you,' he says, his voice bold, and then more gently, 'they'll love you. I've told them that we're going to be living together in Davis anyway, so it's not as though a wedding ring should make much difference.' He kisses me. 'I really think that it's going to be great.'

Looking at him then as he begins to talk about Davis – the house we'll live in, the job he's lined up – I catch his doubtlessness again, his transparency. It's touching, reassuring, but frightening too, prompting a sickness in me, a gag reflex. As he talks I stroke him gently, artlessly, and try to feel sure.

'Steve, my brother, you're going to love him,' he's saying. 'We used to play together all the time when we were kids, he was with me when I fucked up my nose, picked the flap of skin off the ground.'

'Ugh,' I say, with a smiling grimace.

'Yeah, that's a good brother for you, isn't it?'

'Mmm,' I say.

'Anyway, he's twenty-six now and he manages Dad's sports shop. We could probably go to Tahoe with him this winter and you could try some skiing and snowboarding. It'll be great.' He smiles, flashing his gums. 'Macy, Steve's girlfriend, is a fantastic skier. When we were at school we thought that she'd make the Olympic team, but she just missed out.'

As Tom talks, his face pulled close to mine, his fingers dancing over my cheeks as if tracing a map, I duck away gently and under the water again. My eyes shut, hair spreading out, I recall Augusta's face as it was when I left her, the downward pull of it, the wrenching, exaggerated anger. I had seen that expression so often when she was drunk, angry. It would jag suddenly when she was shouting at Ellie. But it had never looked quite like it had then, caught in the thinning rectangle of the doorframe.

I feel Tom's fingers moving into me, grab his hand and hold it. I am still underwater, enjoying the tightness as it pulls across my chest. I remember sitting under our kitchen table with Ellie one Sunday, shelling and eating pistachios, Augusta upstairs in the bedroom. They had just had one of their rows, another argument about me, and watching them through the tablecloth fringing, safe and hidden, I had seen Augusta's face curl and contract with anger.

Six years old, I had held Ellie's hand and cocked my head. 'Why do you stay with Mummy?' I'd said. 'How can you love Augusta?' and Ellie had smiled and wrapped her arms tight around me. 'Not that I want you to go,' I'd added, and she'd laughed and nuzzled my hair.

'You make exceptions for someone extraordinary,' said Ellie.

I come up out of the water panting, to find Tom staring at me curiously, his eyes excited and worried. 'You were under a long time, Moll,' he says. 'I was about to pull you out.'

The bath water has started to turn tepid, our skin wrinkly, and I lead Tom back to bed. We lie there drying quickly in the heat and, reaching for my bag, I take out a sketchpad. Tom has asked me to draw him over and over again, but as my hand starts moving across the page, finding the proportions, recording them carefully, his eyes close with embarrassment. 'I'm not beautiful enough,' he says, laughing, slightly effeminate, but after a while his body begins to relax. It is only when I pull at him dispassionately, arranging him more aesthetically, that his face scrunches up. 'What are you doing?' he says, eyes still shut.

And looking at him for a moment, staring, some images bisect in my mind. Suddenly I realise that Augusta's face, frozen in its jag of anger, is much like Tom's at the point of orgasm.

11

The scrutiny problem

'They're so' – Lenny pauses, the tip of his tongue trapped gracelessly between his teeth – 'so' – he turns to me laughing – 'so rude.'

Lenny has been asking to see my collection of nudes – 'The Tom Portfolio' as he calls it – since I arrived at Carruthers' house three weeks ago, but I've been putting him off until now. It's a particularly bright day, sunbeams piercing through the window, and I've been laying out the pictures one at a time on my bed. We're on to the fourth, Lenny having greeted each with a gasp, a shy foot shuffling and a critic's pose, one hand held effetely to his mouth, the other clutching his elbow. 'I love this one,' he says, as he has about each picture before. This time he peers closer though. 'The genitals are just so, so . . .'

'Big?' I say.

'Well, yeah.' He laughs. 'They're huge.' He looks at me questioningly. 'You're dirty, aren't you, Molly?'

'IT'S ART,' I say, my voice booming, mock-angry, and we both start laughing, tear trails running from Lenny's eyes. Standing there looking at the piece, he takes my hand. Eventually we stop giggling and are still, staring at the picture. As always I am scoping the page for mistakes, false economy of line, too much shadow, depressions caused by leaning too hard. 'It's bad,' I say, almost as a note to myself.

'It's brilliant,' says Lenny, 'I love it.' He pauses. 'Is this one of the ones that Carruthers is buying?'

I nod. 'Yep.'

Lenny smiles. 'I don't blame him.' He turns to me. 'You know, Carruthers is a pretty well respected collector, Moll.'

I laugh. 'I guess so.'

We're both silent for a while, staring, before I go to change the picture. Still holding hands, Lenny pulls me into an awkward hug. I put my arms up around him and he leans in, whispering, 'Why don't you draw me?'

I pull away, smiling. 'I can't draw you,' I say. Then, teasing, 'I thought you said that posing was just for exhibitionists anyway?'

Lenny steps back, his eyes sloping more than usual. 'I think it would be fun,' he says, 'interesting.'

I lean my head to one side and try to look at him objectively, imagining a lens in the way, a frame. There have been moments in Lenny's room with the candles burning (his bulbs have blown) when I've studied the structure of his face, his high browline and pointed chin, his downy white skin. The length of his face gives it character, a sallow quality deflected by his floppy hair and clothes.

I can't decide whether a sitting is a good idea though. The only nude that I've ever drawn is Tom, and that had proved difficult. Sitting still was never a good bet for a climber. I have seen Lenny bare-chested in the past weeks – he seems quite thin, surprisingly hairy – but never naked. When I had started to draw Tom, his body was already familiar. Scrutiny brought a different view, but no real surprises.

Lenny is looking at me plaintively, his eyes puppy-dog wide, chin digging into his chest. He puts his hands together as if in prayer. 'Please?'

I lean my head to the other side, still looking, and laugh. 'All right then, darling, get your trousers off.'

Lenny hugs me again. 'Thanks!' he says. 'Brilliant. It's going to be so much fun.'

He retreats, gambolling into his room, while I clear away the pictures. Looking at them so closely again has been strange, prompting sly memories of the hours spent drawing. Tom had posed for the last one just before the first signs of his depression had set in and its lines veer portentously across the page. I remember how he had fidgeted as I sketched him, mumbling something about going for a run, needing to exercise. To Lenny and Carruthers, the body on the page is an object: provocative, but as simple in its stillness as a bowl of fruit or a vase of flowers. To me the dark, broken lines record discomfort, the unfinished torso a warning.

I am rooting through the back of my closet, retrieving my largest sketchpad, when Lenny reappears, clad in a towelling dressing gown. I turn to see him lean against the doorframe, aping seduction, pulling at a corner of the fabric to show more leg. 'Yes,' I say, matter-of-fact, 'very sexy,' standing up with my sketchpad and picking a set of pencils off the dressing table. I pull my folding chair up close to the bed. 'Get them off,' I say, and motion him to lie down.

Lenny is laughing, nervous. He kneels on the bed. 'You're not going to laugh if I look small, are you? It's pretty cold in here.'

'Only about ninety degrees,' I say. 'I mean, I'll quite understand if it's shrivelled.'

Lenny grins. 'OK. I won't make a big deal of this.' He pulls at the cord around his waist, throws off the dressing gown and lies on his side, head propped on his hand, naked.

I have been determined not to stray immediately to his genitals, have been telling myself to keep eye contact, but as soon as the robe is off my gaze veers down, careering across his body like a car with tampered brakes. As with most American men his age he is circumcised, his head a dark pinkish red. He is a good size and I am fascinated by the way his pubic hair wafts around him, silky and long, freshly shampooed. Tom had always kept his trimmed, partly I think to make him look bigger. Having only slept with five men, I am always intrigued by the differences in their bodies. There's always something surprising, something unexpected to acclimatise to. 'Great,' I say, smiling at Lenny. 'Is that pose comfortable?' He nods. 'Great.'

I start to sketch him, beginning with the most basic outline. Scrutinising him is strange at first but after a few minutes I am deaf with concentration, completely immersed. I begin working in some shadowy details, the nipples, clavicle, pelvis, to be clarified later.

Lenny surprises me with his silence, his concentration, holding it completely for ten minutes. Then, as I pause, leaning back and framing his genitalia with my fingers, he lets out a laugh. I hold up a hand to him. 'Quiet.'

He's bored now though, ready to talk, and as I'm focusing on his genitals, I let him. 'It's so strange to be scrutinised like this,' he says, 'so weird. I feel quite vulnerable, you know, even though it's only you.'

He pauses a second, thinking. 'Did Tom ever mind you drawing him, did he ever find it weird?' He shifts his head a little on his hand, stretching his wrist to calm the ache, careful not to move his hips. 'I guess it wasn't so strange, what with the two of you going out together for so long, huh?'

I smile, not answering as I draw the hole at the tip of his penis, glistening lightly now. I put my pencil down. 'It was pretty strange for him as well, I think. He was really keen that I draw him, but after a while he found it sort of' – I pause, picking up my pencil again – 'intrusive, I guess. I think it made him feel a bit out of control, like you said, vulnerable.' I begin shading the head. 'He wasn't so keen in the end.'

Lenny shrugs, revolving his wrist. There's a deep pink line where it's been bent back by the weight of his head. 'It's like that essay, isn't it?' He closes his eyes. 'You know, that essay by Augusta Flynn. They published it as a book.' He sighs. 'My mind's gone blank.'

My head jerks up and I look at him curiously, trying to work out if he's guessed, whether he's said this for a reason. Over the past few weeks I've wondered whether Lenny's heard of Augusta. Tom had been barely aware of feminism at all, oblivious to its figureheads, scared and impressed when I'd told him of my mother's reputation. Lenny though. Lenny is well read. He knows his thinkers.

'*The Male Muse*,' I say.

He leans his head back on his hand. 'That's it,' he says, 'that's it. A great book. Have you read it?'

'A long time ago,' I say, 'when I was a kid.'

'It's fantastic,' says Lenny. ' I remember talking about it with Bella, the girl who ran the mobile library. I used to call her the missionary.' He pauses. 'She was determined to get all these books out to the people of Iowa, books on gender roles and that kind of thing.' He laughs. 'And what a receptive audience she must have found. She was great. She lent me all these books.' He looks at me intently. 'Julia Kristeva, Andrea Dworkin, Susan Brownmiller. They were fascinating. Have you read a lot of that stuff?'

I shake my head. 'Not much, no.'

'Oh.' His eyes focus on the wall. 'I remember sitting with Bella outside her trailer when I was about fifteen and talking to her about that idea from *Maternities* – the idea that you could take on whatever gender traits you liked.' He smiles, remembering. 'Bella was quite masculine, I guess. She always wore these huge shorts and socks with sandals.' He sighs. 'I loved those feminist thinkers.'

I prod him in the chest, laughing. 'Lenny, you big fruit, you must be the only man who's ever uttered that sentence.' I try to take an authoritative tone. 'Now, come on. Are you going to be quiet for a while so that I can draw you?'

He nods enthusiastically – 'Of course' – but within seconds he's started up again. 'God, it's just so strange thinking about those books. They totally saved my life, you know, Molly—'

'You don't think you're being over-dramatic?'

'Over-dramatic?' he laughs. 'Maybe. But they made a big difference to me, honestly. If I hadn't read those, I'd never have had a sense of life outside that town.' He holds a hand flat against his brow, lowering his voice dramatically. 'I could have been stranded there for ever.' He pauses. 'Augusta Flynn's books especially, they were brilliant. Just so well-written. I mean, all the others write well, obviously, but they're aiming for a more academic audience, I guess. And a lot of them wrote in a way that was really hard to read as a man,' he sighs, 'which is understandable. Augusta Flynn though, she just timed the writing perfectly. She unpicked all the problems that I had with gender, all the problems that affect men as well as women.' He laughs. 'In *Maternities* anyway. Before she went off men.'

Lenny stops talking, caught up in a thought, while I sketch him, my hand shaking. He starts in again. '*The Male Muse* addresses all those things that you said were a problem for Tom though, doesn't it?' He smiles. 'I mean, it's been a long time since I read it – I've got a copy in that box in my room somewhere – but it talks about how being objectified is a feminine experience and how it emasculates a male sitter and all that. Maybe you should have read it to him, made him realise what he was feeling.' He laughs. 'Gender swap.'

I lay my pad on the floor next to me and go over to the dressing table where there's a glass of water. Heading to sit back down, I point at Lenny, laughing. 'Lenny' – I pause – 'you know, don't you?'

He looks bemused and laughs. 'Know what?'

'You know that I'm Augusta's daughter.'

'What?'

'I'm Augusta Flynn's daughter.'

Lenny stares blankly at me for a second, one hand rising to his mouth, the other pointing at me, almost a parody of surprise. 'No.'

I nod, eyebrows raised.

He smiles, laughs, 'No,' and pauses. 'Molly Flynn.' He sounds slightly hysterical. 'You're Molly Flynn!' He rubs a hand across his forehead and then slaps himself. 'I can't believe I didn't recognise you. I mean, I've read all the books on Augusta, I've seen pictures of you when you were a kid. How could I not have recognised you?'

He stands on the bed and starts jumping, his penis as

animated as a small animal, and points at me again. 'You're Molly Flynn,' he laughs. 'That's fantastic.' He climbs down, coming over to hug me, before noting his nudity and cupping his genitals in his hands. He goes to the bed and motions for me to perch beside him. I sit down and Lenny stretches an arm out, pulls me close.

'Molly, why didn't you tell me? That's so exciting.'

I rest my head on his shoulder and smile suddenly at the situation, me fully clothed, Lenny naked. I am relieved that he knows really, had been starting to get confused about the lies I'd told. Anonymity is difficult when you like someone, it starts to lose its appeal. 'You're Augusta Flynn's daughter,' says Lenny again, his voice breathy with recognition. 'Your mom's a legend.'

I sit up and go back to my chair. 'We'd better get on with your portrait,' I say, 'before the light changes. Can you remember the position?'

Lenny laughs. 'As if I feel like sitting now. Your mom's an icon. God,' he sighs, arranging himself obediently, 'I almost feel like looking Bella up and telling her. Me, here, in this room, with Augusta Flynn's daughter. It's amazing.'

'It's nothing to get that excited about,' I say, shifting in my chair, suddenly uncomfortable. 'It's really not that interesting.'

'Are you kidding?' says Lenny. 'It's amazing. Augusta Flynn's one of my idols. She's a great writer, she's a maverick. It must have been so exciting growing up with her. I'm totally in awe.' He laughs. 'Particularly since you told me your mom was a housewife.' He points at me. 'Liar.'

I feel myself turning red. 'Yeah, well, it's not always that easy being known as Augusta's daughter. She's not the simplest person in the world.'

'She's fantastic though.'

'She's a drunk.'

Lenny shrugs. 'So are we.'

'Trust me,' I say, 'she's not alcoholic in that American way that means you like a few beers. When I was a kid she used to drink perfume if there was nothing else in the house.'

'Oh, alcoholic alcoholic,' says Lenny, nodding soberly.

'Yep,' I say, 'full-time.' I start some dark shading on his groin. 'I think she's getting a bit better now Ellie's back but she was really ill for a while.'

Lenny stays quiet for a few minutes, respectful, as I etch his pubic hairs. He can't keep from twitching though, or emitting the occasional awed 'Wow'. I shift in my seat, trying to get a better angle on his chicken-skinned scrotum, and he takes it as a cue to speak.

'So you had a hard time growing up with Augusta?'

I smile. 'Not all the time, not really.' I move so that I can see some of the underside of his right ball, which hangs lower than the left and rests mournfully on its opposite number like a dying soldier. 'It was OK.'

Lenny shifts slightly. 'And did she talk a lot about her work, did she discuss stuff like the porn project with you? I mean, that was pretty controversial, wasn't it?'

I move closer to Lenny and notice that his genitals seem to be shrinking away from me, receding. The skin of his balls especially is changing shape, contracting. I almost reach out to rearrange them, but manage to stop myself. I sit back in my chair. 'She used to talk about stuff at home, yeah.'

'It's so amazing,' says Lenny, his voice breathy.

I start sketching some veins, sighing. I smile. 'You really want to know about Augusta, don't you?'

He grins, slapping his hand against the top of his thigh excitedly. 'I kind of really do.' I grimace and Lenny reaches out and touches my arm. 'I'm sorry. Not if it's too weird for you, of course, but I'm just so' – he laughs ecstatically – 'so excited.' He looks at me, eyes as beseeching as those of a fourteen-year-old girl, alone on Valentine's.

'You promise to stay still if I tell you about her, promise not to get over-excited, because' – I look at the page – 'this is actually going pretty well.' I scrutinise the drawing with an editor's eye, picking out the shading that needs to be refined, imagining the detail that can be added. 'I think this could work, could be interesting eventually. Is that fair?'

'Let me see, let me see,' says Lenny, straining his neck to get a look.

I turn the pad away from him. 'Not until the end,' I say, my voice strict. 'I'll show you at the end. Now will you keep still?'

'Of course,' says Lenny, 'of course.'

'OK then. What do you want to know?' I continue with

the network of veins which, in this flaccid state, create a kind of mottling. 'What's on your mind?'

'OK.' Lenny is smiling so widely, his hand still tapping his thigh, that he looks like he's stumbled across an orgy. 'OK' – he pauses – 'my mind's gone blank.' He glances down, thinking. 'So what was it like growing up with her?'

I smile. 'It was great sometimes. I mean, Augusta's all those things that you say she is – she's funny, original.' I lean back to get a perspective on the triangular creases of skin that link the groin to the legs. 'I guess it was like other people have a favourite aunt or something. Augusta wasn't very responsible but she was fun. She was always making up games for me, stories.'

'What kind of stories?'

'Oh, all kinds. I was reading a newspaper article when I was about ten, a sort of overview of Augusta's life and work, and I suddenly realised how many of the stories she'd told me were made up. I mean,' I laugh, 'I'd kind of figured that she'd invented the more outlandish ones, but realising that maybe ninety per cent were fiction was pretty scary.'

'So what had she made up?'

'Oh, lots of things.' I sigh. 'When I was younger she told me that she was a ghost, a spy.'

My hand ratchets across the page, moving faster now, as I think of the hours each day after nursery school when Augusta would pick me up and we'd walk together through the park. Perched on a bench, she would tell me of elves, satyrs, vampires, each story featuring her in the starring role, me in a short supporting appearance. Convincing me that we were descendants of Vlad the Impaler she had held her hands limp-wristed above her head and lunged for my neck, mouth open, teeth bared. The screams as I ran off, toppling through the trees and down the hill, seemed to echo for hours, the surrounding wildlife fleeing the scene.

'She told me that she was a Russian refugee, a clairvoyant.'

Lenny's laughing. 'She was a bit nutso, wasn't she?'

I smile. 'I guess you could say that. The thing is, it seems funny now, but it was always getting me into trouble. It was a nightmare. I remember, when I was about five, telling one of my teachers that Augusta was a member of Swedish royalty. She shouted at me in front of the whole class.'

I think of that day, standing beside the front desk reading to my teacher before telling her of my royal background. She had pulled me by the arm to stand in the corner of the classroom then, making me stay there from lunchtime until the school bell, my classmates bulgy-eyed at the punishment.

'She called Augusta in and told her that I was a fantasist, that I might have some kind of mental problem.'

'And what did Augusta say?'

'Oh well, I was waiting outside the classroom putting my mittens on, and she just went mad. She told this teacher that she knew nothing about creativity, that I was going to be an artist when I grew up and was more

talented than any other kid in my class. It was so embarrassing. I had to change school after that.'

Lenny reaches to scratch his balls. 'Don't!' I say, holding up my hand to stop him.

He looks down and takes a long breath. 'Fair point.' He
touches himself gently, still breathing deeply. 'I'm fine.'

'Thanks,' I say.

Lenny is staring at me curiously. 'So how did you stay
so sane? It must have been a bit' – he pauses – 'I don't
know, disorienting, to be constantly told different stories
about who your mother was, where you came from.'

'Oh, it was.' I bite the end of my pencil. 'It was pretty
weird, but to be honest, Ellie – you know, my mother's
partner' – Lenny nods – 'Ellie brought me up really.
Augusta was so unreliable. Ellie had to call her from work
every day just to remind her to pick me up from school, to
make sure that she'd got me some lunch.'

'Ellie's not an academic, is she?'

'Oh no, not at all. When I was a kid she was managing
this bar in London. It was pretty cool.' I lean back and
start sketching one of his biggest veins.

'So did she set you straight about all the stories your
mom had told you?'

'Yeah, kind of. She told me that Augusta wasn't a vam-
pire, which was a relief. I remember sitting with her one
Sunday when my mum had gone off to do some broadcasting – I must have been about twelve – and we just
went through all the different stories talking about what
was true and what wasn't.' I start shading the ridge of

Lenny's penis, the point where the head joins the shaft, struggling a little with the proportions. 'I mean, obviously by that age I knew that she hadn't been born to pirates, that she wasn't the Queen of Sweden' – Lenny laughs – 'I wasn't completely backward, but she'd told so many small lies too that I had no idea what was true.'

'Small lies?'

'Yeah, she said that she was born in Edinburgh when she'd been born in Devon. She said that her parents were part-Egyptian, which wasn't true. She told me that she'd been married at Cambridge—'

'To a man?'

'Yeah, to a man, which was just the weirdest story of all. Complete bullshit. She's such a lesbian, I'm sure she's never even kissed a man.' I rub out some of the shading and start again.

Thinking back on all the inventions and revisions of my childhood is quite exhausting. As a kid I had thought that Augusta's compulsion to lie stretched to everyone she knew, but after a while I'd realised my mistake. She'd lie to Ellie, of course, about her dalliances and affairs, but the wild, disconcerting stories were saved just for me.

'So was Ellie able to sort through it all for you?'

'She was really helpful, yeah, as I said, really great.' I remember that day and the shock of Ellie handing me my birth certificate. The father's slot had been left blank, a stark, bright white, with not even a smudge or a blot to act as a clue to his identity. I shrug almost involuntarily. 'She couldn't tell me everything I needed to know – it was impossible to ask all the right questions – so I started to read up what I could about Augusta.'

'Biographical stuff?'

'Yeah, I started to piece things together. There were a couple of biographies that had been published by then so I got hold of those. They weren't great but they were factual. They told me some important stuff.'

'Wow,' says Lenny. 'That's so weird, isn't it? We were probably reading those biographies at about the same time.'

I laugh. 'You've read biographies of Augusta?'

'Oh yeah, like I said, I was completely fascinated by her when I was a teenager.' He pauses shyly. 'I mean, I still am, but at that age I was a bit obsessive.'

'Wow, you poor boy.' I lean forward. 'Can you shift your penis slightly to the right?' He moves it gingerly a few millimetres. 'A bit more? That's great.' I start in on the left ball, squashed as it is.

'So are Ellie and Augusta still together?'

'Oh yeah. They broke up for a few years whilst I was living in California – I think Ellie had just had enough – and Augusta fell apart a bit. It was never going to last though, the break-up. They're such a couple.'

'It's amazing really,' says Lenny. 'Brilliant. I mean, Augusta seems like such a' – he pauses for the right word – 'maniacal person. It's amazing that she's had one partner for so long. It must be – what is it – thirty years now?'

'About thirty-two. They got together in the late sixties some time.'

'That's right. Augusta was studying at Columbia when they met, wasn't she?' Lenny motions to me. 'Could I have some of that water?'

I reach over and pass it to him. 'Yeah, I think Augusta was doing her PhD.'

'And what was Ellie doing? The biogs never really made that clear.'

'Oh, she was looking after her dad. He was Augusta's English professor – he died of cancer in her second year at Columbia, I think. That's how they met.'

'Eyes locked over the operating table?'

I flick my eraser at him. 'You're grim, aren't you? No, I think Ellie's dad had introduced her to Augusta a couple of months before he died and they moved in together a while later.'

I finish shading Lenny's ball and go to the sink in the corner to fill my glass with more water. Sitting back down I notice a shadow starting to inch its way across Lenny's legs, the light fading quickly. I put down my pencil.

'That's it for today,' I say. 'I'm finished.'

Lenny yelps and jumps off the bed. 'Really?'

I nod and he starts to pull his robe around him. He taps my arm, his face mischievous. 'Can I see, can I see?'

I look at the picture for a second, held away from me at an angle. 'Sure,' I say. I turn the drawing to face Lenny and he backs away, sitting abruptly on the bed.

'Wow,' he says, transfixed. 'I have the biggest cock in the world.'

12

Before the fall

The descent, when it came, was quick. Just try diving slowly, I think. Impossible. You can't mess with velocity. I remember my science teacher telling us that a penny dropped from the top of the Empire State Building would gather enough speed to split a pedestrian right down the middle, head to toe. Advances take a long time, I think, scrunched up small, back tight against my bedroom door. Advances take effort and work and commitment. They need a will to direct them, a force, but a descent can be unguided. Just look at lemmings. You never see determined lemmings. Freefall comes easy.

I take another gulp, my glass half-full of vodka. It tastes good, I think, smoother than usual. I consider knocking on Lenny's door to thank him for bringing it back from the store this morning, but decide not to. He's probably asleep by now, I think as I stretch across the wooden floor, turned slightly on my side to drink.

Then again, maybe the descent wasn't so quick. Maybe it had started years before I met Tom, before he was born. Perhaps his foetus, thumb-sucking in the womb, had been predisposed to the madness. There had been the black moods, after all, even when we'd met in Australia. The crying spells followed by weeks of energy, exercise, the climbing trips that purged Tom's brief unhappiness. Maybe those had been the first signs. I shrug to myself. Or maybe they just seemed important now.

Perhaps you were oblivious, Molly, uncaring, I think, as I say my name aloud, lingering over the syllables. Molly. Slowed down and repeated it sounds arbitrary, as all words do, as though it could signify anything – a kind of tree, a chemical cleaner, an animal indigenous to Australia. I imagine a furry creature somewhere between a kangaroo and a wallaby. A Molly, I think, that could be a Molly. I smile.

Dozing, I think of the time Tom's mania had really become obvious, two years after we'd moved from his hometown of Davis to London. I think of the weeks he was someone else. My mind scrolls through the panic attacks – Tom hyperventilating in a corner, crouching for hours, face turned to the wall. These would be followed by a run around the block whenever his breathing stilled, be it midnight, two am, five am. During those weeks of panic Tom had gone completely without sleep and when I'd managed to coax him into bed I would feel the dry heave of his body beside me, his lungs creaking like a pair of bellows. Sometimes I would be woken by his screams too, not the rehearsed shrieks of movie queens but a keening, desperate howl, like a chicken being toyed with by a neighbourhood fox. Caught between its teeth and killed.

There were stomach cramps in those weeks too, vomiting, our supplies of tissue and toilet paper constantly depleted, always some mess to wipe away. And his energy had increased, the midnight runs becoming marathons, our flat sparkling with the polish of nervous excitement. It had built up, built up, the mania, like rainwater lapping at a flood defence, climbing around the sandbags, creeping, creeping, gathering its strength before streaming through the town's windows.

And then Tom had been stranded in bed, helpless even to stand up or talk. Coming home from work one day, a month after the plummet, I had found him sitting on the edge of the bed, shoulders hunched like a shell. He was naked except for a single sock, the other held limply in his hand. This was the state I had left him in that morning. He had seemed a little more together then, intent on getting into work, pulling that first sock on triumphantly. He needed a shower – hadn't had one for three days – but I was so excited to see him out of bed that I had decided to ignore it. 'Great,' I'd said, 'great. You'll feel so much better once you've been to work.'

Of course that sock had always defeated him. Too much of a hurdle. And the shower might as well have been Everest, a cross-Channel swim, forty days in the wilderness. The only way that Tom could manage that was with me acting as a crutch. He would stand under the water, motionless, as I lathered him, washed his neck and swaddled him in a towel. The process took two hours.

When he had seemed a bit better, had been to the Harley Street pharmacologist and started his drug cocktail, Tom had tried to explain it to me – the panic and mania, the breakdown. As we sat up in bed together, his speech still peppered with pauses, his eyes unfocused, he had likened the panic to the feeling that you have in dreams when you find yourself falling, out of control, and suddenly jerk awake. It was like that, he said, except that it extended through an hour sometimes, or a day, and he'd be left permanently mid-gasp, inhaling, suffocating. It wasn't so much that he wanted to breathe and couldn't, Tom said, more that he'd lost the memory of breathing and had to accept that the air would keep filling his lungs. With no idea of anything that might help, his body was locked tight, like a scream, bottled and capped. He'd inhale until he exploded.

I try to imagine panic as Tom described it, but can only recall how good that falling sensation feels. I'm drunk, I think, smiling more. Not panicky or depressed, just drunk. I lie flat on my back, thinking about how much I like sleeping on the floor, supported by the boards.

I am asleep for a few minutes, the ice cubes still melting in my glass, when I hear a knock at the door. 'Come in,' I say groggily, my head jolting up, expecting Lenny.

We had gone out to a local bar tonight but had come back early after he had fallen asleep at our table. He was exhausted after stacking shelves all last night and spending today writing furious, amphetamine-driven prose. Getting in, he had made me a drink and I had slumped off to my room, sulking. 'I guess I'll read,' I'd said over my shoulder, knowing that there was no chance of concentrating and hoping that Lenny would come to my room to entertain me. Eyes dusty with fatigue he had plunked some ice into my vodka and sloped off to bed. 'Good night.'

The door opens and I close my eyes, head hard and heavy against the floor. 'Hi, Lenny,' I say, and notice that my voice is slurred. How strange, I think. 'What's up?' and I feel a hand over my mouth. Opening my eyes I am shocked to find Matt standing over me. I try to say something but my voice is so muffled that all that comes out is a single glottal stop.

He takes my hand and pulls me, quite gently, onto the bed. He starts to kiss me, his teeth painful against my top lip, and I push at him half-heartedly. Lenny and I had been talking about Matt tonight, his looks, his silence. 'He's gorgeous, isn't he?' Lenny had said. 'I'd do him in a New York minute.'

'That would be fun for you both.'

Lenny had hit me. 'I don't mean that the act would be that fast,' he said slowly, 'just that I'd be there if ever he wanted me.'

'I'm sure he'd be relieved to hear that.'

'Well, you'd be the same, wouldn't you?'

I'd thought about Matt's glassy eyes, the wisp of hair across his brow. 'With a bit of mood lighting and some cheap wine, yeah.' We had both laughed. 'Of course.'

'He's so enigmatic, isn't he,' Lenny had said, 'although I always wonder whether his silence comes down to charisma or just lack of vocabulary?'

'Maybe he's actually Spanish,' I'd offered, 'maybe English is his second language.'

'*Sí*,' said Lenny.

Matt holds me down as he lifts my skirt, pulling clumsily at my underwear. Slapping at his hands I try to push him away. 'No.' We struggle against each other for a minute, me scratching his arms, pulling at his ear. There's a small lamp beside the bed and I can just make out his frenzied pupils, dilating like an inflatable ball. I shove at him again more lightly now, sad as I realise my lack of resolution. His hand moves away from my face as he tugs at his belt. 'A condom,' I say, 'a condom.' I motion to my top drawer.

He almost smiles. 'Yes.' Closing my eyes, I steel myself against the strobe vision of nausea. Matt straddles me as he gets ready, opening my legs and feeling between them. I kick at him but he holds me still before pushing hard into me. It's so painful that I bite his hand. My teeth clamp down for five, ten seconds, sinking further and further into him but he ignores me and eventually I stop, scared of drawing blood.

As his body starts slapping rhythmically against mine –

determined, industrious – I have a kind of physical memory. It's a few seconds before I recognise the feeling, place it to the time of Tom's mania, when everything he did was touched by this pummelling determination too, when a fuck was just that. I imagine Matt's torso is Tom's and feel, momentarily, like wrapping my arms around him, clasping each side of his head and stroking the hair at the nape of his neck.

Lying there silent and still, almost numb, I try to pinpoint the start again, the slow plod to the cascades, the wonderless look over the edge and the jump. Was it while we were in America? Could it have been before London? Reading a book about depression recently I had searched each page for clues, like the cheapest undercover sleuth. I knew what I was looking for – a sign that the depression had started in childhood, that it wasn't linked to me. A sign, maybe, that it was genetic, a flaw in his brain that had lain happily dormant until being shaken awake. Perhaps it was that time he'd slipped over skiing, I think. Perhaps that tumble and the spraining of his ankle had made him depressed. Or it could have been dislodged out hiking. Awoken by sheer physical endurance.

Matt is pushing harder into me now. He is propped up, left hand leaning against the mattress, his arm tensed so that he has more space to move. I open my eyes a little, noticing that his are closed and that he's biting his lip. I examine his face, looking for an explanation, but he has the blank, squeezed-dry appearance of someone who has been doped. His features have dissolved.

I feel tears on my face. They had started to slip out like this, so easily, when Tom and I had first arrived in London in 1997. The city had been like a trigger then. We'd been married for three years, had spent enough time in Davis for me to secure a full US visa and now we were free to move between the two countries at will. Although Tom loved Davis – enjoyed managing his dad's store, going skiing, playing baseball – he had been excited about coming to London. He liked to travel, had the easy confidence to meet new people. As we boarded the flight to Heathrow he had been grinning like a loon. This was freedom, Tom said. Not bohemia, but better.

Despite being bored with Davis's small-town eccentricity, I was less excited about the move, more ambivalent. It was partly the cost of the city that put me off. I knew what minimum-wage London could be like. But it was mainly the fear of seeing my mother again, of turning a corner and finding her there, face still caught in gargoyle anger.

As it was, Tom and I had found a bedsit south of the Thames, miles from my mother's house in Islington. There was almost no chance of an unplanned meeting, but still her closeness nagged at me. Since I'd left, Augusta's presence as a commentator, one of Britain's cultural elders, seemed to have grown bigger than ever. She contributed to a late-night review programme now, screened three times a week. Some evenings I would find myself idly switching the channels – as though unaware of the time – and would catch a few minutes of the show. I

was struck then by Augusta's articulacy. I had imagined
that broadcasting would be beyond her now and that her
work would be confined to a few hours of writing each
day. The shock of Ellie leaving seemed to have smacked
her into sobriety though. During my last months in Davis
I had received a card from Ellie explaining that Augusta
was drinking far less and that they were tentatively back
together. She suggested I get in touch. I hadn't quite
believed her, but seeing my mother on TV having lucid
discussions about art and books, I realised it was true.
The recognition made my stomach plummet as though
flying over a speed bump.

I look again at Matt's face, blank, unchanging. It is
Tom's breakdown face, distant and hollow, as though the
brain behind it has been removed and suspended in a jar,
still pulsing. When was the start, I think, staring at him,
when was the start?

The tears seem to be having a thermal effect on my
face and I can feel my skin glowing red. I think of our
bedsit in London, 'our garret' as Tom used to call it.
Moving in, we had been optimistic, sure that we could
transform the musty, ugly room and kitchen into something more promising. After a few months though our
resolve had waned. Despite air fresheners and deodorant,
the room still smelled rotten, as though an animal had
died behind the radiator. Despite cleaning the shared
bathroom ourselves, the tub was still full of suspect hairs
each morning or dark puddles of dye. And the yellow
wallpaper. There was nothing we could do about that.

Patterned in swirling paisley it could have driven the safest psyche mad.

Matt thrusts into me and I cry out, a heaving sob. Looking up, he nods as if to suggest that it's almost over, maybe to reassure me, and cups my face in his hand. I shake it away, but again feel drawn to touch him. I close my eyes and concentrate on the weight of my arms.

The wallpaper, already lumpy with air bubbles, had started to peel after a few months, as mould crept up one wall before spreading virally across the room. Our bedsit was on the ground floor of a converted building. When we moved in, it had no curtains but we had resolved to save for some fabric that would cover the windows – netting at least, or muslin. As it turned out, we were so broke and, later, so demotivated, that it never got done. I lived in fear those years that a man on the street – the faceless, black-hooded man in my dreams – would see me naked and break into the flat to rape, torture and kill me.

It wasn't then that it had started though. Despite the odd snap of anger, Tom was the grounded one then, as focused as ever on keeping us content. I was the one who griped and drank through the weekends, curled up in our dirty duvet. Temping in a call centre, a twenty-four-hour banking helpline for people who'd lost their debit cards, I found the work so frustrating that I used to plot arson, bomb threats, as I answered customer queries. I found it hard, after a few weeks, not to shout at the callers. It wasn't just that they never knew their account numbers or how many cards they had. Some of them had raised vacuity to an art form. One female caller, explaining that she was a customer at our bank, had demanded that I come out and read her gas and electricity meters. When I replied that I could only help renew her debit cards she had started to yell. 'This is a twenty-four-hour helpline,' she'd screamed, 'you're supposed to help.' I had pulled my earpiece out and walked off to the toilets for a cigarette. Away in the distance I could hear her words rattling through the phone. 'A fucking helpline.'

Tom had been more upbeat about his temp jobs, had expressed a shy fascination with office life. His aim – the pinnacle of temping for him – was to secure a data-inputting job where he could listen to his Walkman as he worked. When he finally got the call to say he'd landed one of these Tom was ecstatic. Tearing out of the bedsit, he had come back twenty minutes later, panting and brandishing a biryani. Other than toast and potatoes it was the first food we'd had all week.

I feel the sly twinge of approaching orgasm and wonder how my body can respond so hopefully. Such a betrayal, I think, this physical shift to autopilot, my body following some familiar script and not recognising the discrepancies. I am still nauseous, my head throbbing, attempting to stave off the sickness by focusing on a damp patch on the ceiling. I stare at it for a minute, counting each second firmly and slowly in my head. All right, I tell myself, hands up, I surrender.

The insistent throb keeps coming closer and my back

arches naturally, like a stem in the frost. It was that night
after work, I think, that night when Tom came back late.
That was it. The depression and mania may have been
there anyway, may just have been waiting for a signal, but
that evening set it off.

Matt lies heavily on top of me and squeezes his hand
beneath my back. He pulls me up towards him and I lie,
limp and heavy, a dead weight on his arm, my arched
body the only response to his thrusts. If only Tom and I
had had sex that evening, I think, then the argument
would never have happened.

Tom had just started his data entry job then, working
for a massive company in Shoreditch, three to nine pm
every weekday. Despite the unsociable hours he quite
liked it, coming home the first evening and describing
the row upon row of tall-sided desks and the cricket-like
bleat of the keyboards. I could imagine him and his co-
workers clattering away at their computers like a factory
full of monkeys, just waiting for the day when one of them
would produce Shakespeare. 'It's OK,' he'd said, shaking
his head and laughing at its mundanity. 'It's not so bad.'

Most trains had been cancelled that day – there was a
strike going on – and it had taken Tom two hours to get
across London. Still, he was in a good mood when he
arrived home, looking forward to a baked potato and
some sleep. In the hours since getting back from work
myself, I had been slumped in front of the TV, sinking
glasses of wine as I watched gardening shows. Feeling
bored, picky and over-analytical, I responded to every-

thing he said with a shake of my head or a shrug. 'Do you want to go to the cinema this weekend?' he'd said. 'I think we can just about afford it.'

'About all we can afford.'

It was while we sat eating that I had really started to chip away at him. 'We've just never been very compatible, have we?' I'd said, as we watched a repeat of a comedy show that hadn't been funny the first time round. 'We should probably break up for a while.'

Tom's face had pinched inwards for a second, like a corpse's, before he took my chin in his hand. 'I know you don't mean that,' he'd said, kissing me gently. 'You're a bit drunk, aren't you' – he was laughing at this point – 'we'll go to bed in a minute.'

I had jerked back from him then, laughing too, and insisted that I wasn't joking. 'You were my prop,' I said, 'a great prop.'

Tom had stood up and walked into the kitchen and I followed him, red-eyed and determined. I would tell him now, I thought, tell him everything that he should have known about the reason I'd first left London. Cornering him against our cooker I had proceeded to lecture him, venomous, unpeeling it all like a pomegranate, its seeds turned to mush.

Tom held me as I spoke, trying to calm me down. If I had put my arms up and around him, I think, everything might have been OK. But I kept insisting that we'd never been suited, that he was just a refuge. We had slept naked that night out of habit, our backs turned to each other.

Matt is breathing heavily now, and when he pulls me close I can feel the pulse in his chest. His pounding is even more painful than before. Lying there flaccid, mute, I try to remember why I hadn't explained the rift to Tom when we'd first met, in Australia or Seattle. Telling him about the argument between me and Augusta would have given him the chance to assess my motives then, to reconsider his bent-kneed proposal. I had been evasive from the start, I think, suggesting that my mother and I just didn't get along – no drama – that she was a little crazy, I was a little diffident. Lying in wait that night, I had brought out her screamed threats, the parting, the flight, and let him suppose our marriage was a sham. The way I told it he wasn't a husband. He was an escape route. I think of a book I once read on depression that noted that the worst forms were often caused by humiliation and loss.

I feel the slap of Matt's chest against mine now, the same sensation as the slap of the tide. The tears have stopped – I could never cry for long – and I start laughing, giggling, suddenly almost gleeful. I laugh at everything: Tom's depression and my maudlin anger, the irony that Augusta had paid for his drugs, the strangeness of Matt fucking me. It's just gristle, I think, remembering my mother's description of a penis, tumescent gristle. I laugh so hard that I wonder whether the hysteria, the almost painful heaving, will override any orgasm I might have, obliterate everything in fact. It is like a bombing raid, I think, this laughter, opening my eyes to see Matt staring, still pounding at me, suspicious. Completely hysterical now I suddenly feel it sweep over me. Matt comes, his teeth clenched hard, rearing up and back like a horse, his face mimicking pain. And I come too, a dry spasm, and slowly start to scream.

13

The Bonsai Bride

'So I brought them back with me, these tiny brides. They were all perfect, like' – the man pauses to wipe some salsa from his mouth – 'like bonsai brides. Sometimes I would sit next to whichever one I was with that night and just stroke their hands while they slept. These tiny little girls with their long, thin fingers which you could have just snapped, like that' – he makes a crunching noise – 'if you'd wanted to, of course.' He takes another bite of his burrito and keeps talking. 'They were beautiful.'

'And they were all married to you?' says Lenny. He takes a gulp of beer and lifts his eyebrows at the bartender. 'A Bud for me and – what do you want, Molly? The same?' I smile. 'A vodka and Coke,' says Lenny, 'a double vodka and Coke.'

The man is nodding hard, his jowls like fleshy wings. Looking at him I realise who he reminds me of – a guy I once saw on TV who held the record for the most pegs ever attached to a human face. This man has as much surplus flesh, but he's older, about sixty-five. He's wearing a checked shirt with what look like egg stains down the front, and his jeans sag expertly beneath his stomach.

Lenny and I have been in the bar since mid-afternoon, just after he'd barrelled through my bedroom door, proclaiming himself tired of work. It's a cavernous Mexican joint on the corner of town, fitted in red and orange, with an inept copy of a Diego Rivera mural covering one wall. Until ten minutes ago it had been empty and we were discussing the space–time continuum (a short conversation) and Madonna's film career (a longer conversation). Arriving mid-sentence, this man's body odour had announced his presence immediately and he had launched into his life story.

'Course they were all married to me,' he says, 'in a sense. They loved me so much. Knew they were lucky. They had a much better life than in Vietnam.'

'And how did you bring them over?'

'Oh, different ways. Some of them married my friends. Others came over with false papers. At one time there were twenty of them, all living with me.'

'So' – Lenny puts ten dollars on the counter and gestures at the man with his beer bottle – 'so you're telling me that you lived with all these Vietnamese girls in Eugene?' He pauses. 'In a big house in Eugene?'

The man laughs. 'Not in Eugene, no. I lived with them on a little homestead in northern California.'

'And they were your harem?'

'Harem?'

'You slept with them all? They serviced you?'

The man smiles. 'That's right. We got lots of customers too though. Those girls were so happy. They just used to smile all the time – made them real popular.' He leans past Lenny, takes my chin in his hand and squeezes it. 'This one here. I could make some money out of her if she'd smile more.'

I prise his fingers from my chin. 'Thanks,' I say, 'that's great.' I motion towards a table in the corner.

Lenny nods, before turning and shaking the man's hand. 'Good to meet you.' He leans in with a stage whisper. 'I'll try and convince her to try prostitution, yeah?' The man nods.

I take Lenny's arm and pull him, laughing, to the corner table. 'You bastard,' I say, and we both sit down with our backs to the bar. I prod him hard in the stomach. 'Bastard.'

He puts his arm around my shoulder. 'I was only trying to help.' His eyelashes quiver. 'I think you'd make a very good prostitute,' he pouts, 'really. He's right though – you don't smile as much as those Vietnamese girls. But there's still a market for you, honey.' He smiles at me, his voice emollient. 'Some men love angry women.'

I push at his shoulder. 'Just give me a cigarette.'

Lighting it, Lenny grins. 'I thought maybe we could get a bus into Portland next week and visit that bookstore I was telling you about. We could go in early, spend the day there maybe, get some food. There's this great toy store, all second-hand toys. You can buy robots from the sixties, those plastic ones that come in primary colours with flashing eyes. They're amazing.'

I exhale a thin stream of smoke, nodding. 'That sounds great,' I say, 'but I'm not sure how much I'll be around next week.' I look down. 'I think I'm going to be out of town after Wednesday.'

'How come?'

I stir my drink with a finger. 'Oh, it's nothing. I'm just going on a trip down the coast.'

'Great,' says Lenny. 'Where to?'

'California.'

Lenny takes a long swig of beer. 'Oh, OK. Is that to visit some of your friends there?' I nod and he smiles, the ivory slingshot of his mouth thrown open. He grabs my hand. 'I could drive you if you like – we could visit San Francisco for a few days. Let's do that. It'd be great.'

'I'd love to,' I say, 'love to, but I don't think so.'

'It would be brilliant,' says Lenny, not listening. I watch as he looks up at the ceiling, his eyes glittering like the dancing lights of the Golden Gate Bridge, the luminous colours of the Castro.

'It would be good,' I say, hand clasped over his. 'But I have to see Tom while I'm there – kind of an important visit – and after that I should really get back to London.'

Lenny jumps slightly in his chair, rocking forwards. 'What?'

'I've been here much longer than I planned.'

'But you haven't said anything about leaving. I thought

you'd decided to stay a while. You've got a visa for a year, haven't you?'

I pull purposefully on my cigarette. When Lenny and I had first spoken about my work, about Tom, I'd told him only a few bare details. He knew that our split had included all the classic themes of hate, betrayal and recrimination, but he didn't know the extent of it. He didn't know that we were married, that I had a full visa, that divorce awaited me in small-town California.

'I just don't think it's such a good idea for me to stay here. It was probably a mistake for Carruthers to let a woman work in that house.'

Lenny frowns. 'You've had a falling out with someone, haven't you? I knew something was wrong with you this week, I knew you were acting weird – we haven't been drunk together for days.' He narrows his eyes. 'You can't hide anything from Señor Lenny, you know. Has Ed been bothering you again?' He laughs. 'I came home the other day and four of his friends ambushed me with a fishing net, but it's nothing to worry about. Did they do that to you? They're pretty harmless.'

'Oh,' I say, 'I'm not worried about them. Ed's very sweet – he was showing me that killer whale he's making at the moment.'

Lenny nods. 'Out of cocktail sticks? It's weird how it doesn't have a head or a tail, isn't it?'

I smile. 'Yep, that's it. Very abstract.'

'Like de Kooning,' says Lenny, 'if he'd made sculptures out of cocktail sticks.'

'Absolutely.' I put on a haughty voice. 'It has an elegiac quality, doesn't it? Rothko-esque?'

I smile, watching Lenny laugh. I've spent most of the past week reading in my room, hunched low beneath my duvet. Coming out of the bathroom a few days ago I had heard a mumble behind me – 'Hi, Molly' – and had turned to see Matt retreating down the stairs, the black crown of his hair bouncing happily. I had been sure he was out. Since then I've been more careful to listen for the creak of his bedroom door each morning and the sound of footsteps, the simple proofs of his absence. Yesterday – when I knew he'd left the house – I'd surfaced briefly to share a joint with Lenny, and he had asked why I'd been so withdrawn lately, so quiet. Laughing, I'd made up some lame excuse about menstruation. Lenny had looked at me oddly then but had backed off, digging out a copy of my mother's radical feminist magazine from the late sixties, *Bush Fire*, which he had bought for fifty cents at a thrift store. I couldn't help smiling at the cover picture of her and the other Super Flying Femmes, dancing naked around a campfire. The title was 'The Earth Mother issue'.

I look up as Lenny's laughter begins to subside. 'You can't go,' he says.

I shrug and shake my head. 'It's just that I need to head home. I have to go back some time.'

Lenny stubs out his cigarette. 'Not so soon though.'

A waitress comes over, wiping away the murky liquid rings on the table. 'You want the same?' she says. 'On the tab?'

We nod. 'Great.'

'So why are you seeing Tom?' says Lenny. 'I thought it was all quite acrimonious between the two of you. Won't it just upset you seeing him?' He looks serious. 'Old boyfriends should be avoided.'

'Well, he's not so much a boyfriend.'

'Well, course,' says Lenny, not understanding. 'You split up with him a while ago, didn't you?'

'Six months,' I say. 'That was the last time I saw him.' I pause while the waitress arranges my drink on a coaster. 'We're still sort of together.'

'And you haven't been in touch for six months?'

'Well, Tom's written a couple of times.'

'Still.'

'We're married.'

Lenny spits a fountain of beer across the table. 'What!' he says. He's laughing so much that I can't make out whether the liquid running down his face is alcohol or tears. Catching his breath he looks at me intently. 'Jesus, Molly.'

I give a watery smile and shrug. 'The Flynn family. We're big storytellers.'

I flick my plastic lighter, sending it shooting over the table, remembering the last night in our bedsit, the last time I had seen Tom. Coming home from work, I had found him sitting beside the kitchen sink, legs dangling idly, chin heavy on his chest. He had been there since I'd left, he said, just sitting, thinking about the movement of his legs and monitoring it, analysing the effort that went

into flexing his ankle or his calf. There was a certain
tendon in the thigh, he said, which he'd managed to iso-
late and that had been working well for hours now. He
had been feeling other muscles with his fingertips too,
examining them as they contracted and relaxed.

He hadn't eaten all day, and so, shaking my head, I had
gone to the cupboard to prepare something. There had
been a little left over from the money Augusta had given
us for the pharmacologist and we had bought some
proper food with it – meat, cheese, herbs. I started to
cook Tom a steak and some peas, pushing him up the
work surface so that I had room to get to the hob.

Tom had been silent through all this, still clutching
his legs one at a time and prodding them. 'What herbs
do you want with the steak?' I said. 'I have dried
oregano.'

He stared at me, running his right hand up his thigh.
'Would you like that?' I was determined to be patient.
Tom's mother was arriving from California tomorrow to
pick him up – we were all worried about the plane journey – and I had resolved not to upset him. I tipped in
some oregano and crushed garlic.

A couple of minutes later the steak was done, medium
rare. 'Do you want to eat on the bed?' I said. 'I'm going to
have my crackers in there.' Tom shrugged. 'I'll help you
into the other room, I'll make sure you're OK.' He sat
there, his heel banging against the cupboard door.

'Fine,' I'd said, and went into the bedroom. I switched
on the TV – a succession of news programmes – and

munched my way through the dry crackers. There was
something comforting about the way they stuck in my
throat, reassuringly physical. I watched the images blurring their way across the screen, a famine in Africa,
poverty up north, shovelling the crackers in two at a
time.

Having finished the pack, my throat sandblasted, I
went back into the kitchen. Tom had let the plate slide
from the counter, unbroken, the steak oozing blood
beside it, peas strewn like marbles across the floor. I
dropped to my knees to clear it up. 'Why did you do
that?' I asked. Tom looked at me blankly, his leg still
swinging. 'Don't you want something to eat?'

I had gone over to him then and put an arm up around
his neck. Tom sat there, back straightening, pulling away
from me until I couldn't reach any more. 'I didn't want
that,' he said.

I turned to walk out of the room, to watch more of the
news, cheer myself up. 'I'm sorry you didn't want it,' I
said. Then, crouching, I scooped a handful of peas and
began to flick them at him, one at a time, laughing as they
bounced off his cheeks. Tom stayed motionless.

Reaching out, my fingers folded around his upper left
arm and started to squeeze. At first it was a light touch,
the kind you might offer to a friend whose parent had
died. Then it became a little firmer, my grip tightening
like the black rubber band that tests your blood pressure.
Finally my fingers were pushing into him so hard that I
could see the first shadows of a bruise, a blood vessel

breaking just beneath my fingers. I pushed, both of us silent, staring at my hand. Then I went to watch TV again. Finally. It was comedy hour.

'Me and Tom had some problems,' I say, Lenny nodding, 'more than I told you. He's not well.'

'What's wrong with him?'

'It's a mental problem,' I say. 'Manic depression, they think. He had a breakdown.'

'Oh,' says Lenny. 'Depression.' He smiles. 'What about Prozac?'

I laugh and take his hand. 'Yeah, he has a lot of drugs, but they're' – I pause – 'they're difficult. Some of them dope him up, increase his heart rate.' I pull at the tiny hairs that line Lenny's thumb. 'It's difficult to find a combination.' He yelps. 'Sorry.'

Lenny starts tapping his fingers on the tabletop, nodding to an imagined tune. I smile wider, lips stretching like a rubber band. 'He's not well,' I say, thinking again of that evening, the raised purple lines on his wrists more pronounced than ever.

'So are you planning to get back together?'

I splutter. 'God, no. No.'

'So you're not interested? Even if the drugs worked, got it under control?'

'Well' – I light a cigarette, taking a long drag – 'I don't think so.' I trace my fingers through the spilt beer. 'I don't think it's something that we could' – I pause – 'repair.' I take another drag. 'Even if Tom did get well.'

'Why's that?' says Lenny. 'I mean, you were really into

him before, weren't you? Shit,' he laughs wryly, 'you married him.'

'I know.' My smile is even tighter. 'We were happy for a while, but' – I can feel a pressure at my temples – 'I don't know. Those situations sometimes bring out the worst in everyone.'

Lenny shakes his head.

'We know too much about each other now, I think.' I look down at the cola, fizzing with the movement of my glass. 'It's like looking at a film,' I say, 'and having some kind of X-ray vision that allowed you to see everyone working on the set – the director, the lighting people, voiceover artists.' I pause. 'Too much information spoils everything.'

Lenny ruffles his nose. 'But it's not so bad to know someone well,' he says. 'That could be a good thing.'

'I know,' I say, necking my drink. 'I know. But' – I pause as the vodka floats up to my head – 'I guess I feel partly responsible.'

Lenny stares at me.

'I wasn't very good for Tom.'

'So you think he wants a divorce?'

I shrug. 'His parents do.'

'He's living with his parents?'

'Yeah. They think it's for the best.'

'And you?'

'They're right.'

'Oh.'

'It's the best thing,' I say, my voice shuddering like an

executioner's hand. I motion to the waitress for another drink. 'It's like' – I pause – 'it's like I'm gangrenous.'

'Right,' says Lenny.

'Yes,' I say, sitting up a little. 'It's like I'm Tom's gangrene. I remember going to a science museum when I was about ten with Ellie' – Lenny nods – 'and we spent about ten minutes just staring at this glass-cased waxwork of a man having his leg cut off.'

'Nice,' says Lenny.

'It was hideous,' I say, 'really grim. I guess the scene was set in about the seventeenth century or something. There were a couple of men holding this diseased guy down, a nurse in the background and a doctor going at the offending leg with a saw.'

'A saw?'

'Oh yeah. It wasn't precision work. The card in the exhibit explained that they hadn't developed anaesthetic then, they just sawed the leg off cold.' I pause. 'Actually, I think the guy was holding a bottle of whisky, but that was about it.'

'It's anaesthetised me a few times.'

'Well, yes.'

Lenny stares at me, eyes swimming. 'What's the point of this story?'

'Well' – I think about it for a second – 'OK, it's like this. The amputation was gory, horrible. In the waxwork the doctor was about halfway through the operation and there was blood everywhere, stray bits of flesh on the floor, like chicken. All that kind of thing.'

'Oh, corporeal man,' sighs Lenny.

'Yep, but afterwards, presumably, the man was better.'

'If he didn't die of blood loss.'

'Yeah, if he didn't die of that then he was fine. The break-up between him and his leg was tough, but it left him alive and thriving.'

'If a little lighter.'

'And hopping.'

We both pause, laughing. 'And what about the leg,' says Lenny. 'In this drunken analogy, what happens to the leg?'

'Oh,' I say. 'Well, the leg was diseased anyway.' We clink glasses and I grin. 'It was always pretty fucked.'

14

Gene Genie

'What do you think? Do you want them now?'

Ellie smiles and starts walking towards the staff cloak-room. It's four pm on my fourteenth birthday and I've come straight from school to the bar to meet her and Augusta. As usual there's no sign of my mother, even though her lectures were scheduled to finish at midday.

'I guess there's no point waiting,' says Ellie, emerging with a huge bag of presents. 'I'm sure Augie will be here soon.'

It takes ten minutes to open everything, each parcel eliciting a yelp. The main package is an easel, which I've been wanting for a year now, and when I finish the unwrapping my lap is piled with paints and brushes, pencils, charcoal. Unguents the colour of pearl and mudslides and bluebottle flies.

'Thank you so much,' I say, hooking my arm around Ellie's neck, the paint pot mosaic rolling across the floor.

Holding her face to my cheek, I am already thinking of compositions, subjects. Along our road there's a house I've been planning to draw for a long time now, its garden strewn with three broken Cadillacs in varying shades of rust. The old man who lives there never seems to leave his house, but he often comes to the window when I walk by on my way to school, staring, grim-faced, at my legs. A few times he has smiled, which is more frightening, and I have noticed his hand moving just beneath the window frame. As Ellie kisses my cheek and pulls away I try to figure out whether the graveyard of his garden would look best with him in the background.

'Are they the right things?' says Ellie, standing up and dusting her hands down her legs. 'I spent a while talking to the woman in the art shop—'

'Sasha.'

'—that's right, Sasha, and she helped pick stuff out, but I wasn't quite sure what was best. I didn't know what you needed, but you can exchange anything that's wrong.'

'They're great,' I say. 'Everything's great.' I throw her a grin and she smiles back. Sitting there, as we look at each other, I realise that Ellie would make a great life model. Her skin has aged slowly over the past few years, and her smile, with its attendant wrinkles, is like the curtains going up on a stage. Pockets of skin float beneath her eyes, and her crow's feet are stomping where they used to creep. She is getting old, but with her close-cropped hair and hips she still looks like Jean Seberg. 'You're brilliant, Ellie,' I say. 'Thanks so much.'

She laughs. 'No more thanks, Molly. I'm glad it's all OK.' Standing up, she helps me stack my presents into the bag, then takes my hand and leads me to the bar. 'I'd better get back to work.' She opens the hatch and walks behind the counter. 'Now what do you want to drink? Birthday girl can have whatever she likes.'

I ask for a vodka and Coke. As she throws some ice into a glass, I think about a series of paintings I want to put together, with Ellie and Augusta as subjects. I've been reading a book about Woody Allen films recently, with one chapter focusing in on the kitchen scene in *Annie Hall*. A clutch of live lobsters has escaped, crunching their way around the room, and Woody and Diane Keaton are frantically trying to catch each one. The scene was ground-breaking, the writer says, because the camera had stayed fixed on the location while the actors ran off screen. Woody Allen had let the action bleed out.

And that had made me think about doing some paintings underpinned by the same idea. You could have a person caught in profile, gesturing at someone outside the canvas. Or an empty space in the centre of the picture, with people on each edge running from the scene, their fleeing legs just visible. The paintings would act more like a book than conventional pictures. The figures in them would be a prompt, a clue to the proceedings, but the viewer would have to use their imagination to conjure the whole scene.

'Would you pose for me?' I say, as Ellie hands me my drink and starts filling her sink with water.

She looks up, smiling. 'Of course I would, that would be great.'

'Do you think Augusta would pose too?'

'Would depend what the pose was.'

'Oh, just a series of portraits.'

Ellie starts slopping a cloth around the dirty glasses. 'She might do. Would you make her look good?'

I think about this. 'That would depend on what mood she was in.'

Ellie laughs. 'Oh, I'm sure she'll pose for you if she has time. You know your mother,' she smiles, 'no stranger to vanity. It's just doubtful whether you could keep her still long enough.'

I look at my watch. Four-thirty pm. 'Has she called today?' I say. 'Do you know where she is?'

'She didn't say anything about a problem this morning,' says Ellie, 'but that was at breakfast. I'm not sure where she's got to.'

'Oh.'

It's an hour later when Augusta finally shows up, her hands black with newsprint, white shirt smudged, skin seeping alcohol. Coming close, I taste the faint stench of spirits which I estimate have been fermenting for at least five hours. She hurries over, reaching out to me.

'My daughter,' she says, 'my daughter. You're fourteen and I'm late.' She pulls away and shows me her palms. 'You see this? I've been putting together a board of newspaper cuttings for my students on date rape.' She sighs. 'Always so busy at work. I'm sorry, Molly.'

I shrug. 'It's OK, no problem.' I turn to Ellie. 'Could I have another drink?' I motion to Augusta, who is bending down now, scrabbling in her bag, searching. 'I think I have some catching up to do.'

'OK,' says Ellie, brushing my hand. 'Sure.' She folds her lips inwards, an expression of sympathy.

'It's OK.'

Augusta stands up grinning and hands me a plastic bag. 'Another present,' she says, 'I couldn't come without a present.'

I open the bag. Inside is a box of two hundred cigarettes. I look up at her. 'Are you sure this is the right one?'

She smiles and peers in. 'Yep, that's it. I thought it would be easier for you than buying your own.'

I feel the muscles congregating between my eyebrows. 'Why did you get me this?' Augusta frowns back. 'I mean,' I smile, 'I'm sorry, but . . .' My voice tails off.

Augusta smiles. 'Well, I know you smoke, Molly, so I thought it would put you at ease if I just gave you some cigarettes, made it an open secret.'

'I don't smoke.'

'You don't have to pretend.'

'I don't smoke.'

'But you always smell of smoke.'

I hand the bag back to her. 'That's because I live with you. God, everything smells of smoke. Have you ever stroked Nin?'

My mother shrugs.

'That cat smells like he smokes sixty a day.'

My mother turns to Ellie. 'Double gin and tonic, Eleanor.' I watch as Ellie pours a single. 'Well, I see you're being ungrateful today,' she says to me. 'I thought they'd be a good present. Still,' she smiles triumphantly, 'I guess I'll just have to keep them.'

'Right,' I say. I try to smile at Augusta but I can feel my lips buckle like a bumper on impact.

'Anyway,' she says, as Ellie hands her the drink, 'I paid for the easel. You like that, don't you?'

'It's great,' I say. 'Great.'

We sit there, silent, as the bar fills up. Ellie's shift ends at eight pm and she's booked a table at an Indian restaurant nearby. Looking blankly at the clock I realise that my eyes are ticking away the seconds.

With the place getting crowded, Augusta and I move to one of the red leather booths in the back next to a window. We still aren't really speaking, but instead watch the people walking past – a group of teenage boys in hooded sweatshirts, a girl in platform boots with dreadlocks and a chihuahua. A woman of about eighty-five shuffles along in an outfit comprising various shades of dishwater. She turns to look at us, scowling, and Augusta grimaces back. 'If only people would cheer up,' she says, before smiling pointedly.

Ellie brings over a few more drinks, leaning down to kiss Augusta and glancing at me. 'How are you two?' she says. 'Looking forward to dinner?'

'We're fine,' says Augusta, 'just fine.' She is having

difficulty pronouncing the letter 's' and I smile, realising now why she always seems to hiss in my dreams. Augusta waves Ellie away and turns to me. 'So what's up with you?' she says. 'What did you do at school today?'

'Nothing.'

Augusta smiles. 'Well then, maybe you should stop going and get a job.'

I correct myself. 'Nothing that you'd be interested in. They don't teach women's studies at GCSE.'

'Very clever,' says my mother. 'Very clever.'

There's a pause as we both stare out of the window.

'Actually,' I say, 'something quite interesting did happen.'

'Oh yeah?' says Augusta, staring at a small dog squatting in the gutter.

'Yeah,' I say. 'You know my friend Vaughan.'

'Vaughan? The one with the skin?'

'All my friends have skin.'

'You know what I mean. The one with the boils?'

I kick her under the table and we both laugh. 'They're not boils, it's just that he has a few problems with his complexion.'

'You're so nice,' laughs Augusta.

'Yes,' I smile, 'I am. Anyway, we had this biology class last week where we were learning about genetics and stuff and how your parents' genes determine your, sort of' – I pause – 'physicality.'

'Right,' says Augusta. She looks down into her glass. 'This is very weak.'

'So, anyway,' I say, 'our biology teacher was explaining how eye colour works, and the fact that the character for brown eye colour is dominant to the character for blue eye colour.'

'You're starting to lose me,' says Augusta. She looks around vaguely. 'When are we going to dinner?'

'In about an hour,' I say, touching her hand. 'This is interesting though, listen to this.' Augusta looks up and smiles. 'Basically, our teacher, Mr Jones, explained that if both your parents have blue eyes, then it's impossible for you to end up with brown eyes. That's the crux of it.'

'Weren't we talking about Vaughan for some reason?'

'Exactly. So Vaughan put up his hand and said that that couldn't be true, because both his parents have blue eyes and his are brown.'

'Right.'

'And Mr Jones shrugged and said that maybe one of them had light brown eyes or something like that. Maybe their eyes were hazel and Vaughan was just remembering them wrong.'

'So was that it?'

'No.' I pause. 'Vaughan went home that night and asked his parents about it – he thought he'd stumbled on some fantastic exception – and his parents said that he was adopted.'

My mother smiles. 'No.'

I nod. 'Yeah. It's amazing, isn't it? We were talking about it today at break. Apparently the school are going to send him for counselling.'

We look out at a girl waiting on the opposite corner in a miniskirt. She is smoking a cigarette, her skin becoming more and more ashen as she inhales.

'God, what a strange thing to happen,' says Augusta. 'How does Vaughan feel about it?'

'I think he'll be OK.' I stir my drink with a straw and stutter. 'All the things we were talking about in class though – genetic diseases and the situation with Vaughan – it made me wonder whether there was anything I should know about my father.' I lower my head and look up at her, my sight shaded by lashes. 'I wondered whether there was any way to find out if he's in good health, whether there are any medical conditions in his family.'

My mother starts banging her glass against the table, her drink jumping like a rogue wave. 'I don't think there's anything to worry about,' she says. 'I'm sure your father's just fine.'

'But you don't know that for sure? He could have some horrible condition that's lurking in me now. It might be something that's curable if you catch it early.'

Augusta is still banging her glass against the wood, harder now. 'I wouldn't worry, Molly,' she says. 'Most genetic diseases just affect men anyway. You're fine. Stop being dramatic.'

I smile at her, trying to stay calm, to keep the conversation contained. 'But you were obviously in contact with my father once. Maybe it would be possible to track him down and I could meet him. Or' – I pause – 'I wouldn't have to meet him. I could just speak to him on the phone or something. Just to find out whether there was anything I should know about myself. Anything that might be helpful some time.'

Augusta lowers her glass slowly to the table. 'What makes you think that I don't know where your father is? What makes you think that we'd have to track him down?'

I swill some vodka and Coke around my mouth, mugshots of my mother's friends flitting through my mind. 'You're telling me that my father might be someone I know?'

She smiles. 'I've told you that before.'

I swallow painfully, my throat feeling obstructed. 'You've told me lots of things before,' I say, 'lots.' I point out of the window where a man with eight years' growth of beard and a shabby sleeping bag is walking past. 'Is he my dad?' I look around the bar and start pointing at men. 'Is he my dad? Him?' I stare into the swirling drink in my glass. 'Or is it only famous men who can be my father? Who is it? Norman Mailer, Kurt Vonnegut? You've admitted it isn't Elvis now, which is a relief. Otherwise I'd have a serious genetic disposition to fat, wouldn't I?' Augusta is running her fingernail along the wood, leaving a small superficial scar. 'Who is it this time?'

Augusta holds her hands up. 'Molly, you're being hysterical.' She sighs. 'Stop showing off. Your father is' – she pauses – 'Geoff's your father.'

'Geoff?'

She nods. 'Geoff.'

I start to laugh. 'Geoff's African.'

My mother smiles. 'That's right.'

'You're telling me,' I laugh, 'that I'm half-Nigerian?'

Augusta nods, and I notice a tiny twitch of laughter dancing around her lips. 'That's right.'

'And so Geoff was living in America when I was conceived, was he?' I am laughing loudly now. 'It's weird, because he told me that he spent the seventies in Nigeria.'

Augusta bites her bottom lip. 'OK, so that story doesn't hold up very well.' She sighs as though I've caught her out at Scrabble. 'Geoff isn't your father,' she says, 'although' – she pauses thoughtfully – 'he would certainly make a very good one.'

I am still laughing. 'I can't believe that you're doing this,' I say, 'making up these stories about me and you. Don't you think I've outgrown them, that I'm getting a bit bored?' I pause. 'And I can't believe you've lost touch with my father too. Don't you know how unfair that is?'

Augusta grabs my wrist, her face blank, skin the pallor of baby milk. 'Stop it,' she says quietly, 'or I'll tell you.'

I pull her fingers away and put my hands on the edge of the table, knowing not to provoke her. 'OK.'

As Augusta sits there, mouthing words to herself, I go up to the bar for more drinks. I am so tired of speculating about my father. There have been times when Augusta's seemed to come close to telling the truth, a few moments of sobriety when she's lowered her head and started to outline some details – the fact that I was conceived in upstate New York, born in London, the fact that my father isn't someone she sees regularly. She's ventured these details and then retracted them, spun other lines about me being a love child, an abandoned refugee.

Augusta is still muttering as I head back to the table. 'Not surprising, is it,' she says, 'that men are more affected by genetics than women?' She takes a long gulp of her drink. 'I bet when they know more about how genetics affect behaviour they'll find that it's men who are swayed by them. I bet women are quite capable of defying their genes. Women are so much more directed, they use their free will so much more capably.'

I nod. 'Maybe.' It's seven-fifteen pm and the next forty-five minutes stretch out before me like a threat. 'Maybe Ellie can finish her shift early and we could head off to the restaurant now,' I say.

Augusta looks around the bar. 'I don't think so. She seems to be the only staff here.'

She takes another gulp of her drink, squeezing my hand. 'It'll be all right,' she says. 'We can eat at eight. No rush.'

We sit in purgatorial silence, Augusta staring into her drink, me out of the window. After a few minutes, I turn to ask if she minds me meeting them at the restaurant, but am stopped by her appearance. As she gazes down, her face unguarded, her bone structure seems to have dissolved and she looks about seventy, the baggy skin around her jawline drawn by gravity towards her glass. The haziness, blurring and compressed timescales of

drinking are all made flesh in Augusta. Her whole body
has turned baggy, lost its definition.

Suddenly she looks up. 'I have to go outside.' I watch as
she pushes people out of the way, running towards the
nearest door. Arriving in the street she sits down on the
kerb, spreads her knees and vomits.

I go over to Ellie. 'One of the finest minds of her generation is puking in the gutter,' I say. 'Do you want me to
take her home?'

Ellie shakes her head. 'Oh shit. I'm sorry, Molly.' She
looks around at the customers lining the bar. 'Yeah, you'd
better get her home if you can. I'll go to the restaurant
and get some takeaway for the two of us, OK? I guess I'll
be home about eight-thirty.'

'OK.' I smile. 'Can you bring the presents too?'

'Sure.'

I shoulder my way through the growing throng towards
the door, Augusta still perching on the kerb, her head
tilted forward. As I get outside, I see her put her fingers
down her throat. She turns to me. 'I don't feel well.'

'Really,' I say.

'Shit. I feel shit,' she says. 'Can you get me home?'

I sit down next to her.

'Yeah, I suppose I can.'

She takes my arm. 'Thanks so much.' She looks at me.
'Have you had a good birthday?'

I laugh. 'It's had its downsides.'

'I'm sorry I'm sick.'

I take her hand off my arm. 'Yeah, but you'll always be

sick, won't you?' I look at her, hair falling in her face, lips cracked and bleeding. 'I mean, you talk about free will, about people being – what is it – self-directed? And you' – I feel an involuntary wrench – 'you have no free will at all.'

Augusta looks into the gutter. 'You can't actually talk to me like that,' she says quietly. 'You're not allowed to.'

I smile down at her. 'What are you going to do? You're sitting in the gutter.' I turn, taunting. 'I suppose you could shout at me, but it would be a pretty bad move.' I stroke her hair flat at the back. 'You'll still need me to look after you later.'

Augusta turns to me. 'Don't be a bitch, Molly.'

'You think I'm being a bitch?' I say. 'Oh well. I just think you're fucking it up. Do you think me and Ellie want to look after you all the time?' I pause. 'I was looking at Ellie today and she's still beautiful. Still young enough.'

My mother puts her hands back and pushes herself up. She starts to walk unsteadily along the street and I follow a few paces behind. After a hundred yards she stops and turns. 'I should have listened when they said not to have you.'

15

Selling San Francisco

'They're all human hair, you know.'

Lenny and I back away slightly, sinking as far as we can into the couch, smiling through our bemusement. Ignoring us, Carruthers skips through his wig collection, arms outstretched, hands poised ready to pluck a favourite from its perch. He has arranged forty of them on stands in his lounge, perfectly balanced and brushed. Coming to a sharp Louise Brooks bob, dyed eggshell blue, he stops, sighs, stands on tiptoe and strokes it softly.

'Ah, this one,' he says, 'the hair on this one belonged to Sally originally.'

'Sally?'

'Oh yes,' says Carruthers. He brings a hand fluttering to his mouth. 'Haven't I told you about Sally?'

Lenny and I shake our heads. Closing his eyes, Carruthers begins a slow waltz around the room, arms crooked for an imaginary partner. 'Sally was my manicurist and dance instructor, Tennessee, 1979. Lovely girl.' He starts to hum.

Lenny shifts, uncomfortable, and I elbow him in the stomach. He turns to me, laughing. 'What happened to her?' I say, head cocked with concern.

Carruthers gasps, opens his eyes and comes to sit beside me. 'It was just awful, you know, awful. I'll never forget it. It was a Saturday night, mid-July, and I was at home, recovering from an operation. Sally had called me earlier that evening and said she was going out, and was I able to come.' A sigh rumbles deep in his chest, ending in a belch. It smells of an electro-chemical plant I'd once visited on a school outing. 'Anyway,' he smiles wistfully, 'my spleen was in no shape for dancing, no sir, and so I told her that she should go and have a good time without me.'

A cough turns into a sob. I place my hand gently over his. 'So what happened?'

Carruthers stares at me, his eyes as watery as half-poached eggs. 'You look quite like her actually,' he says and pauses. 'So, later that night as I was getting a massage from my maid, I had a call from Sally's boyfriend to say that she'd been shot in the head during the YMCA.'

'No,' Lenny gasps, reaching to place a hand on mine.

'Yes,' says Carruthers. 'Her boyfriend had started a gunfight and Sally was the victim. It was just,' he sobs, 'tragic.' He stops, brightening a little. 'Luckily she'd cut her hair and given it to me before she died. What was left was in a terrible state after the shooting. I heard they had to winch the disco ball down so they could wash the brains off.'

Lenny and I pull our hands back into our laps, silent, processing this, and Carruthers starts to inspect his wigs again.

'I've never had such a good manicurist since then,' he's saying, 'it's been a blow. Still,' he smiles, cradling the wig in his hands, 'it's lovely to think that I still have a part of her here, a part I can wear.' He holds the wig out to me. 'Would you like to try it on, Molly? It would look much better than that cut you've got at the moment, all those split ends.' He puts his thumb idly in his mouth. 'You'd look so much better with Sally's hair.'

I smile. 'Thanks so much, but I think I'm OK for now.' He shrugs, kicking his right foot across the floor, and turns to pet a deep purple shag.

I prod Lenny's leg, giving him a look of cartoon horror. Arranging this appointment through his occasional secretary, Bette, Carruthers had made it sound official. She had called us on Friday to issue his request for an audience and had mentioned that we'd 'best dress smart'. Neither of us had known what to make of this, but I had conceded a skirt, and Lenny a shirt that required cufflinks. He is using a pair of safety pins.

We had discussed the invitation at length over the weekend, pondering the summons. I had given my seven-day notice direct to Carruthers the week before and he had seemed sanguine about his imminent lack of housekeeper. 'You don't even know where the vacuum's kept, do you,' he'd said.

'We don't have one.'

'Correct answer,' he said, nodding, impressed. 'Well done.'

Still, Carruthers' reactions were entirely dependent on the drugs he'd taken that day. It was quite possible that he'd invited us over to harangue us about our dress sense, cookery skills or sexual behaviour.

'He might attack us,' I said. 'Have you ever met a less predictable junkie?'

Lenny had stroked my arm. 'I think, realistically, we'd be able to overpower him if that happened.'

'What if Bette's there, acting as an accomplice?'

'Have you ever met Bette?'

I'd shrugged. 'No. But she sounds as though she could take us.'

Lenny had stroked my arm. 'She may sound like a pit bull, but she's short' – he motioned towards his knee – 'and blind.'

The threat seemed manageable. Still, although Bette's blindness had made me more positive about the meeting, I hadn't been expecting this – Carruthers at his friendliest.

'What do you think he's taken?' I whisper.

'MDMA?' says Lenny.

'Crystal meth?'

'Could be.'

We watch for another ten minutes as Carruthers tends

his wigs, flicking at them occasionally with a tiny pink brush. 'Beautiful,' he purrs, 'beautiful.' Finally bored, he turns, holds his hand over his head like a mechanical claw and pulls off his own wig – a fifties-style shoulder-length with a fringe. Beneath it is a tight white hairnet. He laughs, sitting down on the chaise longue opposite us. 'I feel so much lighter now.'

We both laugh politely. 'So,' says Lenny, 'what did you need to speak to us about?'

Carruthers pouts slightly, his lips slick with gloss. 'You didn't suppose that I might just want some company from you youngsters?' He smiles, hands held out beneficently. With the white skullcap of his hairnet he looks, for a second, like the Pope. 'You didn't think that I might just like some time with you before you leave?'

Lenny shrugs. 'I'm not leaving. Just Molly.'

Carruthers doesn't seem to hear. His eyes lie closed again and he traces a pattern through the air with his finger. Suddenly his face jerks forward, pupils expanding in the light. 'Yes.' He jabs his hand violently in our direction. 'So I have a proposal.'

'Oh,' says Lenny and we both watch curiously, concerned, as Carruthers shuffles from the room.

'He's going to try and find a way to make me stay,' I say. 'I know it. He'll never find another housekeeper.'

'Yeah,' says Lenny, 'but it's not as though you actually clean.' He takes my hand, his voice mocking. 'You're not actually an asset, are you?'

'I'm a presence,' I say.

'Right.'

Carruthers hovers into the room, sucking his thumb messily, saliva dripping down his chin. He holds out some papers and sits down.

'I thought you might like this,' he says.

I look at the page. Emblazoned across the top is a crest and a Latin phrase, *alere flammam*.

'What does the motto mean?'

'Oh, that's not important,' says Carruthers, waving a hand impatiently. 'It means "to feed the flame". I came up with it when I was younger and thought that Latin sounded authoritative. Now turn over.'

The next page is headed 'The Charles Carruthers Fellowship' and is followed by fifteen clauses of small print.

'You run a fellowship?' I ask.

'I sometimes wonder if you're not terribly bright,' says Carruthers, a sigh breaking across his voice. 'Yes,' he snaps, 'I run a fellowship.' He pulls at the sweaty rim of his rubber cap. 'I haven't granted it to anyone for a while now, haven't wanted to. So many bitches about these days, so much ugly behaviour and vulgarity. So much masturbation in the art world.' He pauses. 'I thought that you two might like a bite of the cherry though. Molly, read out the first clause.' He falls back theatrically into an armchair, a smile creeping to the corners of his face.

'Right.' I bring the print an inch from my face. 'OK. The first clause says, "The Charles Carruthers Fellowship pledges the recipient all funds necessary for them to pursue their chosen career as an artist, without disturbance, over a two-year period."' I smile. 'Oh.'

'Let me take a look,' says Lenny. He starts scanning the page and I feel his hand squeeze between me and the seat, pinching my thigh. I jump, laughing. Lenny leans forward to wake Carruthers, whose nostrils are shuddering gently. 'Is this a serious offer?'

Carruthers smacks his lips together, spitting slightly. 'Absolutely,' he says, 'of course.' He bats his hand back and forth dismissively. 'You know,' he says, mouth held like a beak, 'the Fellowship has so much money floating around, and I'm not allowed a cent of it, not one. I almost went to jail in 1963 when I awarded it to myself, only got off because the judge thought I was pretty. You two may as well have the money. I've been trying to find recipients for a very' – he pauses for effect – 'very long time.'

'So,' says Lenny, and I can hear the patter of a laugh in his voice, 'what are the provisos?'

Carruthers shrugs, yawning. 'Oh,' he says, 'I've told my lawyers to draw up some new contracts with just the first clause on them – that thing's far too complicated at the moment.'

'And there are no other requirements? We don't have to pay the money back?'

'Oh fuck, no.' Carruthers' self-medication is catching up with him and his speech starts to slur. 'The only demand I'd make—' He pauses, slumping.

'Yes?'

He sits up. 'The only demand I'd make would be to have first choice of Molly's work when it comes to selling it. And you' – he turns to wave a finger at Lenny – 'I'd expect you to give up alcohol.'

Lenny smiles weakly. 'Right.'

There's a pause before Carruthers laughs. 'Of course not.' His voice turns serious. 'I'd expect you to work on a proper manuscript though, something you have a chance of finishing.'

Lenny nods and Carruthers stares at us, blurry-eyed. 'Does that sound acceptable?'

I smile, nodding. 'That sounds' – I pause – 'great.' I splutter a laugh. 'Have you ever given the fellowship to a woman before?'

Carruthers points his spidery, shaky finger at me. 'I wouldn't normally give it to a girl, no. But you' – his hand drops to his lap – 'you're good. The exception that proves the rule.'

'What's the rule?' asks Lenny.

'That women are shit artists,' says Carruthers and his face breaks into a smirk. 'And what do you think of the contract?'

Lenny nods. 'Great.'

Carruthers leans his head over the back of the chair, his mouth falling open. 'That's good,' he says, 'very good. You're my children now.' Lenny grimaces at me and our cheeks bulge with silent laughter. 'Bette's having the contracts drawn up with the lawyers at the moment. They should be ready tomorrow morning, before the two of you leave.' His voice cracks with sleep. 'Come collect them then.' He opens his right eye. 'Now go now, go. I'm tired.'

Lenny and I stand up, holding hands. 'Thanks so much.' We edge out of the room, narrowly avoiding the manicurist's wig, and walk quickly down the hall.

Opening Carruthers' front door and letting it swish quietly shut, Lenny turns to me. He jumps down the porch stairs, landing in a crouch. 'Oh my God, Molly.' I trip down to join him. 'This is great.'

We walk next door in silence. Arriving in the kitchen, Lenny uncorks a bottle of wine. 'Do you know what this means?' he says, pouring us each a glass.

'It's unbelievable,' I say, sitting down at the table. 'Are you sure he'll definitely give it to us? We didn't sign anything.'

'It's safe,' says Lenny. 'It's being arranged through Bette. It's fine. And anyway' – he pauses to take a sip – 'that contract looked pretty official. Not the kind of thing that Carruthers would throw together himself.'

We're silent again.

'We don't have to work for two years,' says Lenny.

'It's strange,' I say, swilling my wine absently with a finger. 'Very strange.'

'No more shelf-stacking,' says Lenny, 'no more temp jobs for you.'

I laugh. 'It sure seems that way.' I top up my glass, already half-empty. 'I have to pack anyway' – I pause – 'still have to head down to see Tom.'

Lenny sighs. 'Don't go,' he says. 'We should get the celebrations out of the way first. Why don't you just call Tom's parents and tell them you'll be there in a few weeks?' He looks up at me, eyes pleading.

'Can't,' I say. 'I promised that I'd be there for early afternoon Friday. They'll kill me if I'm late.'

'Why?' says Lenny.

I smile. 'Tom's still very ill, Len, still sort of' – I pause – 'on the brink. His parents aren't too keen on me seeing him. They think it might set him back.'

'I suppose that makes sense.'

'Yeah. I mean, he's been doing a bit better apparently. Going for walks, that sort of thing. I don't want to upset him.'

'OK,' says Lenny. He stands up and puts an arm around my waist. 'Let me come with you.'

I pull away and start to climb the stairs. 'I don't know, that might not be so good. What if Tom sees you and gets the wrong idea?'

'I'll keep out of the way,' says Lenny.

We get to my room, the suitcase laid open on my bed. I go to the wardrobe and start pulling clothes off their hangers.

'And logistically,' I say, 'logistically it wouldn't work.'

'Why not?'

'Well' – I smooth a pile of jumpers and throw them in – 'I was planning to take a night flight out of San Francisco Friday. I wasn't planning to stick around. You'd have to come back here alone.'

'But you don't have anything booked?'

'I've checked availability. It's fine.'

Lenny pushes the suitcase and it lands with a slap on the floorboards. He pulls me down onto the bed. 'I think you should stay in the States, Molly.'

I look at my hands. 'What am I going to do over here? All my stuff's in London, everything. My easel, paints. I have some canvases that I'm working on over there.'

Lenny prods me. 'Look,' he says, 'you've been given this opportunity. If you want to go and collect your stuff from London you can always visit for a week or two and get that sorted out. But where are you going to be more productive, here or there?'

I smile. 'Well, I think there's more material in London than Eugene.'

Lenny smiles. 'We wouldn't stay in Eugene, would we? I admit it's not the most inspiring town.'

'So where would we go?' I pull him towards me and hold his gaze, eyelids fluttering. Then I turn and stretch out, back arching across his lap, left leg pivoting into the air. 'Where would you take me, darling?'

'Well,' he laughs, 'you know how I feel about San Francisco.'

'Huh.' I stand up and start pulling the suitcase back onto the bed. 'Why San Francisco?'

'Have you been there?'

I fold my red dress carefully before shoving it in a corner of the case. 'Yeah, I've been there a few times. It was only about an hour and a half from Davis.'

'That's right,' says Lenny. 'And did you have a good time?'

I shrug. 'Most times we visited it was to see this friend of Tom's from college, Jules.' I pause. 'She was annoying.'

'Oh,' says Lenny.

'We always spent the evenings in her apartment listening as she bitched about her job. It was boring.'

Lenny leans back on the bed. 'Sounds it. Anyway,' he says, 'it's a great city. You'd be crazy to go back to London when we could get a place together there.'

I begin to wedge my shoes along the side of the case. 'Sell it to me.'

'What?'

'Well, you stayed there for a few weeks, didn't you? Sell it to me.'

Lenny sits up and pours us both some more wine.

'OK.' He pauses, head cocked. 'OK, well.'

I point at my clock. 'You have three minutes and then I'm going into town to get some supplies for the journey. I'll tell you the truth.' I pause. 'I think it's a bad idea. If Tom finds out I'm living in San Francisco, he might think I've moved there to get back with him. It'd get messy.'

'He'd never find out,' says Lenny.

'Yeah, until I bump into him and his parents out shopping.'

'It wouldn't happen.' Lenny taps the bed, gesturing me to sit down. His mouth sets into a determined line. 'Three minutes, yeah?'

I nod. 'Three minutes.'

'OK.' He closes his eyes, thinking. 'Well, there's the architecture for a start. They've got all those beautiful houses – blue, green, purple – five-storey mansions with plaster mouldings on the front, mansions that you could just stare at for days trying to work out how they could afford to build so many. They've got the bay, which is pretty, and which looks great from the hilltops, from Coit Tower especially. There are all those weird roads, Lombard Street – the one that's in all the films – Columbus.' He pauses.

'No time,' I say.

'On Columbus,' says Lenny, his voice hurried, 'there's City Lights and Vesuvio's, where all the Beat poets used to hang out, and there's still a good literary scene – Dennis Cooper, Armistead Maupin.'

'Good for you, what about me?' I say.

'I'm coming to that.' He pauses. 'There are beautiful men there, hordes of them, flaunting up and down the Castro.' He leans in to me. 'Beautiful men without inhibitions, men who'd like to be life models.' Lenny smiles. 'There's so much material for you there. Great clubs too, fifties clubs like' – he draws breath – 'like the Hi-ball Lounge. You can dance there,' says Lenny, 'dance properly. You can jive.'

'I can't jive.'

'But you could if you wanted to.'

'I couldn't.'

He sighs. 'How long do I have?'

'Seventy seconds.'

'There's a good cultural scene, lots of second-hand bookstores. There's great Mexican food.'

'We have Mexican food in Eugene.'

'That's mediocre Mexican food.'

'Oh. I thought all Mexican food tasted good if you added enough cheese.'

Lenny shakes his head. 'There's Golden Gate Park, which is huge, and the Haight where you can buy lots of vintage clothes.' He stands up and hugs me close, whispering like the devil to Faustus. 'I know how you love vintage clothes.'

I push him. 'OK, go on.'

He's struggling slightly now. 'There's a drugs problem, a lot of junkies, but that's just good local colour. There's Rice-a-Roni, the San Francisco treat, there are trams and sea lions and tourists.'

'Great,' I say. 'Love those sea lions.'

'And' – he pokes my shoulder – 'how long have I got?'

'Fifteen seconds.'

'There's Alcatraz.' He smiles triumphantly.

'The prison island?'

'That's right.'

I fold my arms. 'That's your pitch?'

He smiles, the corners of his eyes like crepe. 'That's it.'

I start folding my bras. 'Help me pack, Lenny.'

'OK.' He places one of my skirts smooth in the case, building a layer of books on top. I throw a pile of vest tops next to him on the bed and he starts arranging them neatly.

'I'll come, I guess.'

He grabs my shoulders. 'You will?'

I pick up my glass and tilt it towards him in a toast. 'I can't resist,' I say. 'They have a prison island.'

16

The cow's intestines

'What do you want?' says Lenny, leaning through the car window.

'Something healthy,' I say, 'nutritious.'

'That's not like you. Twinkies?'

I grimace. 'Get me a V8, I guess. A V8 and a Diet Coke.' I toss him a five-dollar bill.

'OK.'

I watch as Lenny walks to the store and notice, even from this back view, how he glances slightly to the left and eyes up a suited young attendant stacking wood chip out front. Lenny turns to me as the man bends down and pretends to grab at him.

We have drawn up at a gas station on the outskirts of Davis, the one that Tom and I had come to when I first arrived in town, a week after our marriage in Vegas. The strip mall that houses it still has the same shops: a Rite-Aid chemist, Safeway, a few Chinese restaurants and a video store. The smell out here is the same too – cut grass and rancid mushrooms. Fresh air and mould.

Tom had spent that first drive from Nevada to Davis telling me about his childhood. Listening to him, leaning my head against the cool glass of the car window, I had realised what it must be like to be a teacher wading through those essays on 'what I did in the holidays'. Idyllic childhoods make shitty material. I imagined those teachers getting a secret thrill when they read of a tragedy during a student's vacation – the death of a grandparent, a gut-wrenching disease. At least it must have made for a more compelling read than the endless accounts of sun-blessed beach holidays and ice cream.

'It was amazing,' Tom had said as I scrolled down the window, the glass warm now, 'this one time me and Steve snuck out in the middle of the night with our dog Redneck and backpacks full of food. We had our bikes with us – I had a blue BMX – and we cycled a few miles out to this lake on the edge of town and had a midnight feast. The lake belonged to one of the country clubs so we had to take torches and climb over a wire fence, but it was brilliant. Steve's friend Mickey met us out there and we all went swimming.'

'Right,' I'd said, 'sounds great.' I stared out at another stretch of desert, its barren, sandy carpet suddenly so appealing. 'Is that what the next few years are going to be like? Midnight feasts and bike rides? Maybe I could buy a BMX and we could all go out one night and befriend an alien.'

'Alien?'

'Like in *ET*.'

Tom had punched me lightly on the arm before lifting my hand to kiss it. 'Molly, stop being so cynical, hey? I'm allowed to get excited about my childhood.' We were nearing the town now. 'That's the thing about Davis, it's just such a great place for kids. Really safe and fun, lots of green spaces, good schools. There's a big sporting ethos too – all the kids play baseball, basketball, go swimming.' He had stroked the back of my neck. 'Maybe one day we'll bring our own kids up here.'

I'd laughed nervously. 'That might be jumping the gun a little. I plan to keep these loins child-free for a long while.' Tom had smiled, nodding. 'And anyway, if our kids take after me there'll be no baseball to speak of. Maybe the occasional swim if they're in Barbados or something, but that's about it.'

Of course, it had turned out that Tom's childhood-tinted view of Davis was slightly skewed, reflecting a side of the town, certainly, but one only visible to people under four feet tall. Although the town had a God-fearing, family-friendly population, it wasn't as innocent as it seemed. Beneath the veneer of church fetes and anti-smoking ordinances was a thick layer of eccentricity.

I had noticed this dissolution just a few weeks after arriving in town. Waiting to pay for some milk and cereal in the local store, I had caught the strains of a conversation going on behind me. Turning to look, I saw a police officer speaking to one of the shop assistants. As he told it, the local force – untroubled as they were by serious crime – were stuck in the midst of a puzzling investigation into a string of drive-by gropings.

I had leaned back slightly at this point, not certain that I'd heard him correctly. The shop assistant was confused too. 'What do you mean?' she said, and I turned to see her nose wrinkle until the nostrils were perpendicular with her chin.

'It's been awful,' said the policeman, 'really traumatic for the women involved. Apparently what's happening is that this sicko, this serial groper, has been stopping his car at bus stops or alongside crowded stretches of sidewalk, leaning out, grabbing the nearest pair of ladies' breasts and shaking them.' I liked the fact that he specified 'ladies' breasts' and also the way he held his arms out at chest height, cupping both hands and shaking them at the assistant. 'Like that.'

I had been sceptical about this story until I'd read a long report about it in the local newspaper. 'Look,' I'd said to Tom, 'it's true. The drive-by groper's on the loose.'

Tom had tilted his head back and laughed. 'People have got to take fun where they can find it,' he'd said. 'Just keep away from bus stops.'

Along with its strange sex attackers – men who injected their criminality through a rich vein of pantomime – Davis had other quirks. Many of these were centred around the university campus that dominated the town. UC Davis had originally been founded as the country's premier agricultural college and was still known, appropriately, as a site of technological innovation. Annexed on campus was the prime example of this pioneering spirit, the town's most infamous attraction. The fistulated cow.

'The fistulated cow?'

Tom had nodded. 'You'll get to see it next year when they bring it out for picnic day. It's amazing.'

'Is it a special breed? I don't understand.'

Tom had laughed, his voice drenched with pride. 'It's one of a kind, Moll,' he said, digging into a lamb chop, blood shimmering through the air. 'What the UCD scientists did, a while ago, was to create a cow with a hole in its side.'

'A hole?'

'A hole. It's brilliant. It means that veterinary students and, well, anyone who's interested really, can put their hand into the cow and feel its internal organs.'

'You're kidding.'

'I'm not. You can see the cow when they exhibit it. It comes out every year on picnic day.'

'What's picnic day?'

'Only the biggest day of the year.'

'What happens on picnic day?'

Tom had sighed. 'People eat outside.'

'Right. Cool.'

'Yeah, it's great. There are always queues of people who want to feel the cow's intestines. It's a huge town attraction.'

'Right.' I had given up on my chop. As it turned out, I

never saw the fistulated cow, or its sister attraction – a transparent plastic horse's bottom, complete with vagina. Rumour had it that one of the first year veterinary students (presumably an unpopular one) was forced to sit on a small stool within this structure on picnic day, masturbating a live male horse as it boned the plastic one, thus showing the gathered audience how they collected horse sperm. I was sorry to have missed it.

Lenny leers at me through the car window. 'I'm back.' He climbs in, throwing a can of V8 onto my lap. 'No Diet Coke, and I know how you hate Pepsi.' He's holding something behind him. 'So I got you this instead.' He stands it on the dashboard in front of me.

I look at the small chocolate pig. 'Thanks, Lenny. I can see why you thought that would be a good Diet Coke substitute.' He frowns sulkily. 'Really, thank you.'

He smiles. 'It's OK. Right, are you ready to face the family?'

I push my hands beneath me. 'Not really.'

Lenny squeezes my knee. 'We can always stay here for a while if you want. Maybe we could go and get lunch or something.'

'You're hungry?'

'No.'

'Oh.' I open the V8. 'I should probably just get this over with.'

'OK.' Lenny stares at me, the downward curve of his eyes more pronounced than usual. 'It's going to be all right, Molly.'

'Yeah,' I say, with a faint smile. 'It'll be fine.'

We drive towards the house that Tom shares with his parents, Lenny having agreed to drop me off a few streets away. As we pull into a residential road not far from downtown, I ask him to stop. 'I can walk from here.'

Lenny leans over to kiss my cheek. 'Good luck,' he says.

I smile. 'I'll see you in a few hours. You have your phone switched on, yeah?' He nods.

Walking along the tree-lined street, the sun arcing through the sky to its hottest point, I realise that my legs are shaking. I stand still, holding them straight, and gulp big breaths of air. I start to hiccup.

I remember what I had noted in one of my sketch-books a couple of days after meeting Tom's parents. It was at a time when I still thought I could emulate Jenny Holzer's art – large, nebulous captions on the side of buildings – and I had stencilled across the top of the page: 'The problem with good people is that they make you feel so guilty for hating them'. As art it had been mediocre, I think, but as a statement it still made sense. Good people – teetotallers, charity volunteers, people who recycle – could make the most friendly drunk feel misanthropic.

And Tom's parents were all of these things. He had described them to me on that same drive from Vegas, just before he launched into his eulogy to Davis. 'I know you're going to be part of the family as soon as you meet them,' he'd said, 'it'll be great.'

'I won't have to call them Mom and Dad, will I?'

Tom had turned to me, his toothpaste smile like a beacon. 'You wouldn't want to?'

I shook my head. 'I think I have enough mother already.'

He had shrugged. 'I guess you don't have to then. They won't mind either way. They're very accepting.'

'What does your mum do again?'

He wound down his window to adjust the wing mirror. 'Mom,' he said. 'Oh, she does lots of different stuff now that me and Steve aren't around any more. She helps Dad out with the stores a few hours a week, and she's really involved with the local church. She's always arranging bake sales for them.' He'd turned to me. 'Can you bake?'

I'd laughed. 'You really should have made these enquiries before we got married, shouldn't you?'

Tom stroked my hair. 'Sweetie, I don't mind if you can't bake. It just might be kind of fun for you to help Mom when she's busy getting one of the sales ready.'

'I think I'd rather help out in one of your dad's shops.'

He'd slung me a smile. 'Of course. That would be great. You can help me out with some shifts.'

We had been quiet for a while, my gaze holding the horizon like a kitten chasing string. 'So what's your dad like?' I said eventually.

'Dad? Well' – Tom paused – 'he's quite burly, very good-looking in an old guy kind of way. He was football captain at high school in Davis – we have about ten pictures of him on a wall in the lounge, holding up different trophies.'

'And he likes running the stores?'

'Oh yeah, he loves it. He's quite involved with the church too, he's in the choir, and he coaches basketball at junior high. I just know he'll find you really funny. He has kind of a dark sense of humour.'

'Oh.' Dad sounded more promising than Mum. 'How dark?'

'Well, grey.'

Arriving at their house, we watched as Tom's parents crowded into the doorway, wrapped around each other like Houdini's ropes. Tom poked me and nodded at them, waving and smiling. 'Look at that,' he'd whispered, 'thirty years together and they're still like that. Thirty years and they're still happy.'

I had looked over at them, trying to smile as my top lip configured itself into a sneer. Would that be Tom and I in thirty years, I had thought, holding each other afloat in some Davis bungalow? It was unlikely, I surmised. I'd always had a predilection for space.

His parents hugged Tom – 'you're back!' – before shaking and clasping my hand and ushering us both into the house. They were trying to hide their scrutiny but I kept catching long glances between them, pointed nods towards my legs, hair and nails, as though they were sizing up some prize cattle. 'Did you have a good ride?' said his mother as we came to the lounge, hustling us onto an overstuffed sofa. 'Would you like something to eat?'

'I'm fine,' I'd said, shaking my head guiltily. 'Just fine.' My voice had dropped to a whisper. 'Could I possibly use your bathroom though?'

'Oh Lord,' said Tom's mother, 'that's just fine.' She gave me some directions, pointing – 'up the stairs, first right' – and then watched as I walked out. When she thought that I was far enough away I heard her say to Tom, 'She's so young, isn't she, darling? So fresh.'

There was criticism in the comment, a weighted edge. I hovered in the hall, interested to hear what else she might say. 'She's old for her years,' replied Tom. I started to climb the stairs.

They had always been perfect, I think, as I arrive at the top of the street. Right up until I had married Tom, the four of them had been the most admired family in town. No problems in that house. Or if there were, then they were soluble ones, to be talked over with a cup of cocoa until they diminished, faded and disappeared.

It hadn't helped, I think, that Steve's long-term girl-friend, Macy, was as perky and upstanding as a teenage nun. That first day when we arrived in Davis, she had come rushing around to see us, carrying, of all things, a box of home-baked cookies.

'I made these for the two of you,' she'd said. 'I thought you could use them after such a long journey.' Putting the box on a side table in the hall she had held out a hand. As I went to shake it she pulled me into a hug. 'I'm so excited to meet you,' she said, rubbing my arms up and down fiercely. 'I can't believe you're English!'

We had all sat in the lounge talking, Tom on the couch next to me, an arm draped loosely but possessively around my shoulders. It turned out that Steve and Macy had been prom king and queen in high school, a picture of them sitting proudly in the centre of the mantelpiece. I noted that Macy had sported an ugly perm at the time. 'School was so fun,' she said happily.

As I walk up their drive, I wonder if that photo is still there. I guess so, unless it's been replaced by a picture of Macy and Steve's wedding. I imagine Macy toppling off the side of a mountain, her skis crumpled beneath her.

I knock on the door and stand back. The neighbourhood is quieter than I remember, drab. I hear a bolt being unlocked.

'Hello, Molly,' says Tom's mother, the door opening. 'You'd better come in.'

I walk a little way up the hall and she closes the door quietly before steering me into the lounge. She leads me to the orange armchair in the corner.

'Right, now.' She is standing above me and I notice a nerve pulsing through her eyebrow. 'I need to lay down some ground rules before you can go up to see Tom, young lady.'

I nod. 'OK.'

'Right.' She draws up a foot so that she is balancing distractedly on one leg. 'Now, you're here to arrange some signatures for the divorce papers, aren't you?'

'That's right.'

'Fine, I think that's best for everyone.' She leans

towards me, stumbles slightly and puts her foot down on the floor to steady herself. 'Now, I want you to make this quick. I don't want Tom upset or disturbed. Frankly' – she pulls away – 'from what he's said I know exactly who's to blame for his illness.'

I feel suddenly defiant. 'And who's that?'

Her lips draw back, reminding me for a second of some footage I had once seen of cannons emerging before battle. 'Don't push me, Molly. You're lucky I'm letting you see him at all.'

'I tried to look after him.'

She steps back a few paces, her attack mellowing into disappointment. She motions to the stairs. 'Just go. He's in his room.'

I walk up slowly and knock on Tom's door. His voice from inside – 'come in' – sounds as upbeat and normal as it once was. For a moment I feel hopeful.

I open the door. 'Hi, Tom.' He looks around, surprised.

'Molly,' he says, standing up to greet me. 'Molly.' He holds out his arms and I fall into an awkward hug.

A computer game is frozen on his screen, a Japanese woman in a skin-tight catsuit kickboxing a grizzly bear.

'Doesn't look like a fair fight,' I say, half-smiling. 'Do you want to finish that?'

He shrugs. 'I'll finish it later.'

We sit down opposite each other in office chairs. I notice that despite his mother's home-cooking he has yet to gain any of the weight he'd lost in London and that his facial hair is longer than ever, swirls of it wisping down from his sideburns. 'You look great,' he says.

I smile. 'Thanks. You look much better.'

He laughs, staring at the computer screen. 'I feel much better, Moll. My doctor says that I should make a full recovery.'

I think about what his mother had said to me on the phone, her voice strained as she stressed that Tom could have another breakdown at any time.

'That's good news, Tom. I'm glad.' We sit there, the silence like a welt. 'You know why I've come, don't you?'

Tom glances at me, guileless as ever. The face of an optimist. 'Mom said that you had some official stuff you needed to talk over with me.'

'Did she say what it was about?'

'Nothing specific.'

I lower my head. 'It's about our divorce, Tom. There're some papers I need you to sign.'

We both stare at the computer screen now, the image becoming pixellated, blurring, like the foggy camerawork used to obscure genitalia on TV. I stare at a point towards the centre, the kickboxer's foot high in the air, a flesh-toned blur.

'I don't think we should do this,' says Tom, looking away. 'I think we should talk things through before we make everything final.'

I smile. 'If I thought it might make a difference . . .'

Tom puts a hand on my knee. I shift awkwardly but his hand stays firm. 'We could still work, Moll. I still love you.'

I push at his hand gently. 'I don't think so, Tom.'

'You've met someone, haven't you?'

I shake my head vigorously. 'No, no.'

'Yes you have,' he says, and I hear an unfamiliar note of anger in his voice.

I try to be businesslike, reaching into my bag for the papers. 'I haven't met anyone, haven't been looking,' I say. 'This isn't about me wanting to remarry or anything like that. It just seems to be a good idea for both of us to have a new start.'

'And we can't have a new start together?' Tom's brow has descended low over his eyes, blocking my view of his pupils.

I pause, trying to make the word sound final. 'No.'

'Huh.' He sits back in his chair, takes up the game's keypad and starts playing again. A tinned three-bar melody chimes over the action. I hold the paper patiently, watching as he lays waste to the bear, a hippopotamus and a killer chimpanzee.

About half an hour later, Tom finishes the game, the Japanese girl holding up a trophy, throwing her head back and laughing. Some words start flashing across the screen in pink lettering. 'HOORAY, YOU ARE MASTER OF THE WORLD,' it says. 'GOOD LUCK WILL COME IN ALL YOU DO.'

'Well done,' I say.

He turns to me. 'Maybe you should just go, Molly. I wouldn't mind starting another game.'

'You don't want to talk about anything?'

Tom shrugs. 'You don't want to discuss anything important, do you? There's no point in us chatting.'

'You don't want to talk about the divorce forms?'

He sighs. 'Just leave them here and I'll look at them when you're gone. I don't want to sign them without reading the small print.'

'Right.' I put them on top of his scanner. 'I'll leave them here,' I say, patting them lightly. 'They just need to be sent back to the lawyer in London.' I flick through the papers and point at the address. 'You just need to send them here.'

Tom has already started the next game. 'Sure,' he says, 'it's fine.'

I go to kiss him on the cheek but he pulls away. 'See you later, Molly.'

'Right,' I say. 'I'm sorry.'

Walking down the stairs, I find Tom's mother standing at the bottom.

'How did it go?' she says.

'Not so bad.'

She grimaces. 'I'll bet. And he signed the papers?'

'I've left them with him.'

'Right.' She hurries me to the door. 'I'm glad you're getting this sorted out, Molly. It was all a mistake from the start.'

I stand in the doorway, wanting to explain again. 'I did try to look after him.'

'That's great, Molly,' and the door closes.

17

The flypaper

They watch, silent, huddled in a corner of the quad as Augusta strides towards them, her suit jacket trailing along the ground, cigarette hanging testily from her lips. It's a sunny day, the light having played tag with them as they'd hurried through the cloisters, teasing them with its sudden jousting shafts. Never at ease with the sidelines, Augusta has avoided the cloisters and is walking purposefully, diagonally, across the grass of the quad. Head raised like a salute, she takes the cigarette from her mouth and wafts it playfully through the air as if conducting a phantom concerto.

As she walks, Augusta thinks over recent events. On tour to promote *Maternities*, she and Ellie are spending a couple of days at Vespers, a small private university in upstate New York. One of the richest colleges in the country, it is a haven for the less cerebral of the upper classes. The grounds stretch over 1,500 acres of neatly civilised lawn, the eight hundred students held here partly by the iron fence ringing the land, mainly by the two-hour drive to the nearest city. Despite the college's reputation for intellectual decrepitude, the Dean (encouraged by his wife) had pursued Augusta for a lecture some months ago, promising packed halls and a sizeable fee. She had happily agreed. Perhaps she could bring some stimulation to these students, she had reasoned, something to challenge them.

Augusta knows the microcosmic world of a small college well after her days at Cambridge – the internal politics, the common room tussles, the shrink-wrapped isolation. Some of these students had probably never even met a self-confessed lesbian, she supposed, and the thought of discussing feminism was almost certainly new to them. Calling the Dean to confirm the terms of her visit and to discuss the seminar and lecture she'd be giving, she had commented that 'it might be useful for your students to meet someone radical'. The Dean had agreed. A weary man, a classics scholar worn down by the illiteracy of his students, he was grateful for anyone who might ferment some thought on campus. 'Come and stir things up,' he'd said, laughing. He was thinking, as he said this, about some of his female students. Last year he had called one of them into his study to speak about her dismal mid-term scores and, shrugging, she had told him that she had only come to Vespers to find a husband. The Dean had grimaced. 'Luckily all the men here are wealthy,' she'd said.

Augusta had slapped up against this indifference in yesterday's seminar. The session had been arranged to cater for the cream of the college, a band of fourth year students high up on the honours list. Standing at the front of the class, Augusta had found herself facing twenty excitable women and ten belligerent men, all either staring at their desks, combing their hair or talking, loudly, about better uses of their time. Football. Baseball. Cheerleading practice.

She had slammed the desk lid and started speaking, slowly at first, about the differences between biological sex and gender. The basic premise of *Maternities* – of all her work so far – was that the expectation of certain traits in men, others in women, was entirely unnatural, determined by social precedents rather than biology. It had been in the interests of community elders, argued Augusta, to create a feudal system between men and women, with men playing the leaders, women the weaker halves. Of course, she said, it wasn't natural for women to be servile or decorative or placatory, any more than it was natural for men to be rulers. In line with some of her scientific colleagues Augusta suggested that babies were born with a given sex – male or female – but with a completely clean slate when it came to personality. Given a gender-neutral upbringing, a boy might develop feminine attributes, a girl, masculine traits. Augusta saw this as something to be celebrated – a new era where individuals were truly that, where traits lost their association with gender and women could take up their place on the board.

The class had nodded at all this, heavy-lidded with boredom. There had been silence when Augusta asked for questions, the only sound in the room the dull thwack of a male student chewing his inside cheek. Before he had gnawed right through – and just as Augusta started to talk about her idea of universal maternity – a hand shot up.

A pretty girl, her hair preened into blonde ringlets, looked intently at Augusta. 'If men weren't meant to be the dominant sex,' she said, her hand still raised, 'then why are they usually taller than women?'

Augusta had smiled, walking down the aisle to speak to the girl more directly. 'Well,' she said, 'the difference in physical strength is a cultural construction too.'

The girl raised her eyebrows sceptically, leaning back in her chair. 'How?'

'It's quite obvious when you think about it,' said Augusta. 'As the favoured sex, men have typically been more valuable to their families than female children and have been given more food, more encouragement.' She walked to the front of the class again, turning carefully to face them. 'I'm sure some of the women here will have experienced a difference in the way that they and their brothers were treated at home.'

'I was always fed the same as my brother,' said the blonde girl.

'Absolutely, but you or some of your friends may have found that there was less demand for you to develop physically, more criticism if you climbed trees, that kind of thing.' Augusta stared pointedly at the girl. 'Men are treated to bigger meals, are expected to show more sporting prowess, are encouraged to be' – she paused – 'more.' The blonde girl was smiling now, her eyes moving lazily over Augusta's body, like a puck coasting the ice. 'Just think about the treatment meted out to women in some other cultures,' said Augusta. 'Girl children are regularly starved by their parents or left for dead. If they do survive they're often malnourished. Their physical weakness is determined by their treatment.'

The girl appeared to consider this for a moment, twirling a ringlet around her finger. 'Right,' she said, 'but what about the fact that women act as mothers?'

'What about it?'

'Well, surely that's a strong natural reason why women and men have different traits? It makes sense that a woman should be more nurturing if she's actually carried a child in her body, makes sense that men should be protectors.'

A small ripple of applause came from those sitting around the blonde girl, a nudge of appreciation.

'Does it?' said Augusta. She paused. 'It seems that there's this desire in us to see male and female bodies as metaphors for the way each sex should behave. Because men are usually bigger than women, taller, we attribute strength to them, a protective streak. Equally, because they penetrate women during sex, we attribute power to men, a sort of biological colonialism.'

The girl was smirking at Augusta, her lips pursed with

derision. 'I understand, of course,' said Augusta, 'that the experience of carrying a child can sometimes stir maternal impulses, inspire nurture. But' – she perched on the front of her desk – 'that response is at least partly a product of expectations. Culture tells women that they should love their children and, very often, they do. The actual innate response of each mother can sometimes be different though, but when it veers from social expectations – when a mother rejects her child, maybe gives it up willingly for adoption – that's described as unnatural. Society doesn't allow for different reactions. It's not acceptable to us culturally that some women might not respond to their child as its nurturer. Becoming a mother doesn't presuppose certain traits. Our culture simply expects them, and it damns those who react differently, treating them as pariahs or implying that they're mentally unstable.'

One of the boys started to drum his fingers on the desk. 'How can you have written a book about motherhood when you don't have, sorry' – he paused – 'can't have kids yourself?'

Augusta reached into her top pocket for a cigarette. She lit it, taking a long, wilful drag. 'If you'd read the book, you'd know how I was able to write it,' she said quietly. 'The argument that I make in *Maternities* is partly what we've talked about – the idea that traits exist independently of biological sex. The book goes on to define and analyse the attributes traditionally associated with motherhood, maternity. It looks at our culture – at the workplace, the way we socialise – and suggests that some of the elements of so-called maternal behaviour should be applied to these areas.'

'Yeah,' said the boy, legs stretched out in front of him, tapping his foot, 'but don't you think that you'd be more qualified to talk about this kind of thing if you had kids?'

Augusta blew a smoke ring into the air. 'I'm looking at the traits associated with motherhood, rather than motherhood itself. As I said,' she sighed, 'many mothers might not possess any of the traits that we deem maternal and this is completely understandable, completely natural. What I've done in the book though is to look at those culturally defined traits – nurture, selflessness, strength – and tried to apply them to different male-dominated settings.'

The boy laughed.

'And anyway,' said Augusta, 'I can have children.'

There was silence. 'Without a husband?' said the blonde girl.

'Of course.' Augusta stood up. 'A husband is hardly a prerequisite for having children.' She paused. 'Neither is a male partner.'

The class stared at her, a few muttering towards the back.

'But that's not natural,' said the blonde girl.

Augusta turned around, smiled at the blackboard, walked behind the desk and sat down. She was used to meeting students who were closed-minded – she'd given lectures in Idaho – but this class had been particularly strained. Barracked here in New York State, these girls were obviously preparing for nothing more than marriage, children and a Puerto Rican maid. And the boys. She rarely received a good response from young men, but she'd never come across such antagonism. She scanned the room for a friendly face. There was a boy at the front biting his nails, hair lapping at his collar. He looked interested. Probably gay, thought Augusta. The others were glaring at her like predatory animals. After she had talked about the idea of having children outside a heterosexual relationship, one of them stuck up his hand. Face turned to his desk he said, 'Why can't you just get a man?'

Still, despite the hostility Augusta felt that she had achieved something by the end of the seminar. The blonde girl had conceded that women might want more out of life than a holiday home and the boy at the front had stopped chewing his nails. It wasn't much, thought Augusta, but there was always tomorrow's lecture.

After the seminar she had headed back to the study bedroom she was sharing with Ellie. It was situated in one of the nineteenth-century blocks that flanked the quad, a huge red-brick building, looming and impressive. The room had a high, wood-beamed ceiling, the walls lined with paintings by minor but significant Renaissance artists. It smelled like a shipwreck.

Ellie was sitting up in bed, naked, smoking a cigar and reading yesterday's copy of the *New York Times*. She smiled vaguely as Augusta floundered through the door, before turning back to the paper. Three weeks ago Ellie had caught Augusta undressing an eighteen-year-old student in Iowa, and she had been sulking ever since. 'Hi, sweets,' said Augusta breezily, walking to the bed, sitting down and untying her shoes. She kissed Ellie lightly on the cheek. Not a flinch.

Ellie was being petty really, thought Augusta. Her night with the girl hadn't meant anything, and it wasn't as though she had instigated it herself. Approaching Augusta after the lecture the girl had practically stripped her right there at the front of the theatre, pawing at her jacket and flicking away dust with almost religious zeal. It had been embarrassing but flattering, and she was sure that Ellie would have reacted in the same way given the circumstances. It had just been one night.

They sat there together in the bedroom, silent, Ellie reading, Augusta writing notes for tomorrow's lecture. She tried to come up with fresh material for each one, tried to tie her ideas into current events and keep the subject matter relevant. 'Will you be coming tomorrow?' she'd said, crawling into bed. She put an arm around Ellie's waist. 'I think it's going to be a good one.'

Ellie had shrugged and smiled, her back straight, body unresponsive. 'Well, I don't have anything else to do,' she'd said, Augusta's lips curling like the rim of an oyster shell. Ellie watched her, mildly amused. 'I'm only joking,' she said. 'If you'd like me there then of course I'll come.'

'Good.' Augusta's grip tightened and she leaned in to kiss Ellie again. 'I'm so glad. You'll enjoy it.'

They had slept for a few hours then, resting before a

dinner being held in Augusta's honour. All the senior faculty members and their spouses had been invited – about seventy people – and it was going to be held in the main dining room of the Dean's residence. 'It'll be quite an event,' the Dean had said. 'Everyone's coming. They're so excited to meet you and discuss your ideas.'

Having dusted down her tuxedo and threaded a black silk dahlia through her hair, Augusta had set off to dinner, Ellie in tow. The place had been decorated beautifully, huge bunches of lilies spewing from every surface ('like a funeral parlour,' said Ellie) but Augusta was disappointed to find that few of the guests knew anything about her work. 'They always serve marvellous canapés at these dinners,' said a faculty member, smiling benignly at her as they stood in the hallway, waiting to be seated. He plainly had no idea who she was.

It was half an hour before everyone had settled at the table, the waiters poised to start serving. 'What's the appetiser?' said Augusta, turning to the Dean, smiling.

'Oh,' he said proudly, unfolding his napkin, 'well, it's like prawn cocktail, but it's made with langoustines.'

'Right, sounds good.'

'Langoustines?' whispered Ellie.

'Big prawns.'

As they picked their way carefully through the first course, Augusta muttered about the philistines in the crowd. Waiting for Ellie to collect some drinks before dinner, she had been cornered by a billowy-faced, red-nosed man who had talked to her breasts until the champagne arrived. 'That one there,' she said, pointing at the man, now sitting a few places away from them, 'that one teaches literature but knows fuck all about contemporary writing.' She sighed. 'I mentioned something about Allen Ginsberg to him and he just looked at me like this.' She goggled her eyes at Ellie's chest and stuck a finger in the side of her mouth. Ellie laughed. 'Even the faculty at this college is remedial.'

Halfway through her orange-skinned gammon, Augusta was still smarting. 'It's amazing, isn't it?' she said, breath tickling Ellie's ear. 'Amazing that I can have featured on news programmes and in papers across the country, that my book is on the bestseller lists in all the US cities' ('bar Dallas,' said Ellie) 'bar Dallas, and still these people have no interest in my ideas.' Augusta sighed loudly and everyone within a five-person radius turned to stare at her. She lifted her glass. 'Cheers.'

Still, there had been at least one person who was interested in her work, who appreciated her visit to the college. Augusta smiles as she walks through the quad, and lifts a wrist to her face. She can still just about detect the scent of Magdalena, the Dean's wife, marking its territory.

Magdalena had arrived at the dinner late, slightly flushed from a private tennis lesson. A six-foot woman, slim but muscular, she moved with the silky scorn of a panther. Augusta had smiled at her as she sat down a few seats away from the Dean, resplendent in an orange wrap dress, a Diane von Furstenberg. Magdalena had smiled back, her incisors glinting like the teeth of a small but vicious animal.

After the dinner Ellie had retrieved a bottle of champagne from the table and retreated to a far corner of the room, talking to anyone who approached her, smoking happily when left alone. She could be so anti-social, thought Augusta, standing in the middle of the throng, feeling slightly jealous. She leant against the dinner table and lit up a cigarette whilst the Dean of History started talking about Joan of Arc. She nodded as he laid out the various arguments for and against Joan's claim to leadership ('she may just have been a prominent whore,' he said), too bored to respond. Another argument about prostitution, she thought, that's the way all my parties seem to end these days.

As Augusta struggled to swallow a yawn, Magdalena came powering across the room. 'I'm so sorry, William,' she said, stroking the history tutor's arm. 'I'm simply going to have to steal Augusta away from you for a while. Everyone's just desperate to speak to her.'

He had nodded, surveying the guests (most looking at their watches or attacking their mouths with toothpicks) and turned his back to them. 'I'm Magdalena,' she said, stretching out her hand. Augusta kissed it gently.

'Augusta Flynn,' she said. 'I'm Augusta Flynn.' Magdalena had laughed.

They circled the room then, skirting around the other guests, pretending to mingle. Magdalena was talking about her proposed PhD on feminism in twentieth-century literature. She wanted her doctoral thesis to focus on a single author, but couldn't decide who would be most interesting. 'All the obvious writers are just too . . .' She paused.

'Obvious?' said Augusta.

'Exactly,' said Magdalena. 'There are authors who I'd love to study more – Virginia Woolf, Gertrude Stein – but they've already been deconstructed so often that it seems slightly pointless.' She smiled and cradled her arm around Augusta's shoulders. 'But it would be difficult to sustain four years' research into someone more marginal. It could all be a bit insubstantial.'

On their third circuit around the room, Augusta noticed that Ellie had gone. 'Where's your friend?' said Magdalena with a sly edge to her voice, a petulance that suggested she wasn't too worried. 'Doesn't she want to stay around and make sure you're OK, keep you company?'

Augusta had laughed, magnanimous. 'Oh, you know. We've been keeping each other company at events like this for years now, I don't blame her if she wants to leave early.' She looked up at Magdalena. 'Not that it hasn't been beautifully planned, of course, but it's not really Ellie's scene.'

Magdalena had thrown her head back, hair whipping across her bare shoulders. 'Well planned,' she said, 'but fucking boring. No one could have prepared the two of you for this faculty.' She looked around, unconcerned, to see whether anyone had heard her. She leaned towards

Augusta. 'I'm so sorry to have subjected you to them. Some of these dinners are just deadly.'

'It's OK,' said Augusta. 'Not at all. I've been having fun.'

'Good,' said Magdalena, and she turned and walked silently up a winding iron stairwell in the corner.

Arriving in the middle of the quad, Augusta sits down on a ledge that flanks the statue of the college founder, Anthony Vesper. Crossing her legs and leaning on her knee, she puts a cigarette in her mouth, head tilted, and lights it. She sits, smoking calmly, remembering the night before.

Upstairs, Magdalena had taken Augusta firmly by the hand and started leading her around the wood-lined corridors, the catacomb passages of the attic rooms. She was whispering excitedly, her voice echoing as she took Augusta past portrait after portrait of the college benefactors, each of them whiskery-haired and disapproving. 'Come with me,' she was saying, 'I have my own little room at the back of the house, a corner of the attic.'

On turning thirty earlier that year, Augusta had promised herself that she'd give up her affairs, the one-night stands, and try and be faithful to Ellie. Her behaviour had caused so many problems over the years, particularly the past couple, when she had been working on *Maternities* and Ellie had looked after her, keeping her well-clothed and fed. Since they'd first met, Ellie had amazed Augusta with her commitment, her unquestioning devotion. Sitting at her desk on the eve of her birthday

Augusta had decided that she, too, would try to avoid temptation, would limit herself to eye contact, compliments, the coy repertoire of flirtation.

This was the reality though, thought Augusta, following Magdalena up another flight of stairs. First there had been the eighteen-year-old – sweet and naïve, her body caught up in that coltish, pre-college clutter of limbs – and now there was Magdalena. It hadn't taken much, thought Augusta. Just the suggestion of that body beneath the wrap dress, some expensive-smelling scent. She shrugged in the darkness.

Magdalena's hand was soft, slightly clammy, as she reached out to Augusta. Nerves, thought Augusta, flattered. A small table lamp was flicked on beside a mattress on the floor, made up haphazardly with old sheets and blankets. 'I thought we could have a lie-down,' said Magdalena, the gravel in her voice reminding Augusta of the skin of a coconut, knees grazed on concrete. The voice was calm, steady, innocent. Magdalena had brought a bottle of champagne upstairs with them and she began to tear at the gold wrapping with her teeth, mouth gnashing like a dog tearing through meat. Removing the paper she smiled at Augusta, handing her the bottle. 'You pop it.'

As Augusta struggled with the cork, Magdalena walked to a part of the room where she could stand up straight and stepped quickly out of her dress. Looking up from the champagne, Augusta couldn't help laughing. 'You're naked,' she said, her giggles running unsteadily through a scale, like a small child at the piano, 'fuck,' and the cork went flying up into the roof, ricocheting through the beams and back down.

Sitting on the ledge, smoking her cigarette, Augusta smiles at the thought of last night. Magdalena is an anomaly here, she thinks, unsuited to college life: the ennui, the repression. She thinks of what Magdalena had said after they'd had sex, stretched out beside her on the grubby mattress smoking a joint, her breasts laid flat against her chest. 'Coming to this place was a mistake,' she had said, 'so bad. You wouldn't know it' – she turned to Augusta – 'but my husband is a really interesting man. Very clever.' She ran her palm across her belly, her skin still sticky with champagne. 'I feel like I spend my days' – she had paused – 'trying to find ways to breathe.' She put a finger in Augusta's mouth. 'It's like living in a display case. You can see your breath against the glass.'

It was a little after five am when Augusta had crept from the Dean's house back to her room. Ellie was in bed, still awake, the cigar in her mouth burning its last. Augusta could just make out the tip in the curtained room. 'Did you have fun?' said Ellie, stubbing it out. 'I was wondering where you'd got to, whether I should put the authorities on red alert.'

Augusta had laughed. 'Nothing to worry about.' She undressed and climbed into bed. Ellie had turned on her side now, her body coiled like an insect being poked with a stick. Augusta stretched an arm out, tried to pull Ellie towards her.

'You smell of sex,' said Ellie.

Augusta had lifted her hand away then and lain on her front. 'You're so paranoid,' she said, feeling Ellie curl even more tightly beside her. She had sighed, kicking at the sheets to straighten them. 'You really should keep your delusions in check.'

Recalling it now, Augusta feels slightly guilty about that comment. It had been unfair, vindictive. She would never have been so snappy and defensive when they were first together, she thinks, but then Ellie had been more open-minded at the start, more self-confident and generous. There had been times in those first years, Augusta guesses, when Ellie had known about her affairs, had realised that her early morning appearances in their flat weren't just due to late nights at the library. She'd never spoken about it then, thinks Augusta, or made it into a serious issue, blown it out of proportion. She knew the significance of their relationship, the fact that she was Augusta's linchpin.

And staring out over the bright lawns of the quad Augusta realises that perhaps her relationship with Ellie is reaching an end, has been toppling from the precipice for some time now. That's the pattern, thinks Augusta. The excitement of a new body, the altitude sickness, the fall.

With Ellie it could all just be dealt with quite cleanly. Deft movements, thinks Augusta, precision. No need for too much shouting or analysis. No need for heaving shoulders in darkened rooms. Just a simple split.

Sitting there, adjusting a crease in her trousers, Augusta thinks about the problems between them. The main one, she decides, is Ellie's lack of ambition. Her stints at bar work, shop work, the voluntary stabs at teaching adult literacy would be all very well, thinks Augusta, if only they weren't so – she searches for the right word – temporary. As it stands though, it's difficult to connect with someone who has no ambition, who spends their time inking price labels.

I need to free myself up, thinks Augusta, need to buy some space to enjoy the adulation. She stretches her head back to feel the sun on her face and laughs. She has just finished giving the promised lecture to 600 students in the college auditorium – the bulk of the student body – and she feels happy that it has gone so well.

Stepping onto the stage, her notes laid neatly in front of her, Augusta had felt confident that she could win this crowd, proud of her material. As she scanned the audience, she had spotted Ellie in the back row, knitting, Magdalena towards the front, subtly adjusting her bra. It always bothered Augusta to think that Ellie could be content to knit while she was talking onstage, had seen it as an affront. It seemed so obtuse. How could she be more interested in that ugly scarf, thought Augusta, than in what I'm saying? Still, she had shrugged, it was her decision.

Lighting a cigarette, she had skimmed her notes before walking to the front of the podium and starting to talk. The crowd had been chattering peevishly until now, like sparrows around a birdbath, but as Augusta spoke they began to hush. She started the lecture with reference to Vietnam, the gender politics of war. After a few minutes, some of them started to lean forward, moving closer as she talked about the tropes of attack, the symbolism of force. It was simple stuff, Augusta realised that, easy to outline the meaning of dominance in these terms, too basic for a sophisticated audience. Given the crowd that had assembled though, she thought it best to start with simple material, easing them all into the lecture gently, greasing them up for the distance.

And standing on stage, talking about some of the ideas in *Maternities*, the subtle and explicit, minor and totemic creation of gender, talking about its deconstruction, the fact that it could be squeezed like an accordion, whining, until it was flat and boxed away, Augusta had felt powerful, happy. She had always been able to do this, command attention, had always been capable of impressing an audience. Since she was a kid she had known the power of ideas, had watched herself, almost objective, as she pulled her arguments tight around her peers, stifling any objections they might have, weaknesses they might exploit. She had always known her abilities, the bubbling potential of her words.

Standing at the front of the stage, hands clasped to her hips, she had spoken about the media portrait of women, of men, of her. She talked of the challenge offered by her looks, the fact that her physical attractiveness forced people to accept that she wasn't lesbian through any want of male offers. She had spoken for an hour and a half and they had all listened, rapt.

It had been a very successful lecture, she thinks again, taking a final toke on her cigarette before standing up and stubbing it out. A successful lecture on a successful tour. Aside from her concerns about Ellie, it had been a hugely profitable few months all in all – funny, exciting and drug-fuelled. As the tour continued, *Maternities* kept selling by the crateful and the media attention spun on. Apparently *Vogue* was interested in interviewing her and *Cosmopolitan* had commissioned a piece from her about gender for their January issue. The article – which asked readers whether femininity was a given or a choice – was part of the magazine's 'New Year, New You' edition.

Striding again across the grass, Augusta smiles widely, her cheekbones swelling high on her face. Only three months to go, she thinks, and then it will be 1975 and her new plans can get under way. Augusta has spoken to her publisher about her second major book, most of which she intends to write this winter, when she holes up in New Mexico for a couple of months – with or without Ellie. In a history of the free-love movement, she plans to look at whether sexual promiscuity is truly liberating for women. I'll have to attend some swingers' parties before I start, she thinks, have to interview some of the partici-pants. It should really capture the world's imagination, this second book. The most explicit analysis of sex yet undertaken.

And walking across the grass, through the corner gap

in the cloisters, the light suddenly blinding, Augusta feels
a wash of happiness. For a moment she knows she is
invincible. It has been an emotional few days – the pout-
ing criticisms of her seminar group, her guilt over Ellie,
the visceral excitement of Magdalena's honeyed limbs –
but she knows that she can take it now.

She only catches sight of them for a second as she
rounds the corner, a well-framed glimpse before they
spray the liquid in her eyes. They are wearing black
hoods, the four of them, the holes in their balaclavas cut
so far apart that only the corners of their eyes are visible.
They look like flies, she thinks, with those big holes on the
side of their heads. Flies looking around for somewhere to
land.

One of them jumps shakily towards her as she starts to
run, grabbing her wrist so that she falls forward, his grip
tightening quickly. She pulls away, wrenching hard, and
gasps as she tastes the liquid being sprayed in her mouth.
Her lips purse as she crawls a few paces, and she spits at
the ground. It smells like ammonia, she thinks, blinking
wildly, a few blurry shadows in front of her, and then
nothing. Just that final image.

She knows, of course, what is going to happen, knows
as every woman before her has. She is glad that she can't
see them as they drag her fast along the gravel, hefting her
like a piece of roadkill. They pull her to what she supposes is a bush, somewhere hidden. Her hands feel the
ground surrounding her, small mounds of grass and peb-
bles, what feels like mud. One of them bends towards

her, clutching at her hair, so close that she can just smell his breath through the stench of ammonia. 'Shut up,' he says, and Augusta feels something cold against her neck. 'I'll fucking kill you.'

It is with this warning that she screams loudest, her mouth opening so wide that the flesh at each corner seems to tear. 'They'll kill me anyway,' she is thinking, defiant, 'but at least if someone hears they might catch them. They might find my body more quickly, cover it up, give me some dignity.' She finds herself obsessing then, strangely rational, thinking about them getting caught. She concentrates on their voices, trying to pick up what they're saying. Two of them are whispering a few paces away and she listens intently. Nothing. Their voices are low and indistinguishable, each with the same clipped rattle of the East Coast upper classes.

She hears a ripping sound, a faint trickle of liquid and a balled-up cloth is shoved into her mouth. Augusta gags as the sharp, dull taste spreads across her tongue. She bangs wildly at the grass. Her trousers have torn up the front of her calves, gravel inching under her skin, and she feels the cloth being ripped by a pair of hands.

Struggling to swallow, she veers in and out of consciousness, head bumping against the ground. As she comes to – tides of nausea slapping up every few seconds – she tries to stay awake. She waits for another voice, something to record, to make these boys human. She can just make out their mumbling as one kicks her hard across the face, can feel her cheekbone shatter. Augusta coughs, vomiting, the cloth still stoppering her mouth. She swallows, retches, swallows, retches.

How do I survive this? she is thinking, feet scrabbling for a foothold as they pin her flat. She feels the inevitable rip of her waistband, her trousers being pulled off. They are clumped halfway down, Augusta exposed to the knee, when she hears muttering at her elbow. 'Should we do this?' one of them is saying, his voice small, uncertain, his grip loosening on her arm. Augusta's head starts jerking back and forth and she tries to grab his hand. He's the one, she thinks. This is how I'll survive. His voice is wavery though, shot through with indecision. She feels a sharp tug at her underwear. 'Do it.'

Naked from the waist down, her legs are forced apart. She feels a tug and somehow remembers her mother, for a second, standing by the sink, telling her that she'd been cut open during childbirth. Augusta feels something wet crawling over the top of her thighs, presumes it to be blood. Nothing hurts so much now. Where's Ellie? she thinks.

One of them is on top of her, a knee pushing deep into each thigh, and she feels something being forced into her, something metallic. Her body bucks at the pressure, the pain real again now, and she realises that she's stopped breathing. She used to do this as a kid, used to enjoy the feeling of standing out in a field and holding her breath until she passed out. Now, though, she knows that if she faints they will have killed her. I'll suffocate, she thinks, choke on my own vomit.

'We're doing this for you,' says a voice, soft and laughing in her ear, 'we're doing it to make you realise.' The metal is pulled from her with a small sucking noise, replaced almost immediately by something human. She feels the boy pushing into her, his hands hard on her covered breasts, holding them flat and bruised. It is over quickly, she supposes, a few thrusts and something wet on her stomach.

Augusta passes out. Coming to she feels someone else inside her, her shirt ripped open now. There is something sharp against her chest and she feels a trickle of blood, realises that they've stabbed her, a shallow cut. 'I can't do it,' one of them is saying, 'we'll kill her.' She can feel his breath heavy on her ear.

'Do it,' the one on top of her is saying, his voice strained. 'We're not leaving until you've fucked her. If she dies, she dies.' He pushes into her so hard that she thinks she feels something inside her rupture. Her head falls back again.

She wakes to find Ellie pawing at her clothes, covering her up, the rack of her sobs like a pulse. 'Wake up, Augie, please wake up.' The cloth is out of her mouth and she turns her head robotically to the side to vomit. Ellie lays a hand flat against her face. 'Augie,' she says, 'can you hear me?' Augusta nods.

18

The performance artist

'I think I'll just send her some flowers,' I say, looking around for the cleanest table. Lenny and I are in All Day Donuts, a café opposite our apartment on Market Street. I notice that Stan, one of the smack addicts who lives at the bottom of our stairwell, is sitting at a table beside the window. Lenny and I had seen him shooting up in the street earlier this afternoon, injecting the underside of his foot, and his high has obviously kicked in. A croissant sits uneaten in front of him, while his eyelashes flutter gently.

Lenny and I have been living in San Francisco for a few weeks now, renting a spartan apartment above an Indian restaurant. Although we've been trying to work (suffering faint twinges of duty), the hours we're keeping are nocturnal and unsuited to hard labour. The few times that we have emerged before late afternoon – the light still good enough for an hour's drawing – Lenny has pulled me

away from my sketchpad, taking me shopping in North
Beach or for long walks through Golden Gate Park and its
hemline stretch of beach.

I choose a table next to a pillar, brush away the crumbs
and place napkins over the wet circles of coffee. Lenny is
collecting drinks at the counter.

'A Diet Coke for you, and a Grand Royale Chocolate
Delight.'

I yelp with excitement as he places the doughnut in
front of me. 'I hadn't expected this.'

He shakes his head. 'A surprise.'

'Thanks so much.' I pull it apart and let the chocolate
hazelnut filling run out. 'Shall we go halves?'

Lenny shakes his head. And then, 'OK.'

We sit in silence savouring the first bite, the sugary
dust melting into the cheap, creamy chocolate. Both of us
have the empty sickness of a hangover after a night out at
Vesuvio's. Arriving there early, Lenny had spent hours
glancing around, anxious for a sign of Lawrence
Ferlinghetti, talking vehemently to tourists and regulars
about the Beat Generation. 'I love *The Dharma Bums*,'
he'd said to a blank-faced Australian girl before she and
her friends moved quickly upstairs.

'That's gorgeous,' I say through the mouthful.

Lenny nods and swallows. 'Mmm. Anyway' – he takes
a quick sip of his coffee – 'you're not going to call your
mom today?'

'Back to that?' I sigh, opening my Diet Coke. 'No, I
don't think so. It'll just end up in an argument.' I take a

gulp, before saying regally, 'Which is not what one needs.'

A few days ago the papers had announced that Augusta was to be the first recipient of a major new award for services to women, which recognised her 'exceptional contribution to women's global rights, as well as her ongoing work as a theoretician and provocateur'. Lenny had caught sight of the story as we walked down Haight, my mother's picture emblazoned on the front of the *San Francisco Times*. Picking up a copy outside a convenience store, he had read the article intently as Augusta stared out at him, sanguine and serene. 'Look at her,' he'd said, 'she's fabulous.' I had pulled the paper away, carefully inspecting the photograph.

'It looks like she's had a facelift,' I mused, 'but it must just be giving up the booze.'

Lenny has been pushing me to call her ever since. 'You're going to send flowers?'

'Yeah, a nice bouquet, something flamboyant. She'll probably like that.'

Lenny is quiet for a minute, blowing tiny ripples across the surface of his coffee. 'Huh,' he says, and then, 'So why did you stop talking to her?'

I take another bite of doughnut. 'It's not as though I don't talk to her,' I say, mouth muffled, 'it's just that we tend to keep our communication quite' – I pause – 'minimalist.'

'When was the last time you spoke to her?'

'Before I came away. I called to say that I'd be in

America for a while, that I was going to sort things out with Tom.'

'And what did she say?'

I swallow the doughnut. 'OK,' I confess, 'I didn't actually speak to her. I called and left a message' – Lenny looks disapproving – 'but I would have spoken to her if she'd been there. I did call.'

Lenny stares at the pillar behind me.

'Anyway,' I say, defensive, 'it's not as though you speak to your parents.'

He sighs. 'I know, but' – he waggles a finger in his coffee to test the temperature – 'ouch. But I never got along with my parents.'

'Well, how do you know that I got along with Augusta?'

'It's obvious, isn't it?' he laughs. 'You have all these stories about the things you did with her as a kid, getting drunk together as a teenager. I didn't do things like that with my parents.' Lenny pauses. 'I don't think I have a single funny story involving my mom and dad.' He laughs and shrugs. 'Tragi-comic maybe.'

I think of the nights when Augusta and I had gone out dancing when I was fourteen, fifteen, the nights she had managed to hold herself together. She was like a flame in those darkened rooms then, always holding court at a large table and letting my friends flutter around her, laughing.

Lenny takes a mouthful of coffee. 'I just don't understand why you don't get along with her any more. I mean, I know she has a drink problem, but that's not what's stopping you speaking to her, is it?'

'It's not that I don't get along with her.'

'You just don't talk to her.'

'I do sometimes. It's just that we had a big falling out and we haven't really talked much since. It was before I went to Australia.'

'What was it about?'

I pause, taking a huge bite of doughnut, chewing slowly and gulping it down. 'It's complicated. Boring and complicated.'

'So tell me.'

I excavate my teeth with the tip of my tongue, upending the morsels of cake. 'You really want to know?'

He laughs. 'Of course.'

'OK.' I pause. 'Well, it happened when I was seventeen.'

'Right, and what was it about?'

'It was' – I gulp my Diet Coke – 'it was about the whole mystery of who my father is.' I sigh, embarrassed. 'All that blah, blah, blah and the rest.'

'So why did it come to a head then?'

'Oh, well, Augusta finally decided to tell me who he was.'

'Wow.' Lenny goes quiet. 'I'd always just kind of assumed that it was some anonymous sperm donor, someone Augusta didn't know.'

'Yeah.' I lick my finger and pick crumbs from the plate. 'I'd thought that for a while too. It seemed so weird for her not to have told me otherwise, you know, if my dad was someone she knew.'

'So was he just a sperm donor?'

'Well, not really.' I pause. 'Kind of. In the July before I left London Augusta and Ellie found out that one of their friends, this performance artist, had died in New York. It was an AIDS-related illness.'

'Right.'

'So they went over for the funeral, left me for a week or two on my own.'

'OK.'

'And when they came back they told me that the guy who'd died, Bob Farago, had been my father.'

'What?'

'Well, exactly. They showed me a letter that he'd written a month before – it's in a drawer somewhere in Augusta's house – saying that he wished he'd had a chance to get to know me, that he felt proud to be my father, all this stuff.'

'So had he and Augusta had an affair?'

I laugh, and notice Stan twitch violently. 'Fuck, no, they never slept together. In that respect it was just a donation, a turkey-baster affair.'

'What, him masturbating into a cup?'

'Yeah, a romantic beginning, isn't it?'

Lenny looks down at his coffee, tapping his fingers on the table. 'God. So were you shocked?'

'I was. I was devastated really.'

'It must have been a relief to know who your father was though.'

I laugh. 'Well, yeah. But he was dead, wasn't he?' I

think back to the blow of finding out about Bob Farago. All those wasted years that Augusta had spent weaving stories – that I was the last tsarina, a magical sea creature, a ghost. All that time I could have been getting to know him, visiting him in New York, taking carriage rides through Central Park.

I sigh. 'It just seemed unfair, you know.'

'So is that when you and Augusta argued?'

'Oh no. I mean, we had a bit of a fight then, but it was a month or two before it went nuclear.'

'Why?'

'Oh well, I don't know.' I look down at my hands, rubbing at what looks like a cigarette burn on my thumb. 'I think we both acted badly.'

'What happened?'

I laugh. 'You're very nosy, Lenny, you know that?' He smiles, nodding. 'I felt freaked out by it all, I suppose. It wasn't just that I'd found out that this guy was my father. I started to read about him and his work and' – I pause – 'I don't know. It wasn't what I'd been expecting.'

Lenny kicks me gently. 'Did you have some image of what your dad would be like?'

I laugh. 'Yeah, of course. It seems stupid now, but I really did. I was always making up stories in my head about how I'd find him and he'd be' – I bite a piece of skin from my lip – 'I don't know. Tall, I guess, and masculine and upstanding.'

'Like a film dad.'

I hit the table. 'Exactly. You know how in films and TV

there are those generic "good men", and they're always defined right from the start by their job?'

'Like who?'

I try to think of an example. 'Like Bill Cosby in *The Cosby Show*. You always knew that he was a good guy because he was a doctor. Or all those films where the leading man's an architect. There was a big trend for architects for a few years.'

'So you thought he'd be generic film guy.'

'Yeah, I really did. I used to imagine that he'd be the kind of dad who would take me out for long walks and give me advice – how to handle Augusta, what I should choose for my major at university. And he'd be protective. He'd let me go out with boys, but he'd be kind of weird about it, a little bit overbearing.'

'All very Freudian.'

'Yeah.'

'So what was Bob Farago like? Do you know much about him?'

'Oh yeah.' I pull at my fringe. 'After my mother told me, I went to the library and looked up some of the obituaries that had run.'

'And what did they say?'

I lay my hands flat on the table, bang my head hard against them and look back up at Lenny. 'He was a freak! A complete oddball, even weirder than Augusta.'

Lenny is laughing. 'What did he do?'

'Well, like I said, he was a performance artist' – I raise my eyebrows appreciatively – 'which was interesting, granted. He centred all his work around his sexuality, and a lot of it was quite ground-breaking, I think, quite challenging. There was a play he wrote, *Ego Massage*, about the gay scene in the seventies. It's pretty funny, it did well on the fringe.'

Lenny smiles. 'He sounds great. Why do you think he was a freak?'

I laugh. 'Oh, I don't, not really, but the thing he was best known for – in New York especially – was this video performance called *The Fairy Prince*. They show it every now and then at the Museum of Modern Art.'

'And what's it about? Is it a proper film?'

I shake my head. 'No, no, it doesn't have much of a storyline or anything like that, it was just this act that he created where he would dress up as a fairy – you know, wings, sparkles, a star-capped wand – and waft through some woodland. Anyway, it starts with him alone, dancing, and then he gets approached by these really butch men dressed in leathers and moustaches, all that stuff.'

'OK,' says Lenny, 'and does that lead to some horribly sordid sex scene?'

'Oh no.' I put my head in my hands, laughing. 'Thank God I don't have footage of my dad having sex. No, these guys approach him and he just starts beating them up. I think there are about seven guys in all and he just lays waste to each and every one, annihilates them. It's quite gory, a lot of fake blood. I heard an art critic talking about it once on the radio and apparently it's meant to be quite a transparent piece about breaking down gay stereotypes.

Bob was hoping that it would reach a wide audience, might make it into some suburban homes, but I'm not sure whether it did.' I shrug. 'Interesting though.'

'He doesn't sound freakish at all,' says Lenny. 'Certainly not compared to you, Ms Molly, with your dirty little collection of penis portraits.'

I smile. 'Fair point. But, you know, when I found out about him I was only seventeen and I think I was hoping for a bit of conformity on that side. Augusta was really wired at the time and the first picture I found of my father was the one that they ran with all the obituaries – a bearded guy, fully made up, sitting beneath a tree in a nest of scarlet tulle.'

Lenny hides his hand behind his face but I can see his torso shuddering. 'Not quite the father figure you had in mind.'

'No. Not what I was expecting.' I am laughing now too. 'But I'm grateful really. Apparently he was a lot of fun.'

'You hadn't ever met him, when you were a kid or anything?'

'Yeah, apparently when I was about three he came over to do a performance in London. I don't remember much about him except his beard and that he had quite a big tummy. Nothing too specific.'

'Oh.' Our laughter dies down. 'So what happened for you and Augusta to argue so badly later on?'

'Well, I decided to give up school and go to Australia for a year.'

'And she wasn't happy about that?'

'Oh, we never really discussed it. I never sat down and told her.' I pick at the label on my Diet Coke. 'She and Ellie were out at work most of the time so I just left school without telling them.'

'So when did they find out?'

'Oh' – I pull the label away from the plastic bottle – 'well, I told Augusta on the day I was leaving. I was really looking forward to one of those big showdowns, you know, I was hoping that she was going to cling to me and ask me not to leave. All that.'

'And she didn't?'

'Oh no. People never give you the showdowns you want.'

'So how did she react?'

'She went mad. Honestly.' I think of Augusta's face during the argument, the crack of her jaw and the screams that had eviscerated our house. Her eyes were just black slits then, her cheeks red and pricked with moisture, veins popping in her neck. I'd seen her rage before – she'd been sacked from a college job once and had shrieked for days – but never this. I look up at Lenny. 'She just started bellowing, incredible. Her face was about an inch from mine, yelling. She told me to fuck off.' I shudder. 'She was calling me all these names – a bitch, a whore – all the obvious things, until she just stopped making sense. She stopped forming words. Her voice was just sort of' – I pause – 'throwing up consonants.'

'And what were you doing?'

'Oh, I was standing against the door, crying. She told me that she didn't want to see me again, that she wasn't my mother.' I laugh. 'She told me I was devil spawn. It got kind of over the top.'

'And then you left?'

'Yeah, she was going on and on, just repeating that I wasn't her daughter, that she shouldn't have had me.' I think of how bloodshot her eyes had been when they'd finally flown open, like the pained pink irises of an albino. 'Ellie pulled her away and into the kitchen after a while, just as she was about to start back in, and I left.'

'Oh.' Lenny looks into his drink. 'Had you asked Ellie why your mom had kept Bob a secret?'

I nod. 'Oh yeah. I asked her a few times in that last month, but she never gave me a good answer. She just said that it had been Augusta's prerogative to tell me and that they felt they'd done the right thing. She asked me to go easy on Augusta.'

'So when did you speak to the two of them again?'

'Well, apart from postcards and Christmas cards, that kind of thing, I wasn't really in touch until Tom had his breakdown.' I pause to finish my Diet Coke. 'Augusta was good then, really supportive. She seems to have sobered up a lot recently.'

'Which is why you should speak to her,' says Lenny emphatically. 'Maybe she could come over, she could stay with us.'

'You just want to meet her, don't you,' I say, teasing.

'You just want to tell her about the crush you had as a teenager.'

Lenny pouts and laughs. 'I'm doing this for you, Molly.'

'I know.' I take his hand. 'I think I'll just send flowers.'

19

The dragon lady

I feel something whip against the back of my legs, like an invitation to a play fight. The man I am talking to – dressed as a tiger, complete with whiskers – laughs as I spin around unsteadily to catch the retreating tail of a large Chinese dragon. It is one minute to midnight on Millennium Eve, and the seventeen-strong conga line beneath the red paper costume has obviously visited a clutch of parties before arriving, finally, at this one. The crepe is dirty with scars, scuffed against brick walls, wet with spilt beer. A rip runs along its right side revealing a phalanx of mouths, laughing as they weave deftly through the warehouse.

I grab at the dragon's tail, tripping along behind as it rattles through a beaded curtain to the dance floor. Champagne splashes up and over the rim of my glass as we veer past the guests. A man by the bar is sporting a snail costume, ready to retract into his lacquered shell at any moment, while a shoal of women flit rhythmically towards him, their tropical fish outfits topped off with flowery swimming caps. Despite their costumes, everyone on the dance floor is trying to move as naturally as possible to the hip-hop being pumped through the venue. The only one who seems unhappy is a man who stands against the wall, his arms folded, forehead scored with lines, his painted monkey mouth set in a permanent grin.

I glance around at the curtain as it settles, the printed image falling slowly into focus. There are three of these curtains in the warehouse, with a different picture of Tom digitally scanned and transferred onto each one. The first that visitors come to, the one that covers the entrance, shows the only full-length portrait of him, my name and the exhibition dates (31 December 1999 – 4 February 2000) printed in bold white capitals underneath.

The owner of this gallery had originally planned to have the space empty for a millennium party that he was holding, the theme: come as your favourite animal. It had taken some expert wrangling by my dealer, Frank, to convince him that he should exhibit my work, but the cajoling had paid off. The animal party had become a launch.

Stumbling along with the conga line I peer up at the pictures, suspended above me. A computer has generated copies five times the size of my original drawings, and these have been laminated and hung from the warehouse ceiling on long steel wires. They swish slowly back and forth as we pass under them, the subject matter of each one almost obliterated by its size. I watch as the gallery's pink flashing lights pick up details at whim. A vaguely mottled thigh. The simple coil of an ear. A stray square foot of pubic hair.

I gulp the last of my champagne, whirling now, alone, laughing as my head whips around, the childhood rush of dizziness. I feel relieved. Lenny and I had arrived at the warehouse early this evening, drifting through the exhibition arm in arm as it filled up, trying to avoid overheard criticism. Still, while Lenny shouted encouragement over the crescendoing dance music – 'They're beautiful. Transcendent. Big' – I had found myself mesmerised by a lonely iguana looking up sadly at a nude of Tom. He seemed so disappointed. And why was the blue fluffy bear gnashing his teeth in the direction of Lenny's crotch? 'Don't worry,' Lenny had said, snaffling drinks from a passing waiter, 'they're just jealous of my cock.'

I stand still a moment, my head spinning, before catching the dragon's tail again. Stroking the peacock feather in my hair, I wave to Carruthers and Frank, who are leaning against a wall in the far corner, their faces serious. Dealmaking at a party, I think, how dull. The pair have known each other for years now, decades, and Carruthers had recommended me to Frank as soon as I arrived in San Francisco. Mumbling about 'the death of figuration', Frank had nonetheless taken me on after a first viewing. 'They're different,' he'd said, nodding, 'interesting.'

Carruthers had flown down from Eugene yesterday, buying up most of the exhibited work and taking Lenny

and me out to dinner. He had been planning his outfit for
weeks, enlisting Bette's help as a seamstress. His butterfly
costume accentuates his paunch, the padded satin leotard
set off with iridescent blue wings and springy antennae.
His feet are clad in a huge pair of flippers. Frank's costume is simple in comparison – a pinstriped suit with a
pair of white rabbit ears. 'Come as your favourite fucking
animal,' he'd grumbled. 'I don't have a favourite animal.
I don't like animals. If I liked animals I'd be a fucking vet.'

Carruthers waggles a hand at me and smiles, pointing
up at one of the portraits that he has bought. It shows
Tom naked, lying on his side, his hips undulating against
the page, strangely curvy. I remember drawing it in our
South London bedsit, soon after we'd moved there. It was
a sunny day and we'd had lunch in a park, locked together
in the shade of the trees. Coming home he had stripped
off for me, laughing, compliant, as I pulled his limbs into
the right position. He was reading a book as I drew him,
a biography of a famous explorer I'd never heard of. While
I stared vacantly at his groin, trying to sketch a firm outline, Tom read passages to me. 'God, it's horrible,' he'd
said. 'He was separated from his party at one point and he
ended up having to dig himself a pocket in the snow,
nestle there for a few days until his nose fell off.'

I had looked up. 'What?'

'Well,' Tom laughed, 'his nose didn't actually fall off,
not the whole thing, but most of the skin on it came away
when they found him, I guess through frostbite.' He
flicked back through the pages. 'Let me find you a bit—'

As he searched for the details, I had laid my sketchpad carefully on the floor and wrestled the book away from him. 'OK,' I said, 'enough for today.' His kiss tasted of our lunchtime sandwiches.

I had called Tom's parents when the exhibition dates were confirmed, wary that Tom would catch a notice for it and panic. When they'd put him on the line though, he had been calm, congratulating me. 'That's great,' he'd said, 'I'm so glad everything's going well.' I had listened for a bitter edge to his voice. 'I'd like to come and see the exhibition some time,' he said, leaving the phone a second to find a pen. 'Where's the venue?'

The countdown to New Year has started, people shouting the seconds until midnight. I feel something tap at my back and turn to see the head of the dragon bumping against me. It veers around, circling the dancing creatures like a predator eyeing lunch. Watching its glittering red body snake through the room, I have a glancing memory of the trip I had taken, aged ten, with my mother. A four-month tour to promote her porn project. We had stopped all over Europe, the Far East, Australia, the Americas. Augusta had a few days free each week and she had heaved me off to tourist spots, the two of us hand in hand, ignoring the explanatory placards and making up elaborate stories about the background of each place. On a special trip to Pompeii we had both lain on the floor, perfectly still. 'Imagine you're fossilised,' said Augusta, 'preserved in boiling lava.'

I had been suffering bouts of insomnia for a couple of

years before the trip and the disruption of the different hotel beds had made it worse. It had been brought on initially by my friend, Jack, who would watch horror films – sometimes ten in a weekend – and then describe them to me in graphic detail. In my imagination the vivisections, rapes and murders multiplied, unchecked.

As the dragon sweeps again past a llama, a sheep, a yawning tortoise, I think of those nights spent sleeping with my mother, the two of us huddled together in a hotel bed. She had held me tight against her stomach, her body warm and intransigent, the horrors in my head ebbing away. What did I have to fear from razor-fingered rapists, brain-eating vermin, lovable pets that would decimate you after dark? I would shift back further into the cradle of her curled body until nothing could catch me.

The voices are getting louder now, the shouted numbers more insistent. The dragon stops as they reach number three, the costume thrown off and left like a snakeskin on the dance floor. I start laughing as the people inside shake themselves down, sweat flying from them. A waiter approaches with champagne and they form a parasitic swarm around him.

I see Lenny running towards me, his feathered wings flapping, holding my cellphone at arm's length and bobbing his head to the music. He has a wraparound smile and kisses me hard on the cheek. 'I spoke to her,' he shouts ecstatically over the noise as people clasp each other. 'Happy New Year.'

I jump on the spot, holding his hands as the forgotten

lyrics of 'Auld Lang Syne' start murmuring through the crowd. 'It's going to be a great year,' I say, 'great.'

Lenny nods, laughing loudly before holding the phone up to his ear. He looks stricken as he ushers me to the edge of the dance floor. 'Are you still there?' he shouts. 'Hello?' He looks up at me. 'Shit.'

'What is it?'

He puts the phone to his ear again. 'Hello?' and his face relaxes. 'Thank God,' he says. 'I'll pass you over to her now, here she is.'

I take the phone, excited. 'Who is it?' I shout. 'Who is it?'

Lenny smiles. 'Augusta.'

Acknowledgements

Many thanks: to my agent, Darley Anderson, for his unflagging encouragement and support, and to his team, for their organisational skills, enthusiasm and general brilliance.

To Kate Lyall Grant, my editor, for taking the book on at a fledgling stage, trusting me to come up with something coherent and giving fantastic advice. Also, to everyone else at Simon & Schuster for their confidence and help from the word go.

To Mike Butler, for seeing a faint glimmer of potential in me as a kid and sponsoring my education.

To some of the female mentors I've had the luck to run into – Maria Lauret, Sheridan McCoid, Sarah Baxter, Eleanor Mills and Tiffanie Darke.

And finally, to Louise Byrne, Mark Atkins and (especially) the indefatigable Colin Midson, for reading parts of the book for me and being supportive way beyond the call of duty.